THE SUMMER OF US

LILY MORTON

Warning

This book contains material that is intended for a mature, adult audience. It contains graphic language, explicit sexual content and adult situations

FOREWORD

This book is a spin-off from the Beggar's Choice series, and although it features characters from the series, it can be read as a complete standalone.

However, if you are reading it as part of the series, chronologically it's set during Bram's book 'Keep Me' in the year when Bram and Alys weren't talking.

PROLOGUE

John

I FIRST MET the members of the world-famous band Beggar's Choice when their lead singer tried to punch me in the face over a girl. The next time I met them, they hired me as their lawyer while two girls fought on the floor.

I thought that was a big enough lifestyle change, but little did I know that the biggest change was already happening. I just didn't know it at the time.

I stand in the kitchen of a penthouse flat belonging to Bram O'Connell, the bass guitarist for Beggar's Choice, watching the two women roll about on the floor and feeling slightly helpless. I'm clutching a sheaf of legal papers guaranteeing the silence of one of the girls who is currently trading slaps. She'd signed them and agreed not to ever talk about her relationship with Bram, before being tackled to the floor by Bram's lodger, who had taken umbrage at her.

My eyebrows rise before I can help it. This doesn't normally happen when I'm dealing with land and property disputes, and then

I snort at the thought of Michael, our senior partner's face, if it did. He might even put down his copy of The Times.

Looking up, I catch the eye of Matt Dalton, Bram's assistant. Wearing dark-blue jeans and a faded denim shirt, he is leaning against a kitchen cupboard, and rather than watching the floor show he is watching me, the customary look of disapproval of me once again written all over his face. I sigh, because we'd got off to a terrible start last night.

I'd met him when he'd opened the door of Charlie Hudson's house last night. The lead singer of the band had formed the completely mistaken impression that I was with a girl he was in love with, and I'd gone round to try and sort the problem out. Matt had leant against the door looking at me enquiringly, which was justifiable as it was one in the morning, and obviously not normal visiting hours.

I remember blinking slightly at one of the best-looking men that I'd ever seen, lean and tall with shaggy-blond hair, a face with high cheekbones, full lips, and a friendly, open look that had made me instantly warm to him. Unfortunately, his face had kept this friendly expression right up until I'd announced my name, and then I'd had to watch his warm brown eyes ice over.

Once I was in the house the situation with Charlie had improved drastically when I'd explained that under no circumstance had I ever touched a hair on his girlfriend's head, or hair from anywhere else for that matter, although that remark had received a frown. The rest of the band had quickly warmed to me after that.

Everyone, in fact, apart from Matt. From that first second he'd judged me, and every time that I'd opened my mouth afterwards, a dark look had formed on his face. It had pissed me off so much that I'd done my normal thing and lapsed into coldness with him, my voice sounding even more cut glass than it normally does. I don't know why it had hit me on the raw so much, because I have a knack of pissing people off at the best of times, but it *had* flicked a nerve.

Coming back to the present, I try a humorous quirk of my mouth at him, hoping I don't look like I'm trying to be superior, which has been said before. However, he just shakes his head as if I'm making light of the situation, and then wades in to try and stop the fight. When the girls have finally been separated, I clear my throat and motion for the paperwork to be signed by the witnesses.

Job done, I button up my suit jacket and shake hands with Charlie and the others. Then, to my surprise, Matt comes up to walk me to the door. I frantically rack my brain for something to say that will make him soften towards me, and unfortunately my mouth opens independently of my brain's orders. "Some people use pay-per-view for that." I hear the words come out with an internal grimace of horror. He obviously disapproves of the fighting.

He turns his head slowly to look at me. "For *what*, exactly?" His voice is cold, and yet still my mouth babbles on.

"Two girls writhing around on the floor. It's the stuff that dreams are made of. Even better if their clothes had dropped off and they'd been oiled up." Oh my God, I want to punch myself in the fucking throat to stop talking. I sound like a total public school douchebag.

"I wouldn't know," he says stiffly. "I'm gay. I don't watch your weird, straight-boy porn."

I open my mouth to apologise and to tell him that I don't even watch porn. I don't have bloody time for it, to start with. However, I run out of time to halt this disastrous impression that he has of me, as he opens the door for me and gestures me through like I'm a fucking door-to-door salesman.

My next words come out clipped and cool. "Well, I'm sure I'll see you around."

"Hope not," he says just as coldly, and shuts the door in my face.

1

Five Months Later

John

I LEAN BACK in my seat, dimly aware of the jaw-dropping view of London's skyline from my office window, but focused more on the husky voice of the lead singer of Beggar's Choice, Charlie Hudson.

"So let me get this straight, you've bought, sight unseen, a villa in the hills above Cannes, which you've now found to be a crumbling wreck that requires an extensive building overhaul before it's even remotely liveable?" I say slowly.

There's a small pause and then he laughs. "Well, when you put it like that it does sound a bit fucking stupid, but mate, the view is to die for."

"Yes, but the lack of windows does tend to detract from that."

He pshaws. "That's just details, John. Nothing that a little money thrown at it won't help."

"A *little*? This is the South of France we're talking about. Enjoy being a multimillionaire while you can, Charlie, because when this is finished, you won't be."

"Blah blah blah, you're such a fucking pessimist, John."

"That's what you pay me for, Charlie, and why am I only hearing about this now? As your lawyer, these tiny, frivolous details about buying houses tend to be quite interesting to me."

"I paid cash, mate. Mabe and I had a weekend there and came across it. My wife took one look at it and fell in love with it instantly, so I tracked down the old man that owns it. He inherited it from an aunt and never lived in it, so it's been empty for years. I offered him money and after a bit of haggling he took the offer, and he's bought himself a modern house in the city instead."

"How much haggling?"

"Well, I had to promise him our firstborn, but you know, I think Mabe will be fine with that when she sees the *view*."

"You're so funny. What did she say when you unveiled your grand gesture?"

There's a pause. "Well, she doesn't exactly know yet."

"Why?"

"I want it to be a surprise. You know the South of France was where she first told me that she was in love with me, and it might be silly and sentimental, but I want to produce it on our anniversary as her present. Obviously, it would be better if her first anniversary present wasn't a crumbling wreck."

"First anniversary present is traditionally paper, isn't it? That could be your divorce papers if you leave her in the dark on things. You know how she is about grand gestures and keeping secrets."

"Sometimes I hate that you know us so well."

I smile because I do know them well. In fact, I count them amongst my closest friends, not that there's too many of them. I'm too private and contained a person to embrace vast groups of friends. However, the members of the band are definitely in there. "I do know you well, which is why I'm wondering why you're ringing *me* with this fait accompli."

"Ooh, fancy words. Bet you're wearing a three-piece suit while you speak."

I smirk. "No, only a studded thong. You've interrupted me in my lunch hour."

I hear the sound of fake gagging and laugh out loud before glancing round self-consciously to check that no one heard me. I don't know why I do this when I have a private office, but old habits die hard. "Spit it out, Charlie, because this call is costing you three hundred pounds an hour."

"You've got me on a *meter*?" he says in an indignant voice which is spoilt by the thread of laughter running through it. "Okay, the thing is I may own the villa fair and square, but there's going to be a lot of paperwork and building regs if I'm going to get the work done, and I'm sort of on a time limit."

"What time limit?"

"Three months."

I sit bolt upright. "Three *months*! Didn't you mention some slightly long-winded projects like a new roof?"

"Yep, and I don't have anyone to ask advice from."

"I'm not licensed to practice law in France."

"I know. I've got a French lawyer for that. Bill, our manager, got hold of him for me, but you speak fluent French, don't you?"

"I do," I say suspiciously.

"Thought so. The point is, I'm not going to be there, and I may be a debonair multimillionaire and a devastatingly handsome man, but I'm also not a twat, and no one is going to swindle me."

"Charlie, you're not asking me to oversee building work, are you?" I ask disbelievingly, but he laughs.

"Fuck, no. I can't picture you doing that. I've got someone else in mind for that. What I need to know is whether you're still taking that sabbatical to write your book and prepare for your visiting lectures?"

"I am. I just never realised that underneath that ditsy exterior you actually listen to the words that I say."

"Fuck off," he says peaceably. "What I'm getting round to asking is whether you're still planning to decamp to your place in France?"

I have a villa in the hills above Cannes, which is actually where Charlie and his wife Mabe first got together. I'd loaned it to her and my best friend Viv, who's a paralegal in the law firm at which I'm a partner, and also Mabe's best friend.

"I am. I leave next week and I'm staying there through the summer, before coming home in time for the lectures in October at University College in London."

"Would you be okay to be on the end of the phone if there are any problems or documents that need a second look at?"

"Of course I will, Charlie. I'll help in any way I can, you know that."

"Thanks, mate. I knew that you'd help."

"Who have you got to oversee the building work? I might know someone if you're interested. The bloke that did mine was very good."

"No need, mate. I'm going to ask Matt to go over. I'd trust him with my life."

I'm startled. "I'm surprised Bram's parting with him without a fight. What will he do without his assistant?"

There's a long pause before Charlie speaks, and when he does there's an undercurrent of laughter in his voice. "I'm not sure *anyone* tells Matt what to do, John. Especially Bram. You'll find that out."

My eyes narrow in confusion and I'm about to ask what he means, but another thought occurs to me. "Where are you putting Matt up? It's busy at this time of the year."

"I'm not sure yet. I'll sort something out."

My mouth opens, and to my utter astonishment I hear myself say, "Don't worry about it, he can stay with me if he wants to."

There's a pause. "Are you sure, John?"

No, I'm not. This is utterly unlike me. I like my peace and

privacy, and I adore my house in France because it's my home and my sanctuary, and I don't let others into my space easily. However, my mouth opens independently again. "It's not a problem. The villa's big so I'll hardly know he's there, and at least he can find me easily if he's got any queries."

After wrapping up the conversation and giving him permission to tell Matt, I hang up and swivel my leather chair to look out over the city, but my attention is elsewhere, and my mind instantly conjures up the events of the last few months.

After that inauspicious first meeting with the band I'd thought that I'd only see them again for legal matters, but instead it had led to a surprising raft of friendships with the men who proved to be friendly, sociable, funny, and loyal. I'd therefore come into contact a lot with Matt because he's one of Bram's best friends. He's known the group since they were kids, and so is firmly in their inner sanctum.

However, while the other men had warmed up to me he hadn't, and he'd remained distant and wary of me. Watching him with the other men I'd quickly realised that this wasn't normal for him. He's funny, laid-back, and extremely sociable with a warm manner that people love, but with me he'd maintained a wary distance.

The knowledge had been surprisingly sharp. I'm not an easy man and there are plenty of people who don't like me, but it had stung slightly that this man who liked everyone, didn't like me. I therefore can't believe that I just invited him to stay with me for the summer.

My thoughts are interrupted by the buzz of my intercom and my secretary Carol's voice. "Mr Harrington, your wife is here."

It's on the tip of my tongue to remind her that she's my ex-wife, but I hold my fire as bitterness won't get me anywhere, apart from embarrassment in front of my secretary. I depress the button. "Show her in, Carol."

There's a soft knock on the door and the middle-aged figure of my secretary pops her head around the door, her mouth twisted into a slight moue of displeasure. She hates Bella and always has. I smirk at her as I stand up, buttoning the jacket of my three-piece, navy pinstriped suit before moving forward to greet the figure of the woman who I swore to love and honour four years ago, before she shafted me.

She wafts into the room on a wave of expensive perfume. Her hair is perfectly coiled on the back of her neck, and she looks cool and beautiful in a lemon-coloured sheath dress which highlights the length of her legs and the fullness of her breasts. "Bella," I say coolly, sliding my hand around her waist and pressing my lips to her cheek. She's cold to the touch. Sometimes, towards the end of our marriage, I'd found myself wondering whether there was any part of her that was warm, or if she was ice all the way through.

I dismiss that traitorous thought, and motion her to the seating area positioned in a corner of the room looking out over the city. "Sit down, Bella, and tell me what's brought you here."

She looks at me coyly. "Do I need an excuse? I've never needed one before."

"Of course not," I say urbanely, resisting the urge to say that had probably been before she served me with divorce papers.

I settle down on the chair opposite her, looking at her blankly until she squirms. *Interesting.*

"I saw your mother yesterday," she says hastily.

"Oh yes?"

"Yes, she was at a lady's luncheon that I attended. She asked me to say hello to you."

I stare at her, wondering whether she thinks this is normal behaviour. A mother passing on a 'hello' message to a son who she hasn't seen in months, through his ex-wife who she sees most weeks. I look at Bella. Of course she doesn't think it's odd. She and my mother are cut from the same cloth.

I become aware that she's been talking and has now stopped, waiting for an answer. This time I don't make an excuse for my inattentiveness, and interestingly she doesn't become angry like she used to. I'd swear she's also sitting a bit closer.

I want to smile because the old adage of 'treat them mean, keep them keen' clearly runs true with Bella. She wanted nothing to do with me when I was bending over backwards to please her and slaving to make her happy, but as soon as I became cold she heated up.

This is all part of my plan to get her back, but for the first time the thought occurs to me that maybe relationships shouldn't be such hard work. My thoughts shift to the men from the band. They are in relationships, but they bear no resemblance to the ones in my life. Theirs are warm, and brimming with humour and love and care. I dismiss the thought because that's their world and not the world I was born into. I just want my old life back.

I'd been flabbergasted when Bella asked for a divorce. I knew that our relationship was cool, but it had always been like that, and it mirrored the marriages of our friends and families. What surprised me most was the feeling of failure that had fallen on me. I had never failed at anything in my life, and that it happened in my marriage in the full view of everyone was humiliating. I'd fought against it, trying everything to persuade her to change her mind, but her smugness and resolution had increased exponentially with my pleas, so instead I'd backed away. Now, I'm trying another way. I will get her.

"You are distracted, darling," Bella coos, and I look up at her.

"I'm sorry, Bella. That was rude of me. What did you want from me?"

She sits forward, deliberately letting me look down her top. *Hmm, and I never even had to open my wallet* I think cynically, and then jerk. These rogue thoughts are coming thick and fast lately. I must be overdue for a holiday.

I focus on her again as she speaks. "I wanted to know whether you fancy taking me over to France to Daddy's house for a few weeks in the summer?"

House. It's a fucking estate, I think, but smile. "Darling, you are aware that we're divorced, aren't you? I don't think going away together is something that most divorced couples do."

She runs her fingernails down my arm. "Sweetheart, I think

there's a few things we've done that aren't part of the divorce process."

I think back to the weekend we'd spent fucking. The memory should fill me with heat, and it did before, but for some reason now it just makes me feel weary. She's good in bed, but it never felt totally real to me, more like an act she put on. But then, who am I to judge? Sex with her was always lacking for me, so maybe it's me. Sex has never been something to seize me, but rather just an itch that needs to be scratched. I'm sure that some people feel it deeply, but not me. I don't think that I feel anything deeply.

I mentally slap myself. I'm in the middle of the longest play that I've ever made. I want her back. I'm not used to failure, and to fail at my marriage is embarrassing and humiliating. None of my family have ever divorced, my father told me when I gave him the news. I don't wonder that he's bitter. If I'd been stuck with my mother all these years with no chance of parole, I'd have been miserable, too.

However, he had a point, so a few months ago I set out to win her back. I used studied coldness and being seen around town with a friend of hers to whet her appetite. Now, here she is, a sleek blonde shark nibbling at my bait. I want to fist pump.

"Bella, you know that I'm at the villa," I murmur. "And after the summer I'm lecturing for a few months."

She makes a moue of displeasure, and then smiles invitingly at me. "Maybe I can visit you there then, if you're not going to put out now, sweetie."

"Maybe," I murmur, and then stand. "I'm so sorry, Bella, but my next appointment will be here any second, and I've got to get things ready."

She rises gracefully and then comes towards me, gifting me with a cool kiss on the cheek. "Good to see you, John," she says gracefully, and I nod as I see her out of the door.

Once she's gone I throw myself into my chair and do a quick fist pump, which attracts a disapproving huff from Carol as she puts some paperwork on my desk.

"What's that look for?" I ask idly, as I grab my pen and start checking the deeds.

"I'm not sure that you know what you're doing," she sniffs.

"Carol, sometimes I marvel at how the rest of the staff are so wary around me, but you, however, treat me as though you used to change my nappies."

She sniffs haughtily. "I might not have changed your nappies, Mr Harrington, but I've certainly cleaned up some shit for you over the years."

I roar with laughter and pretend to swat her backside. "Never leave me, Carol," I say, smiling winsomely, and she smiles that wide, maternal smile that had made me hire her over the hundreds of other, more nubile applicants.

"One day I will," she says solemnly, and I frown. "And then what will I leave you with? Madame that's just gone? I might just as well stick you in a deep freeze and leave you to it." She looks at me searchingly. "I'd like to see you happy before I retire, John."

"I am happy," I protest, and she smiles sadly.

"Sweetie, you wouldn't know happiness if it came up and bit you on the arse."

I smirk. "I would if it came in the form of a size eight blonde."

She sniffs and leaves the room, but after she's gone I let the pen fall to the desk. *I am happy*, I tell myself. My plan is coming together, and I'd be prepared to bet good money that Bella will be back in my home and by my side by the end of the summer. Then my life will go on as before, with no disappointed or pitying looks.

The thought occurs to me as to whether I actually *want* my life back the way it was, but then I huff and pick up my pen again, determinedly drawing the paperwork back to me. *I just need the villa*, I tell myself. *I need my holiday to get my mind back on track.*

Matt

I sigh heavily into the phone. "Just sort it out, Ed. You made this mess. Apologise to the customer and make it right."

He gives a petulant snort. "Matt, if you met them, you'd understand how I feel."

"I have met them, Ed," I retort sharply. "I met them when they signed the contract for a new, discreet PA, and I recommended you. I really got to know them when they deposited an exorbitant amount of money into my company's bank account." I pause, and my voice hardens. "That's really all I care to get to know about them. I've informed Mrs Armitage that the matter will be sorted and that your offensive online rant about them will be taken down from Facebook immediately." He says nothing, and my voice goes sharp. "*Immediately,* Ed. I mean it."

"Matt," he says apologetically, and I instantly interrupt.

"I don't want to hear it. I think I'm an approachable man and I do understand that clients can be difficult, but we're professionals and this sort of behaviour reflects badly not just on you, but on me as well. I've worked too fucking hard to make the business a success for you to fuck it all up in a petulant temper tantrum. Now take the fucking message down, and that's an end to it."

Silence falls. "An end to what?" he finally asks in a sharp voice, and I pause for a second, wondering whether I'm really doing this. Then I think of how very fucking high maintenance he is and how many of these conversations I've had lately, and my resolve firms. "Everything, Ed," I say firmly. "We're done, and you're done."

"For fuck's sake, Matt," he shouts. "You don't mean that."

I sigh. "I really do, Ed. Look, this hasn't been working for a while and you know it. This is just the final straw."

"Matt, it's just business."

"No, it's *my* business, and I expect to be able to trust the person I'm with, with something that means a lot to me. When you posted that message you weren't just saying fuck you to Mr and Mrs Armitage, you were saying it to me." My voice goes harsh and I wince slightly, but it doesn't stop my next words. "I may be laid-back, but I'm not a twat, so don't treat me like one."

The phone goes dead and I swear under my breath. Taking out my keys, I let myself into Bram's flat. "Honey, I'm home," I call out sarcastically. "And I bring a shit-ton of paperwork and your dry cleaning."

Bram's Irish voice calls from the lounge. "In here, my dearest darling."

I snort and unload the junk onto the side table in the foyer and then cavalierly throw his dry cleaning onto a chair. The fucker can put that away himself. Taking off my jacket, I rub the back of my neck which feels strung tight with tense muscles.

"Tell me something stupid that you've done to cheer me up," I call out, and then come to a stop when I see both Bram and Charlie sitting on the sofa, beers in hand and wearing identical Cheshire Cat grins. "Oh, shit," I mutter. "What have you two done, and is there time to call your impossibly bossy lawyer before the police arrive?"

Bram snorts, and Charlie stretches and gives me a very knowing grin. "You're looking very spiffy, sweetness."

I look down at the navy suit trousers and white shirt that I'm wearing, and then throw the jacket onto another sofa, closely followed by my body. Lounging back on the supple leather, I remove the red tie that appears to be trying to strangle me, and kick off my shoes.

"Comfortable enough?" Bram smirks, and I smile at the best friend that I have in the world. I've known the members of the band since childhood, but since the first minute that Bram and I met we just clicked, and we've been inseparable ever since.

On the surface, I operate as Bram's assistant. This is because every other person, male and female, that I sent for the job, fell in love with him. The women he shagged, the men he befriended. Therefore, to stop him operating some version of a medieval court in his flat, I volunteered myself as the one person who is immune to his charms.

The arrangement works because I really am immune, as he's a brother to me, and also because he's one of the most laid-back people that I've ever met. He tolerates me spending two days a week in the office and then running my business from my phone, because when we're together it's just like we're back in school, messing about and piss-taking.

I realise that I've tuned out and focus back on them. "Why the fuck are you grinning like some nutter?" I ask Charlie, and the lead singer laughs. Then he bends forward, looking at me winsomely. "Oh, fuck right off," I say, alarmed and sitting up straight. "Don't look at me like that, Charlie. Last time you did that we nearly got arrested in Germany."

"That was a total misunderstanding," Charlie protests, and then smiles again. "I just wanted to ask you a *teeny* favour. That's all, Matty."

"Oh, please don't call me Matty when you're smiling like that," I say faintly, and Bram bursts out laughing. I steel myself. "Okay, ask me."

"Don't look like that," he says indignantly. "It's a good favour, honestly."

I stare at him. "Charlie, I have had a shit day so far. I was called into work to sort out an extremely irate customer, which led to me kissing arse for hours, and not in a pleasurable way. As a direct result of this I was forced to sack Ed, not just from his position in the company, but also as my boyfriend. Now, I'm faced with the two of you sitting there looking like Statler and Waldorf. Spit it out."

"Not something that you normally say, Matt. You usually go for the swallowers," Bram says comfortably, and I glare at him. He smiles lopsidedly. "I can tell you're not happy today, babe, but can I just say that I'm fucking ecstatic? I fucking hated Ed. He was such a whining motherfucker all the time, and seriously money-grabbing." He puts his hand to his chest in a horrible facsimile of a pouting debutante. "Oh Matt, please buy me that. Oh Matty, my childhood was so appallingly bad that we could never afford Louis Vuitton."

"Oh, shut up," I say, but a grin is playing around my lips.

Charlie laughs out loud and then stops. "Actually, that makes what I'm going to ask you so much easier." He pauses. "In fact, so much easier I could actually make out that I'm doing you a favour." I stare at him and he slumps. "Okay, I won't bother with that." He straightens. "I'm just going to ask you outright. How do you fancy a three-month paid vacation in the South of France at not one, but two luxurious villas?" Bram snorts disgustingly, and Charlie slumps slightly. "Okay, *one* luxurious villa and one broken-down money pit."

"You're not making any sense," I say calmly, pulling my legs up and settling comfortably into Bram's sofa. I think I might sleep here tonight, rather than go home and confront a hysterical Ed.

"Well, you remember how much Mabe loved the South of France?" I nod. "And how I will do anything to make my wife happy?" I nod again. He might be overdoing it slightly with the dramatics, but Charlie adores his wife. "Well, I've bought a villa."

I look up. "Well, that's good, right, babe? She'll probably be cross with you for spending money, but who can resist a luxurious villa?"

Bram laughs and Charlie shifts uncomfortably. "Well, the one I've bought isn't exactly the *luxurious* villa. Mine is more the run-down money pit."

I smirk. "Okay, that sounds like you, but why are you telling me this?"

"I'm having it done up, money no object, but I'm on a time limit of three months and I need someone to oversee everything."

I sit up. "You're not suggesting what I think you are, are you?"

He nods emphatically. "You're perfect, Matty. You deal with people so well. You're calm and organised. You speak French and you spent that year working on that building site, so you've got loads of building knowledge."

"Charlie, I was brick carrying because I had no money. I wasn't designing and building the fucking Sistine Chapel."

He shakes his head merrily, ignoring me. "You're perfect, Matt.

You're the only one I can trust. Anyone else and I might worry that they'd shaft me and do a shitty job."

I turn my head and look at Bram, and he shrugs. "Might be good fun, babe." Only Bram would describe a building site as fun. He carries on. "I mean, you've just broken up with Ed. The South of France for three months sounds fantastic. You've been moaning for a while about being tied to your desk so much. This would be outside and involving people which is really your strong point. Work's fine, and Lana's doing great as your office manager, isn't she?"

I nod because Lana *is* fantastic—organised, clever and switched on. She could definitely carry the business if I was away. She's done it before when I've joined the lads on tour.

Realising that I've fallen into a trap somewhere, I sigh wearily and look at both of their matching bright smiles. "Okay, in theory I could go. Sell me on it some more, Charlie, because if the villa's such a fucking wreck, I'm not feeling the idea of sleeping in a sleeping bag with no electricity or water. It's like a particularly bad camping trip that Bram and I went on once when we were seventeen."

Bram sighs, looking nostalgic. "Ah, happy days."

I shake my head, and Charlie leans forward, nearly falling off the sofa in excitement. "But that's where the other luxurious villa comes in. It's a fucking beautiful place, Matt, high in the hills above Cannes. It's huge, got an amazing pool, and you could drive to my place in five minutes. I loved it the week that Mabe and I spent there."

I stare at him, my mind working furiously. "Hang on, the only villa that you two have stayed in belongs to—" I pause, and they nod together, looking like complete idiots. "Not *John's* place?" I say in a disgusted voice.

Charlie nods. "Bingo. He says you can stay there, and he's going to be around to offer advice if you want it on building regs and shit. I've got an expensive French lawyer, but John's better."

"No, Charlie," I groan. "Not *him*. Tell me he isn't staying there, too? You know I can't fucking stay there if he's there."

"Well, it is his house," Charlie says primly. "It'd be a bit awkward to ask him to move out just so that you can move in. Have some heart, Matty. Dumping and sacking your boyfriend in five minutes has made you into a really hard bastard."

He looks at Bram, who instantly holds his hands to his heart. "I remember, Charlie, when Matt was such a sweet, giving person. Money has made him into a completely different person." His voice goes quavery. "I miss the real him soooo much!"

I lob a cushion at him. "Shut up, you fucking twat. Now be quiet and let me think."

I stand up and wander over to the windows looking out over the River Thames. I stare at the slow-moving river, thinking hard.

Three months away does sound good, and the idea of getting my hands dirty also appeals. I've been stuck in my office for months now, and it doesn't suit me, as I'm active and sporty by nature. I know that Lana could cope, and I'm only on the end of a phone and Skype if anyone needs me.

The only fly in the ointment is John. I think back to the night when Charlie and Mabe had imploded, helped along by Charlie mistakenly thinking that John was involved with her. We'd spent the night at Charlie's house stopping him from charging round to where Mabe was staying, and John had arrived that night to try and clear up things.

I'd taken one look at him and embarrassingly gone hard straight away. He's utterly gorgeous with dark hair, piercing blue eyes, a sharp nose, and a hard, long body that screams plenty of time spent exercising. He looks like a very hot David Gandy, if he could possibly be any hotter. However, the mistaken belief that he'd fucked up my friend's relationship, followed by five minutes in his abrasive, bossy company listening to his public school voice, and I'd taken a complete, instant dislike to him.

I see him a lot now because he's become very close friends with the lads and has been accepted into our inner circle, which doesn't happen to a lot of people. However, every time I'm around him, and no matter how much I resolve to try and get to know him, I've found myself jittery and antagonistic, which is so unlike me it's a joke. He gets under my skin in some way that no one ever has before, but to really ladle on the irony, he's straight, so I can't even fuck this feeling away.

So, three months doing something I'll enjoy, that will also challenge me, spending my time in a beautiful country that I love and sleeping in a beautiful villa. But also spending my time with someone who completely rubs me up the wrong way. I shake my head.

Becoming aware that I'm under the focus of two pairs of sharp eyes, I turn around and sigh. "Okay, I'll do it."

2

John

I LIE BACK against the cushioned lounger, feeling the sun baking down on me and sending everything behind my eyelids a golden black. For the first time in months, I take a deep breath and inhale the scents of lavender and suntan lotion. I exhale, feeling like all the tenseness is flowing out of me in that one breath, and then I lie there listening to the shrieking of a lone seagull and the lapping of the water in the pool against the steps.

I have a thousand things to do, a book to write and a series of lectures to prepare for that I've been asked to give at University College. I have emails to answer and phone calls to make, but today I refuse to do any of them. Instead, I seize the peace that I have only ever known in this place. This whitewashed villa, high in the hills around Cannes with its view of the sparkling sea and its fragrant grounds hidden down a winding road and behind high gates, is the one place in the world that I can really call home.

I have a very expensive penthouse flat in London in a desirable location and kitted out with everything that any man could want, but nothing rivals this place. I'd found it quite by accident when I was taking a short weekend away to celebrate making partner. I'd always loved the South of France from the holidays that I'd spent here as a child when something about the place had imprinted on me—the winding roads with their jaw-dropping views down to secluded coves lapped by the blue sea, the little villages with crooked paths redolent with the scents of fresh baking bread and garlic and the sheer profusion of scented plants everywhere. It's no wonder that the place is the centre for perfume making, because every breath that I take here is redolent with some blowsy new fragrance.

That weekend I'd been puttering around in an old Citroën, enjoying kicking back and feeling the excitement of having made it at becoming the youngest partner in the firm's history. I'd come across a fork in the road and some instinct had made me take the left-hand turn, leading me down a winding narrow lane towered over by tall cypress trees, broken occasionally by the quick glances of a sparkling Mediterranean sea.

I'd followed the road to where it ended in a dead end. Swearing under my breath, I'd just been about to execute the world's tightest three-point turn when I'd spied a sign attached to a rickety pair of old iron gates. It read 'For Sale' in French and curiosity had bloomed, and I'd found myself turning off the engine and getting out of the car. The gates had been secured with a huge, brand-new padlock, but looking up at them they'd looked sturdy, and feeling strangely compelled and ignoring the vision of making partner and being locked up in a French jail on the same weekend, I'd reached up and climbed over them.

I'd dropped down into a wilderness of overgrown greenery and the most startling colours and scents imaginable that overwhelmed the senses, so that I'd inhaled greedily. I've always had a weakness for scents and have always insisted on fresh flowers everywhere, so this was like paradise. Seeing what looked like a drive which was pitted with age, I'd followed it around until it led out onto a circular fore-court in front of an old derelict house.

It looked like an old Provençal style farmhouse, two storey with tall windows, but the paintwork had faded and chipped, and the windows were either dirty or broken. Following the house around, I saw that the path ran down the side of the house, and I followed it only to come up short when I saw the view. Beyond a swimming pool, which was empty apart from a few inches of stagnant water and copious amounts of ivy, was the most spectacular view of the Bay of Cannes curving around to Fréjus. It was an endless view of the sea sparkling under the fierce sun so intensely that I had to put my hand up to my eyes to shield them.

I'd turned back to the house and noticed what looked like an old broken-down veranda next to the pool, and instead my imagination had supplied a wide terrace around the pool, big sun loungers with bright cushions, and a rebuilt veranda covered with bougainvillea and shading a huge table and chairs for outside eating and looking out over that view.

I'd inhaled the sharp scents of lavender and eucalyptus, and I'd felt a peace stealing across my soul that I'd never felt before and certainly never since. It felt like this place in some strange way had been waiting for me, and that's why I hadn't taken the piss out of Charlie too much because I, too, fell in love with a tiny corner of a foreign country and had to have it.

I'd put in an offer that weekend using some of an inheritance that my grandfather had left me, finding and cajoling the estate agent out of a lazy Saturday with the promise of a huge commission. I'd pushed the sale fiercely, finding myself in the unique position of wanting something desperately. That attachment has never wavered over the years, and although I'd let Bella have our house without any argu-ment, she'd known not to go after this place. I'd have fought and won over that.

The distant chime of the doorbell startles me from my sleeping dream and I jerk, cursing softly. I wait for a second, but nobody is going to get that because Odell, my housekeeper, has gone home for the day. The bell sounds again, and I slide off the lounger, dragging a towel over my torso which is still wet from my swim but that will have to do, as whoever it is at the door will have to take me as I am.

I pad down the cool entranceway over the tiles and swing open the heavy wooden door, only to stand there open-mouthed. "You!" I say in consternation.

Matt stands there dressed in closely fitting, cuffed grey jogging bottoms paired with white Converse and a crumpled white t-shirt, and looks off-puttingly good-looking and cool. Half of his hair has been pulled up into a top knot, leaving the rest to fall around his face and neck in shades of blond and sand, and his eyes are covered by silver aviator sunglasses.

I run my hands over my own wet hair, feeling the wet strands hit the back of my neck, very aware that I'm standing in only a damp pair of swimming shorts. I'd hoped to meet him dressed properly and feeling put-together because something about this man makes me utterly discomposed. "You're early," I blurt out and then groan. "I'm so sorry. That came out so rudely. Please come in."

He smirks at me and shoves his sunglasses up over his hair, pushing the wavy blond strands back and revealing a pair of piercing brown eyes that are regarding me in an amused way and making my hackles rise again. I remind myself that I have to find a way to get on with this man because we're going to be sharing a home for the next few months, and really because I want him to like me, damn him. He likes everyone.

I stand back and he brushes past me, gifting me with the scent of coconut and a light trace of sweat. I gesture to his battered leather holdall. "Let me take that."

"Thanks, mate." His deep voice still bears the trace of North London where I think that he and the other men grew up.

"Let me show you to your room. I think you'll like it. It's got a wonderful view of the sea." *I'm babbling. I never fucking babble.*

I become aware that he's stopped moving and I turn back to him, raising my eyebrow queryingly. "I think that we should talk," he says, not perturbed by the eyebrow raise. *Damn, that's one of my best weapons.*

"Oh, yes?" I put his bag down.

He smiles and it looks almost nervous, but then I dismiss that thought. "I think that we got off to the wrong start," he says abruptly.

"You do?"

"Yes, and so do you." I smile involuntarily and his lips quirk. "Listen, I know you think that I don't like you."

I cover up my jerk of reaction with a shrug. "Well, you don't." I stop talking, aware that the thought hurts my feelings in some way. This man likes everyone. How unlikable must I really be if he doesn't like me? I have very few friends, and perhaps that's why. Perhaps his reaction is the true one. I feel my face close in the cold façade that I wear a lot to hide my soft side, but I'm amazed by his next words.

"I don't make snap judgements, John, but I did that night, so I'm sorry. It was a tense night and you came in so composed and controlled that it rubbed me up the wrong way, and I decided that I didn't like you." I don't think that my wince is covered up, because his eyes sharpen and then he shrugs. "But that was more about me than you."

"It's not me, it's you, then?" I ask wryly and he gives a startled laugh, making his eyes crinkle and his whole body relax.

"I've used that one a few times, but in this case it's the truth. I disliked you on sight because I mistakenly thought that you were fucking Mabe, and it solidified afterwards because I'm usually the one that sorts everything out and you stepped on my toes with your take-charge attitude." He shrugs. "Your porn joke didn't help."

I groan. "Oh shit, I was so embarrassed by that. I wanted to punch myself in the throat to stop talking." He laughs. "No, I really did. I'm not that sort of person at all, and I knew that you didn't like me, and for some reason my mouth decided to cast me as an immature wanker."

He laughs, his teeth gleaming white in his tanned face. "I knew that afterwards when I had the chance to think about it. You looked far too horrified for it to be true. The boys all really liked you as soon as they met you." I warm inside at this and give him a small smile which his eyes seem to stick to for a long second, and I wonder whether I've ever smiled at him before. He clears his throat. "I didn't really give you a chance, which was a shitty thing to do, so I'd like to give us a second chance to become friends. After all, we're going to be spending a lot of time together, and it would be a lot easier if it's not in conditions that would have made Stalin uncomfortable."

I give a startled bark of laughter, throwing my head back, and when I straighten it's to find him staring at me, his face curiously blank. I quickly offer my hand for him to shake and then swallow hard as his long fingers encircle mine. Something about the feel of his warm dry skin makes this seem almost portentous.

Dismissing this thought, I smile. "Okay, we'll give it another shot. Now, how about I show you around the villa and then to your room? You can have a shower and freshen up and then meet me downstairs, and I'll make you something to eat and we can go over the paperwork."

He nods and follows me out and through the villa like a lithe, blond shadow.

Matt

I follow him through the villa, marvelling at the size and also the comfort that it exudes. If you'd asked me a few months ago what furnishings he'd favour I'd have said leather and steel, practical and functional and cold. But that's not in evidence here. Instead I pass light oak furniture, a huge beige sectional sofa with deep cushions, comfortable chairs, and massive modern art hanging on the walls. Everything is done in shades of sand and cream and blue, echoing the colours of the sea that can be seen from nearly every window.

I pass light oak shelves stuffed with books, and not just the heavy legal tomes that I'd expected. They're there, of course, but they share space with battered paperbacks of thrillers and biographies.

We go up a marble staircase to a long hallway lit by large picture windows looking down on to the garden where I see the turquoise of an infinity pool, and I whistle under my breath. A house this big takes some serious cash, but I know that he's loaded, not just from his job as a lawyer, but also through his family who have a lot of money. If I remember rightly, Bram told me that his dad was something big in the city and his mother's family are landed gentry.

He shows me to a big white door which he opens and gestures to me to precede him. I edge past him, feeling the incredible heat that his tall body is giving off. I inhale subtly, smelling the scents of suntan oil and sweat. It makes my head swim, and I concentrate on the room. "It's lovely," I say simply. "Your home is gorgeous, John." He grins the same wide grin that he gave me earlier, which makes creases appear at the sides of those piercing blue eyes and the whole of his face light up.

I clear my throat. *Concentrate on the room,* I chant inwardly, *not on how much you'd like to lick him.* Luckily the room is beautiful. A massive bed with a tall petrol-blue fabric-covered headboard is made up with masses of pure white sheets and big fluffy pillows. It faces a pair of patio doors that let out onto a balcony, and when I wander over, I see that it runs the length of the house. I look down at the view of the sea sparkling in the sun with boats skipping along it with their sails out.

"Bathroom's through there," he says, his rich, deep voice making me jump at his nearness.

Turning, I almost overbalance as he's standing very close behind me, staring out at the view. I put out my hands to steady myself and swallow hard as I feel the sleek satin of his skin, still heated from the sun and slick with sun lotion. I move my hands away quickly, but the slickness of the lotion makes the gesture more of a caress than I'd intended, and I swallow hard as the atmosphere for a second seems to thicken.

Then his eyes crease in confusion and I make myself laugh carelessly and stand back. It's harder than I anticipate because he draws me like a magnet. "Sorry, I'm a bit of a klutz sometimes."

He clears his throat. "No problem. I'll leave you be, shall I? Come down when you're ready and we'll have a drink."

The door closes behind him and I fall back against the whitewashed wall, looking out at the sea but seeing instead that beautiful body clad only in navy checked swim shorts. He's broader than me, with big shoulders and a heavily muscled stomach leading to a mouth-watering 'v' and cut hipbones from which his board shorts hang. They'd been tight enough to be able to see the length of his cock occasionally.

My mouth waters and heat flushes through me at the thought, and without thinking I reach down into my jogging bottoms, digging into them and withdrawing my cock which is embarrassingly hard, drawn tight and throbbing with a drop of pre-come already glossing the mushroom head. Feeling like a total creeper but unable to stop myself, I spit into my hand and shuttle my hand firmly along my length. Just that one touch and the thought of his wet, hot body, and I feel my balls draw up and a jolt of electricity in the base of my spine. It only takes a few rough strokes and then my back arches and with a muffled grunt I come into my cupped hand, long and hard.

For a second I lean against the wall, panting like I've run a race and feeling the slickness of my come cool in my hand, and then I sigh. Wanking over my very straight housemate is never a good way to start things off.

John

The next morning, I sit under the veranda by the pool, reading a newspaper and drinking coffee while listening to the distant sounds of Odell bustling about in the kitchen. I think back to last night. Matt had come downstairs after an hour, hair loose and still wet from the shower, smelling of something citrus sweet and dressed in khaki shorts and a navy v-neck t-shirt.

He'd unloaded what looked like reams of papers tied up in red string from a leather document folio. I'd pushed my finger into the pile, tracing one document which bore the stamp of the French government, and indirectly the scent of endless bureaucracy. I'd looked up at him and his lips had twisted into a wry shape. "Have at it," he'd announced blithely, and then thrown himself down in the chair opposite me and poured himself a glass of rose from the bottle sitting next to him.

He'd then proceeded to chatter away about anything and everything, making me laugh quite a few times, and so the evening had gone over dinner and another bottle of wine until we were left with a potential hangover emerging, several neat piles of documents spread over the dining table, a battle plan for the weeks ahead, and what I feel to be the start of a tentative friendship. I hope so, because he draws me to him the way that certain people do when you meet them where it's an instantaneous feeling of kinship. I don't have enough friends, I think with a sense of sadness, and I'd very much like him to be one.

My thoughts stray to that moment in his room when his hand had slid down my arm. I'd felt instant scalding heat spread down in the path of his fingers, and his eyes had seemed to darken. I dismiss the thought as soon as it enters my head, as it did all last night lying in my bed. I know that he's gay; I have no problem with that, but apart from a few incidences of shared jerk-offs at my exclusive boys' boarding school, I'm definitely not gay, so I've decided that it must be due to my recent dry spell.

In my desire to win Bella back I'd recognised that sleeping with other women would be counterproductive, and so I've had several months of keeping company with my right hand, and obviously that's backfiring on me. *Bella will be back home soon,* I tell myself. *Just wait.*

My thoughts are interrupted by a husky-voiced 'good morning' from behind me. Putting my cup down, I turn and nearly swallow my tongue at the sight of him. Wearing only a pair of orange and white checked shorts and carrying a black t-shirt, his long body is on display.

He has a runner's physique, lean and tightly muscled with well-built long legs dusted with golden hair, and surprisingly elegant feet. Becoming aware that I'm staring at his body, I resolutely look at his face. "Do you run?" I ask inanely, but he smiles, throwing himself down in the chair opposite me and pouring himself a cup of coffee from the cafetière.

"I do."

"I thought that you must. You don't have the body of someone that sits in an office."

He laughs. "Unfortunately, that's all I have done lately, so this job is a nice change." He flicks a quick look at me. "Anyway, you can talk, your body is insane."

I look down at myself, oddly flattered and pleased that my daily gym workout is working. "I go to the gym every night," I admit. "I feel ratty if I don't get any exercise."

He nods. "I hear you. I run and I like the gym, but I mostly like anything that keeps me outside, so I try to go surfing in Cornwall most weekends."

"Whereabouts?" I ask idly. I'd been to Cornwall a couple of times as a student and enjoyed the wild beauty.

"Polzeath," he smiles. "I have a little house there."

I'm startled. "Being a PA must pay well," I say tactlessly, because property there is expensive. He looks up sharply, but rather than looking angry at my tactlessness, which sounds judgy to me, he grins. The smile elongates his eyes and picks out well-used lines at the side of his eyes which look like he's spent his life smiling. I like that, and I like his face with its high, sharp cheekbones, firm jawline covered in blond brown stubble, and full mouth. His face is full of life and energy and a smile that constantly hovers on his lips. He has a scruffy charm about him that I think I envy.

"I bought the house years ago, and it was in really bad condition

THE SUMMER OF US   31

then. I've spent a long time renovating it, and I suppose if I wanted to sell it I'd make a lot of money, but I love it too much to let it go." He looks at me as if considering something, and then says slowly, "I'm not just Bram's PA."

I jerk, afraid that he has taken umbrage after all. "There's nothing wrong with it," I say hurriedly, but he shakes his head.

"No, there isn't, and I do a PA job for Bram because he's my best friend and I love him, but unfortunately so does every person that has ever worked for him, some a bit too robustly."

"Not you?" I ask almost involuntarily, and he shoots me a very sharp look before taking a sip of coffee. "No, Bram and I are brothers in all but name. We've gone through a lot of shit together and we're as close as two people can be, but I've never fucked him, if that's what you're asking."

I swallow hard at the thought of that long hard body fucking anyone, but cover it with a sip of coffee. "I'm sorry, that was nosy." He shrugs lazily and I hasten on. "So what do you do if you're not just Bram's PA?"

"I own The Dalton Agency."

I put my cup down sharply, rattling it on the saucer. "You *own* that?"

He laughs. "Yeah, don't I look like your image of a boss?"

"Not really," I say honestly. "You look more like a surfer."

He throws his head back, laughing hard and making me smile widely at the sound. "Well, I suppose I am that, but it *is* my company so I can look how the hell I want." He stretches and pulls his t-shirt on.

"That's one of the biggest suppliers of quality, discreet staff, isn't it? I think that my secretary Carol came from there, and you've supplied staff to my parents."

He smiles. "I've supplied staff to a lot of people that you probably know, and Carol did come from me. You're very lucky to have her."

I smile. "I know, and she lets me know it as well." I lean back. "Well, well, you're a man of hidden talents."

He stretches languidly and reaches out to the plate of croissants, choosing one and tearing a piece off before popping it into his mouth with a throaty murmur, making me shift slightly. "I am, and one of those hidden talents—according to Charlie—is that of master builder, which must have been really well-hidden because even I didn't fucking know about it."

I laugh out loud. "Masturbator, more likely," I say, and his eyes seem to darken.

"Aren't we all?" he says slowly, staring at me hard before sliding his Oakley sunglasses down over his eyes.

I swallow and change the subject. "So, do you still want to go and have a look at the house?"

He laughs. "Might as well, mate. That's going to be my remand sentence for the next three months."

"Okay, finish up your breakfast and I'll take you."

He looks up, startled. "Don't be silly. I can do that. I know that you're busy."

I shrug and then shoot him a smile. "Not that busy, and anyway, I'm nosy. I fancy a peek at this house that made them fall in love with it at first sight."

He stares at me, his eyes hidden by the dark lenses. "Well, okay then, but be warned, Charlie has very odd tastes apart from Mabe. It could be anything."

An hour later we pull up outside what could best be classed as a ruin. We both get out of my car and stand staring open-mouthed at something that seems to be just a few walls and half a roof. Matt slowly lowers his glasses. "Oh my God," he says faintly. "Did they knock it down already?"

I look at him and suddenly give an enormous snort, and before I can say anything we both break into hysterical laughter, falling against the car and clutching our sides. Finally the laughter dies, and Matt straightens and walks towards the house, and I fall in next to him.

It's very quiet, apart from the sound of the cicadas, and I smell an herby fragrance that rises in the air as our shoes crush small plants into an old stone path. It feels like we might be the only two people in existence, and the house gives off a melancholy majesty which renders me silent for a minute.

We beat our way past some oversized lavender bushes into the back garden, and stand staring at the fantastic view of the Mediterranean. It's a clear day, and from here you can see the islands of Lérins in the distance. Matt looks sideways at me. "Well, he was right about the view," he offers, giving me a lopsided smile.

I turn back and look at the house objectively. "I think he was right about the house, too. Underneath all that ivy it looks like an Aix farmhouse." He looks at me in query. "A style of house. This one looks quite old. When done up they're usually very warm and welcoming."

"Like Mabe and Charlie," he murmurs, and I nod.

"They could have a nice place here."

He nods determinedly. "They will."

Something tells me that when he puts his mind to it he's an irresistible force, for all that laid-back charm. "So what's the plan?"

He sits down on the side of an old swimming pool, empty now, apart from a couple of inches of dirty water and a ton of ivy and weeds. Swinging his legs, he contemplates the house. "I've called a meeting here for the main contractor and his project manager. They're in charge of the major aspects of the build."

"English or French?"

"Both. They've got projects in England and Europe. They come highly recommended."

"And they know the time constraints?"

He nods. "They do. Charlie's offering a heavy bonus for completion, and I'm here to oversee everything and push what needs pushing."

I lower myself next to him, and for a minute we sit staring at the house in an easy silence. I shift and my arm brushes his, and I stiffen as what feels like an electric shock runs down my arm. His head shoots round and he stares at me, his expression hidden by his shades, with only the twist to his lips to indicate that he felt it, too.

We stare at each other for a second that stretches too long and I notice his chest rise and fall sharply, but then a loud cry from a seagull wheeling above seems to jerk him out of the awkwardness and he rises up from his sitting position, lowering his hand down to help me up.

For a second I stare at him. His outstretched hand seems like a challenge, so immediately I reach out, letting him pull me to my feet. However, as I stand I catch my foot on some ivy and my foot slips out from under me, and I waver on the edge of the pool, feeling myself begin to fall back. I close my eyes involuntarily, but before I can shout out he jerks me back, his lean form obviously concealing a great strength. For a second I rest against him, getting my breath back and feeling the warmth of him.

"Jesus Christ," he mutters, the vibrations of his voice seeming to flow through my body. I nod, unable to speak or move away from where I rest against him, his arms around me almost as if embracing me. We stay like that for a few seconds before he grabs my shoulders and eases me back. "Are you alright?" he asks, lifting his glasses to reveal stormy brown eyes. "That was a fucking near miss, John. You might have smashed your skull in on the bottom."

I feel my face flush and I stand back as he lets his arms fall away, seemingly reluctantly. For a second I feel cold without his warmth encircling me, but then I curse myself for a fool. He must think me a complete twat. One minute an arrogant overbearing tosser, according to him, and the next second falling over him like a delicate flower.

I lift my eyes reluctantly, already feeling that cool armour settling around me. "I'm fine," I say dismissively. "Nothing to get your knickers in a twist over."

His face twists at either my dismissive tone or words, and instantly his own cool expression slides over his face and I see a trace of the man that I'd met the first time. "Okay," he drawls, the word seeming to have ten more syllables than it normally does, and I flinch slightly, already missing that easy feel of before. His eyes sharpen for a second and his eyes seem to flame as if they're lasers seeing right through my coldness, which has put so many people at arm's length throughout my life, to the real me.

He stares at me for a long minute, and then I almost sag in relief as the coldness in his face slides away, replaced by the friendly amiable smile that crinkles his eyes. I think he notices the relief too, to my embarrassment, but I'm too relieved to have him looking at me like this again to really feel stupid.

"Well, if you're not swan diving into an empty pool, I guess the entertainment part of the afternoon is over," he drawls. "Let's get back to summing up just how much more work is actually involved than Charlie quite covered with his offer of a three-month luxury holiday away from my troubles."

Matt

That evening I stand against my balcony looking down at the lights of Cannes that twinkle in the distance. The sky is a soft velvety blue, and a refreshing breeze blows in from the sea, tousling my hair and drying the drops of water on my body left from my shower.

I push my hair back with a sigh and then brace my hands on the balcony, looking down at the lone figure standing in the garden against the backdrop of sea and lights. He stands dressed only in a pair of blue shorts looking out in a contemplative silence, and I stare at him, enjoying the opportunity to look my fill without making him uncomfortable.

He's such a gorgeous man. I'd seen that at first glance, but every minute that I spend with him makes me more uncomfortable at the way that I misjudged him. I'd seen only the confident, arrogant way that he held his body, and heard only the arrogance in his clear, upper-class accent. I hadn't seen the vulnerability that lies under-neath, or maybe it wasn't there for me to see then. Maybe it's only now when he's at home that it shines through.

I'd thought him a careless man whose way through life had been easy, greased by his looks, money, and family name. I don't think that anymore, and it's an opinion firmed by this afternoon. More and more I've seen a loneliness in him that's soul-deep. He holds himself separately, I think, not because he thinks himself better than anyone else, but because he sees no value in his own company.

My interest sharpens because I've always been attracted to the lonely ones, the ones that need care. Something in them calls out to my nature, and it's always made me happy to look after people. The problem with that, according to Bram, is what I see as a misunderstood soul, the rest of the world sees as an unmitigated twat.

I stare down at John again. I don't think that about him. I want to know him. I want to search out his secrets and find out what made him like this. I want to watch him bloom, to see those crinkles at the edge of those vibrant blue eyes grow deeper as the years go by, showing that he finally knows how to laugh at life, rather than be buttoned down and ready for what it throws at him.

I sigh, because unfortunately this impulse comes hand in hand with others. While I want to teach him to let go and smile, I also want to slide my cock into his warm body until he screams. I want to fuck into him until he comes like he's never come before.

I shake my head because this can't go anywhere. I've slept with supposedly straight men before and the sex was fantastic, because introducing a man to what his body can really feel like when a man takes hold of it is a thrill in itself. However, that thrill never lasted after the next day when they crept back into the closet, shutting the door behind them and leaving me feeling used and slightly ashamed.

John's straight, and I have to get this thought set firmly in my head, because no matter how curious he might be about me—and he is, I can feel it—he is still apparently in love with his ex-wife, according to the others. I don't want to be a curiosity anymore. I want to matter. I want to be loved and love in return.

I take one last look and then move silently back into my bedroom, leaving that lonely figure still staring out at the sea, lost in thought.

3

John

TWO WEEKS later I sit on the patio in the early evening sun, sipping Pastis and keeping an ear out for the return of my housemate. I haven't seen much of him since the afternoon that we'd gone to look at Charlie's house.

He leaves early in the morning and comes back late, usually filthy dirty and knackered. We have a drink and he eats and then retires to his room where, he informed me yesterday, he literally passes out from exhaustion until the next morning.

The house has seemed incongruously empty without him, but part of me has been relieved not to see him. In some way, I've felt almost embarrassed since that afternoon. It feels like I let him see under my armour, and now I'm curling away under my shell from that penetrating gaze of his that sees things that others don't. I take a hefty slug of my drink, wincing, because even thinking this makes me feel like a completely feeble twat.

I have, however, managed to fit in a lot of work, so his absence has had a positive effect. I've traipsed off to my study as soon as he leaves in the mornings and I've stayed there resolutely at my desk, which I'd deliberately positioned years ago to face away from the view. If I was looking out at the sea I could quite easily spend hours daydreaming, and, as my father has always pointed out, daydreaming doesn't sign cheques.

He'd been particularly concerned when I was young because I was a huge daydreamer, drifting along happily in a daze. I'd always completed my homework, but it was at a pace known only to myself and a few snails. That had stopped when he'd sent me to boarding school at the age of seven in the hope that it would snap me out of my bad habits. Needless to say, it did, and now I'm renowned at work for the hours that I log in at my desk.

My thoughts are interrupted by the sound of the gate and footsteps sounding out on the flagstones. Against my will I feel my heartrate accelerate, and I rub my chest absently. I really must be starved of friendship if just having someone's company leaves me like this. My thoughts are forgotten, though, when he rounds the corner of the villa and I burst out laughing.

"What the fuck have you been *doing?*"

He smirks, his teeth shining whitely in his tanned face which is now covered by a thick layer of dirt. He's half-naked in just a pair of cargo shorts and battered old combat boots with his t-shirt hanging around his neck, and the same dirt coats his arms and legs and lean torso, clinging to the sweat covering him. "Had a bit of a messy day," he laughs, coming to one of the patio chairs where he hovers, looking helplessly at the scarlet cushions.

"Oh, for fuck's sake, sit down. The cushion will wash."

He shrugs and settles down gingerly, and then relaxes back against the chair with a throaty murmur of pleasure which hits me in my belly. Pushing it aside, I pour a glass of Pastis for him and push the jug of water towards him. This has become a bit of a ritual lately, in that we meet like this every evening sitting over the Pastis and chatting about our day. I'm almost embarrassed to recognise how much I look forward to it.

I wait until he's taken his first sip and lit a cigarette before speaking. "So?"

He inhales sharply on the cigarette and sends a swirl of smoke into the air. "We were looking for the water supply and it's taken all day. Apparently the French authorities don't see a legal need to register water systems and septic tanks on private property, which is why the plumber and I have spent all day traipsing all over the property looking for water. I felt very Russell Crowe from 'The Water Diviner' after a bit. I just needed some angle rods."

I laugh out loud. "Didn't Charlie give you the title of Overseer? Doesn't that mean that you sort of oversee, maybe by floating around with a clipboard and looking official?"

He grins. "Yes, Charlie did give me that title, but unfortunately I think that he and Mabe might want to actually bathe when they stay here, and you can't find water with a clipboard. I know that because I've tried every other bloody way known to man today."

I laugh, and a companionable silence falls for a few minutes as we stare out at the late evening sun hitting the sea and making everything look golden. Finally I stir. "Fancy doing something different tonight?"

He looks sideways at me, his cigarette hanging loosely from his full lips. "Different from falling into bed and being asleep before most old-aged pensioners? You fucking bet I do. What have you got in mind?"

"There's a firework display tonight in Cannes for the opening of a new casino." He smiles and I hasten on. "I know it sounds a bit childish but it's a big deal round here. The fireworks are usually spectacular when they do this and it's a nice night, so I thought we could drive out and take some food to a little beach near here because it'll be difficult to get anywhere near Cannes tonight." He smiles at me and I try to glare. "What?"

"I just never pictured you for the firework and picnic type of person. I thought that you'd be more gentleman's clubs and casinos."

"Like James Bond?" I raise one eyebrow and he laughs.

"Less Roger Moore and more Sean Connery."

I try a Scottish accent. "I'm flattered."

He stares at me for a second. "You should be," he says in a low voice, and then his face clears. "Please don't ever do a Scottish accent again. You sound like you come from Birmingham."

I laugh and stand up. "Go get showered, you dirty bastard, and hurry up because the fireworks are waiting."

"You sound like a little kid."

"One that's about to have a tantrum if I don't get my fireworks and food."

"Okay, okay." He stands up and stretches lazily before wandering inside, dirt falling from him at every step. I stare after him, marvelling at how he's changed me. A few weeks ago my OCD tendencies would have seen me following him with a sweeping brush and dustpan, but now I just take another sip of my drink and look up at the sky flaming with colour.

Matt

An hour later, showered and dressed in a red polo shirt and stone cargo shorts, I'm sitting beside him as he throws his car round the tight bends of the coastline roads. The top is down and the wind blows my hair around.

I'm trying hard not to look down at the steep drop by the side of the road, but if I'm not looking there then I'm being a creeper, because I'm drawn to the strength of his tanned hands as they grip the steering wheel and the veins that show in his arm as he grips the gear stick and easily changes gear. I can't help but wonder what those long fingers would look like curled around my dick, and then curse myself and shift in my seat as my dick hardens.

Catching my movement, he looks sideways at me and smiles a

mischievous smile that I'm seeing a lot lately, the one that elongates a pair of dimples that I have never seen before. "Scared?" he asks in his deep, rich voice.

I clear my throat from the thick heat that's lingering there and put my feet up on the dashboard. I'm aiming for a dash of insouciance and a whole lot of concealing my hard-on. "Not at all," I murmur. "I've driven with Bram in Italy, and he's got the attention span of a flea."

For a second I'm sure that he's going to tell me to take my feet off the pristine interior of his Jaguar E-Type, as he's always seemed like the ultimate in tight arses to me and not the good kind, but again he surprises me when he laughs and ignores my feet in their red, white, and blue checked Vans. "Is he really that bad?"

I'm confused, my thoughts scattered by the sight of that wide, joyous smile and the sound of his laughter. "Who?"

He shoots me a quizzical look. "Bram."

I relax. "Oh yeah, definitely. He's very absentminded. He parked his Porsche in a short stay car park at Heathrow Airport once and forgot it."

He whistles. "Was it while he was away for a few weeks? Because my God, that's expensive!"

I shake my head. He really doesn't know Bram. "No, three years."

He laughs out loud, and then slows the car before pulling it over to the side of a road and tucking it under a wide tree. He turns to look at me.

"Here?" I ask stupidly.

He shrugs. "Like I said, the beaches at Cannes will be full and I know this beach well. I've been coming here for a walk for a few years and I've never seen another soul here, and it will have a perfect view of the fireworks. I know, because they went off one night when I was walking and I nearly shit myself."

I laugh and he opens the boot, removing a picnic basket and grabbing an old plaid blanket, and then he nods towards a narrow path. "We go down that way."

I wander over and peer down before stepping back quickly. "Fuck, that's a steep drop."

He walks up next to me, cocking his head appraisingly. "I think that's why it's usually deserted. There's a lot of these little coves dotted around here."

"Waiting for mountain goats and you, I should think. Well, come on, then, I'm fucking starving." He smiles and hands me the blanket and goes back to retrieve a cool bag before locking the car. I look at the assortment of bags. "Are we picnicking or moving house?"

"Shut the fuck up. You'll be glad of these later."

I open the cool bag and see a couple of wine bottles, their glass glistening with cold. "Yep, you've got that right. You see, this is why I'm gay. If I was with a woman, some valuable alcohol space would have been wasted on candles."

"And that's the only reason that you're gay? I didn't realise it was mainly a packing and alcohol dilemma."

I lower my sunglasses and give him a long look, trying hard to ignore how good he looks in a pair of navy blue shorts and red checked shirt. "No, there's a much *bigger* reason." I want him flustered, for some reason. I need to see this confident man on the back foot, something that doesn't happen very often. But yet again he surprises me by laughing with no trace of embarrassment.

"Those who boast most usually have the least, as my old nanny always used to say. Come on, maybe your extra limb will help with your dexterity."

He saunters off down the path leaving me laughing, and then I hasten to catch up with him, feeling the lingering heat from the sun still warm in the enclosed cove. I stop a second to admire the golden sand and the water sparkling red in the last few minutes of the sunset. "This place really is beautiful," I murmur, inhaling the scent of eucalyptus and salt that's heady in the air.

He looks back at me, his face softening. "It really is," he says happily. "I try and come here most mornings for a swim before I get the newspapers."

"*That's* where they come from. I thought that you had them delivered and Odell had been up all night ironing them. Felt a bit like 'Downton Abbey' in my head."

He shoots me a glare and I throw my head back laughing, and follow him down the steep path. "Seriously though, John, I'll come with you in the mornings if you don't mind the company. I love swimming in the sea first thing. It wakes me up."

He looks back at me. "I'd like that," he says, almost shyly. "I've never had company before, but I forgot your love of the sea."

I shoot a look at his back when he faces forward again. I've noticed this last couple of weeks that he always seems surprised if I express pleasure in his company, and I vow then that I'm not going to just fuck off to bed from now on, no matter how knackered I am. I like this man, and I want to spend more time with him. I also want him to share this place with me because I get the feeling that he shares very little with people, not from natural distance as I'd originally thought, but because he's unaccustomed to doing it. I refuse to think too much about how much I enjoy him. *He's a friend to me,* I chant inwardly, as I've found myself doing a lot.

We make it down to the beach and I humour him by spreading out the blanket to military precision and then setting out the picnic basket. I think of my weekends surfing when dinner might be a bag of chips eaten happily with a beer, in my wetsuit sitting on a damp towel. However, when I look into the basket I see cold roast chicken and salad, some of Odell's white bean tapenade to spread on baguettes, as well as her gorgeous yoghurt cake which is arguably better than chips. Eating the food from the plates that he produces with a flourish is also much more civilised than eating with my fingers. However, while I sip rose wine from a crystal wineglass, I still make a mental vow that if we become friends then I'll take him to Cornwall and make him eat chips on a soggy towel.

I snort at the thought, and he looks quizzically at me where I'm lounging back on the towel, replete and content to lie with my head cushioned on my rolled-up hoody, talking occasionally and then lapsing into what, with him, are comfortable silences. With him I'm never stuck for conversation, and even when we don't talk, he doesn't feel the same need that Ed did to fill every second with noise while missing out on the beauty that a night like tonight brings, with the sun vanishing and letting Cannes come out to play like a funfair with twinkling lights and the sound of music drifting on the breeze.

"What?" he asks, and I stare at him for a second. He looks utterly content to sit back lounging against a rock staring out to sea, and I see that all the little lines on his face which come, I think, from stress, are utterly smoothed out like the sand when the tide retreats.

Then I realise that he's asking me what I'm laughing at, but I shake my head, and instead ask the question that's been at the back of my mind since we came down to the beach. "You mentioned a nanny. Did your mum work?"

He snorts. "No, of course not. My mother has never worked a day in her life." He pauses. "She sits on committees."

"Sounds painful," I comment, and he roars with laughter.

"I know. I just had a mental image of her squatting over some terrified members of the Women's Institute. Scary." He looks out of the corner of his eye at me. "The committees kept her too busy to look after me and she wasn't naturally maternal." He smiles. "Or warm, either, so we had a succession of nannies."

"A succession? Were you that bad?"

He shakes his head and an almost angry expression crosses his face. "No, I was good. It was my *father* that was bad."

"Oh? *Oh.*" I realise what he means.

"Yes. I was actually quite glad to go off to boarding school, to be honest, because home was never much fun with heated recriminations flying around along with the family china, and yet another nanny packing her bag."

"Not exactly 'Mary Poppins' then?" I muse, and he snorts out a laugh.

"Fuck, no, very far from it. More like Confessions of a Domestic."

He pauses and then shoots me a surprised look. "Bloody hell, I think that's the first time that I've ever laughed about that."

I shrug. "Don't feel guilty, if that's what's on the tip of your tongue to say. It wasn't your fault, and you either laugh or cry."

"Is that how you've lived your life?"

I think back over the years and the mess of my childhood, and then I think of Bram and the boys and nod slowly. "I suppose when you look at it, yes, that's what I do. It's what we've always done. If you can laugh then they haven't won."

He stares at me for a long second as that blunt little statement folds into the ether, and then something else drags my attention. Really, he's a source of immense interest to me. I want to hear all about his life. I want to know everything. Curiosity about people has always been one of my vices. One of them, anyway—I have many. "When did you go to boarding school?"

He looks out to sea. "When I was seven."

"*What?*" The volume of my voice scares away some seagulls loitering nearby in the hope of pinching any leftovers.

He smiles. "You heard me."

"Fucking hell, seven. That's young."

He shrugs, getting to his feet and brushing the crumbs off. "Not really. Amongst my mother's family that's about normal. Shall we go for a walk?"

I forbear from pointing out that there's nothing fucking normal about sending a baby away from home that early, and instead let him pull me to my feet, feeling the warmth and strength in his hand. I want to ask whether he would send his own child away at that age, but I don't bother because I think that I already know the answer in the form of the decent and honourable, if stern, man walking away down the beach.

I catch up with him, making sure that I kick some water up the back of his legs, hitting his backside.

"Twat," he says affectionately, and then bends down and catches a big handful of water, scooping it up and throwing it at me.

"Fucking hell," I shout, backpedalling and joining in with his helpless laughter, glad to see his sad look gone. I don't like to see him sad.

We exchange some more sallies, and then by unspoken agreement we walk on. It's beautiful out here now with a huge yellow moon making it almost as light as day, and the only sounds are the lap of the water, the crunch of the sand, and the distant sound of music from Cannes. He looks sideways at me where I'm looking out at the bright lights. "So that's my fucked-up childhood, what about yours?"

I hesitate because I never tell anyone this, ever. My life began when I found my real family in the boys and I don't like to dwell on what went before, but something about the quietness and not looking at each other helps when exchanging secrets. Something in this man makes me want to let him in, to tell him things about myself that I wouldn't tell anyone else. It's not the way that I do things. I keep the secrets, including my own.

He must take my hesitation for refusal, because he shakes his head a little sadly. "Never mind. Not my business. I—"

I interrupt. "No, it's not that, it's just hard to remember and speak of it because I tucked it away a long time ago." I pause and then go on, my throat thick. "My family are very strict Roman Catholics." He looks at me, waiting, and I swallow hard. "As good abiding Catholics they disapprove of homosexuality."

He looks as if a lightbulb has turned on. "Ah! Oh, Matt."

I nod, determined to get this out quickly. "As such, when I came out to my parents it wasn't exactly a Hallmark moment." I pause and laugh. "Well, not unless that Hallmark moment includes punching your son in the face."

"Jesus fucking Christ!" He paces back to me, water splashing around his ankles and glowing bright in the moonlight, and I gulp as he gets close. "What happened?" he asks fiercely.

I shrug. "He got in a few good punches because I was too surprised to do anything." I'm ashamed that I feel the need to justify my failure to hit back and he must sense this, because he's shaking his head before I can finish the sentence.

"Matty, it's a rare son that hits back the first time that his father lifts a hand to him." I look up, caught first by his use of the nickname that Bram uses for me, which sounds different and somehow *more* when said in his rich, deep voice. I'm held, however, by the odd note of conviction in his voice, as if he knows. "What happened then?" he asks.

I look at him, the moonlight catching in his hair making his eyes look almost black. "He threw me out of the house," I say quietly. "With only the clothes I had on. I had to leave that night."

"How old were you?" he asks fiercely.

"Fifteen."

"Fuck," he exclaims. "What sort of person does that to their own child?"

I shrug. "A heavily religious one?"

"Where did you go?"

I smile more genuinely at this. "I went to Bram's house, confessed I was gay, answered his highly involved and intrusive questions, and then he snuck me into his room to sleep for a few nights and after that whenever he wouldn't get into trouble." He looks at me and I shrug. "Another story."

"So what happened? When did your father have you back?" I stare at him and he seems to fold in slightly. "He didn't have you back, did he?" I shake my head. "What happened? Did social services get involved?" He hesitates. "Did you go into care?"

I shake my head. "I never reported it and nobody in authority guessed."

"*What?*"

I smile at his indignation. Nobody apart from the lads has ever seemed this bothered by my upbringing, and they were all going through their own shit, anyway. "I didn't want to report it. If I had, I'd have been taken into care and I could have been moved anywhere. I didn't want that."

"Because of the lads?" he asks gently, and I nod.

"Exactly. They were more my family than my own parents were by that point. I couldn't bear to be taken away from them."

"So what did you do?"

"I only had a few months left at school, so I forged signatures on school letters and slept on Bram's floor for a few nights at a time, and at Charlie and Sid's house for the rest. Their mum, Jen, was the best. She used to feed me and let me sleep there. When I left school I got a job on a construction site and got a bedsit, and repaid the favour to Bram by letting him bunk with me when his home life got too bad."

I forbear from mentioning sleeping on benches before I started work, but he shoots me a keen glance as if he suspects that more happened. "Did you ever reconcile?"

I shake my head. "My dad died three years ago and my mum forbade me to go to the funeral. I haven't seen her since I was thrown out." I swallow hard at the thought of the mum that I'd loved so much as a small child. She'd been warm and loving and everything to me and I'd thought that she'd always protect me, but she didn't even protect me from my father, and my last memory is of her standing silently and stone-faced to one side as my dad grabbed me by the throat and threw me out like a piece of rubbish for the bin men.

Suddenly heat surrounds me and I gasp as John stands close and pulls me against him in a tight hug, one hand curled around my skull keeping me against him as I stiffen in surprise. "I'm so sorry, Matty," he whispers, and I stand still for a second until against my will my body suddenly slackens and I let my full weight slump against him, feeling his weight and knowing with a deep certainty inside me that he will hold me up.

We stay like that for what feels like forever but is actually only a few minutes, him offering comfort and me taking it without any need for words, until a sudden massive bang makes us jump apart and the sky above us explodes in reds and golds and greens.

"Fucking hell, I'd forgotten the fireworks," he shouts, holding his hand to his chest like a little old lady, and something in his indignant expression that says how dare the fucking world have restarted itself without his express permission, makes me start to laugh. Once I start I can't stop until he joins me, touching my shoulder as we bend double laughing until tears slide down our faces as Cannes sets light and colour to the night.

4

John

A FEW DAYS later I sit on the patio, cradling a cup of coffee and staring out to sea. However, I don't see the view that normally calms me because of the image that's still in my head of a young, bruised boy limping back to his best friend because his bastard of a dad couldn't see what a wonderful man he was bringing up. I grip the cup tighter. I'm so angry that a man like Matt had so much thrown at him at such a young age, and then I wonder whether the man he became is actually *because* of that treatment.

He'd risen like a phoenix from the ashes of his childhood, had really made something of himself and drawn his own family to him, and I feel an odd sense of pride in him. Odd, because I don't normally delve into the deeper feelings and motivations of people. This probably makes me sound like a complete bastard and maybe I am, because people's feelings are so fucking messy at times and they cover you in feelings that are sticky.

I spare a second's thought as to why Matt is different, but I don't know the answer, and that fucking irritates me as well. I like being in charge of my destiny, secure in my ability to handle events and people. Matt's like one of those rogue breezes that appear out of nowhere and knock everything over and mess things up. I snort, and then jump as I hear his sleepy voice behind me.

"What the hell are you laughing about by yourself, you total weirdo?"

I laugh. "It's not weird if the imaginary people laugh back."

He sneers at me and yawns widely, his eyes barely slits as he flings himself down into his customary chair, taking the coffee that I hand him and then snatching a croissant from the basket that I proffer. I smile evilly at him as he suddenly seems to catch onto the fact that I'm second-guessing him and he shakes his head and yawns without covering his mouth, showing a pink tongue and white teeth.

"Why are you up?" I ask, eyeing his half-naked body clad only in a pair of pink patterned board shorts, before tearing my own croissant up and adding some of Odell's homemade jam to it. Delicious. "You're surely not at work this weekend, are you? It's a French bank holiday. Nobody will be at work."

He shakes his head wryly. "And that makes it different from any other day how?"

I smirk. "Having problems with the French workforce?"

"Well, the half that actually turns up." He flails his hand slightly. "They do an hour or two, tops, and then it's like a buzzer goes off and they down tools, take out tables and chairs, for fuck's sake, and all this bloody food and wine. Lots and lots of wine, and that's it for at least two hours. They even have *serviettes*." I laugh out loud and he sneers. "Oh, laugh away. I don't take that much care or that much time to eat when I'm on *holiday*, for fuck's sake."

I shrug. "They'll probably live longer than you and I. They've maybe got the right idea."

He smiles. "Probably, but if Charlie wants to get this villa done before he draws his pension, which, by the way, is going to be a small one the way that we're going, then he'll have to bring some other workers over to supplement the lunch hour alone."

I smile. "You'll get there. They like you."

I'm speaking the truth. The French workers can be insular and take a while to warm up to people but they have warmed to him, as I'd seen when I'd visited the site a few days ago to find him sitting in the middle of them. He was filthy dirty, telling scurrilous stories in his quick French with a wide white grin as they roared with laughter.

I think some of it is because he speaks French and is happy to have the piss taken out of him for getting words wrong, but also because he works hard. He could totally sit back in the shade with his feet up, supervising, but instead he's hurled himself amongst them and no job is too dirty or tiring for him. Men appreciate that, and the fact that he's funny with this warm, scruffy charm doesn't hurt, either.

The ringing of his phone interrupts my thoughts, and he lifts his narrow hips, pulling his phone from his back pocket. He looks at the display and a wide smile curves his mouth as he answers it. "Dude, you so can't live without me." He laughs loudly at the reply and then casts a glance at me and mouths 'Bram' which for some reason makes me relax. *What the fuck is the matter with me?*

I become aware of him gesturing to me. "What?"

He covers the mouthpiece. "It's Bram. He's coming over to visit for the weekend."

I smile. "He really can't live without you."

He shakes his head dismissively. "Is that okay with you?" he asks seriously.

I'm puzzled. "Of course it is, Matt. He's your best friend. He'll stay here, of course?"

"I'd thought that he'd stay at a hotel, but that's a much better idea. Is that okay with you, though?"

"Of course it is, I wouldn't ask otherwise." He looks at me, seemingly oblivious to the stream of words still coming from the phone.

"Really," I say when he still hesitates. "I never say anything that I don't mean. I don't make idle gestures."

He stares at me for a second and something in him seems almost startled as if that's a novelty to him, before he nods and smiles widely, his teeth white in his narrow, tanned face. "That's great, John. It's perfect timing for a weekend. We can all go out."

I nod and my surprise must show in my face because he looks fully at me. "Surely you didn't think that I'd leave you out, Johnny," he says affectionately. "I'd never do that. You're my mate."

I warm inside at the thought of meaning something to him, and then grab his arm as he turns back to his phone. He stills abruptly, apart from a jerk that runs fully down his body like a wave breaking the stillness of the sea, and I still at the charge that runs through my body. I exchange a long look with him which I think adequately conveys that I have no fucking idea what just happened, and then I grab at my thoughts which have scattered.

"Tell him to bring Viv," I say quickly, my tongue feeling a bit thick. He raises his eyebrows in question, a flush sitting high on his cheeks. "She sounded down when I spoke to her yesterday. I want her here where I can keep my eye on her." He looks at me, and I shrug. "Okay, so that I can interrogate her."

He laughs out loud and ruffles my hair with an affectionate hand before turning back to the phone excitedly, and I sit for a long second, staring at someone who I'd rather look at than a view that I spent millions on obtaining. I shrug. *What the fuck is happening to me?*

FIVE HOURS later we stand at the door and watch a taxi pull up the drive. "Jesus, he doesn't waste time, does he?" I murmur, and Matt laughs happily.

"Never has, never will. He gets an idea and he just goes for it. Apparently that's why he's so 'successful.'" He says the last bit in air quotes and I laugh before turning back to the taxi where a long pair of jean-clad legs are emerging, followed by the rest of the bass guitarist. He's a very good-looking bloke and constantly in the papers for his exploits, but at the moment his face is split wide in a massive grin as he drops his bags and races to meet Matt, who's also rushing forward. They collide and Bram wraps his long legs around Matt's waist, sending both of them plummeting to the ground in fits of laughter.

The driver emerges, looking at the two of them with a raised eyebrow before taking the bags from the boot. I smile at him, but my attention is mainly fixed on the woman emerging from the taxi clad in a long burgundy maxi dress, her silky dark hair flying in the breeze.

"Hi, sweetheart," I call out, opening my arms wide for her to step into and then hugging her tightly, resting my head on hers and inhaling the scent of her shampoo and feeling that sense of comfort that I've always had with her.

I'd first met Viv when she arrived as a secretary at the law firm at a time when I was still doing the grunt work as an associate. We'd quickly bonded over long nights in the office and eating takeout when most sane humans had left work and were tucked up in bed. She'd become someone that I viewed as indispensable, to the extent that as I rose in the firm, I took her with me and championed her being trained as a paralegal. She now works with me full-time.

Bella had never liked her, but that's because she'd never got to know her. Viv could never have been a threat because she doesn't poach other women's men and she's hopelessly in love with someone else.

She sighs heavily and nestles close. Something about her body feels tight, and I notice with concern that she's lost weight. "Going to tell me about it yet?" I ask, raising her chin up so that I can see into her deep brown eyes, but she just smiles and shakes her head.

"Nope. I'm fine, babe. I'm just glad that this happened. I need this time away, and I just want to lie in the sun and get drunk."

"No change, then, from any other day." I snort and contort myself away from her as she aims a punch at my midriff. Looking up, I still as

I see Matt leaning against the car, staring at us with an inscrutable look on his face. I smile, but instead of his normal wide grin I get a half-hearted tip of his lips before he turns back to Bram who's collecting the luggage. I wonder what's upset him, but I don't get a chance to ask as they join us and I'm swept up into the house with everyone talking at once.

Matt

I lie in the sun, enjoying the rare opportunity to just be still without being either filthy or so knackered that I'm nearly comatose. I can hear Viv talking in the lounge and the occasional sound of John's deep chuckle, which never fails to make me smile.

Bram's Irish lilt comes from my right. "What's given you that oh-so-very big smile, Matty darling?"

I laugh. "It must be because you're here. You know how your very presence has the power to lift my day."

"I do," he says in a lordly fashion, and I open my eyes to see him settling next to me on a lounger. "Don't worry." He pats my leg comfortingly. "You're in a group of billions with those sentiments."

"How cosy."

We're silent for a second and then he shifts, never content to sit still for long. "How's the building work going?"

I seesaw my hands. "Somewhere between crap and diabolical."

He snorts out a laugh. "Fucking hell, Charlie really shafted you with this." I lower my glasses to give him a long look and he shifts uncomfortably. "I mean, how *great* is it that Charlie obviously trusts you with something that means so much to him?"

I hold my nose in the universal sign for bullshit, and he laughs but looks strained. To everyone else, he would look his normal easy-going self, but I know him inside out and the signs are all there—the fidgeting and the over-bright remarks that can only mean one thing. "How's Alys?" I ask, and then sit back and wait. The response about his lodger isn't long coming.

"Do you know what she did this time? She only told some bird that I'd brought home that I'd got a mad wife locked up in the attic who was violent with a habit of setting fires, and that I was planning to marry the bird without telling her about my first wife."

"Isn't that the plot for 'Jane Eyre'?"

"*Exactly*," he says indignantly. "I told the girl that, but she still didn't get it. Why don't they make models read more?"

"It might make their brains heavy," I say comfortingly and he laughs, but it dies quickly and he rubs his hand along his leg fretfully. "I'll say this again, Bram. How's Alys?"

He looks away over the gleaming blue of the pool. "She hardly talks to me now, and she's rarely at the flat." He shrugs clumsily. "I just miss her, you know?"

I sigh. "Bram, I don't know what happened and I know that I'm not going to find out, which says to me that you've done something very silly, or otherwise you'd tell me." I pause, staring hard at him, and he fidgets nervously. "Or," I say slowly. "She's hurt you in some way. That's about the only thing you won't cop to because let's face it, silly behaviour is the norm for you."

"Hey!" he says crossly, but I ignore him.

"Bram, babe, you have to talk to her."

He shakes his head stubbornly. "She's made her mind up, so I'm just getting on with business now."

"Stupid whoremongering business," I mutter.

"Speaking of business," he says, changing the subject adroitly and gesturing to the lounge. "What's going on here? Have you turned another one, then?"

"Oh my God, please don't say that," I groan. "And especially don't say that to John."

"Why?"

"Because you make me sound like a fucking wizard from Harry Potter."

He smirks. "Bet you've got the biggest and prettiest wand, baby."

"Oh my God, please stop," I groan, but the twat keeps laughing at his own silly joke.

Finally he sobers and stares at me hard. "Seriously, though, I'm glad that you're getting on better with him. John's a bloody great bloke, but he's just a bit uptight when you first meet him. Although really it was only you that had the problem with him, anyway."

I shrug. "I've just got to know him, I suppose."

"In the biblical sense?"

"Fuck off." He must hear the edge in my voice because he pauses and looks at me closely.

"Matt, you seem very close with him, and I've certainly never seen him this relaxed. You look together." I say nothing and he looks worried, sitting up and grabbing my knee. "I just don't want to see you get hurt, babe, because I saw the way that you looked when he hugged Viv."

I feel a flush on my cheeks, because for one brief second I'd been levelled by jealousy. I'd wanted to reach over and pull his arms away from her and grab his attention back, which is ridiculous and alarming in one go. I become aware that he's still talking.

"It's just that he wants to get back together with his ex-wife, and I know you, Matty. You're not a relationship wrecker. You'd hate yourself if you did that. You've been with other supposedly straight men but those were just one-nighters. I've never seen you like this before, and I'm fucking worried."

I stare at him for a second, wanting so much to confide in him the horrible mass of feelings that are bubbling up in me all the time, but I can't articulate them properly in my head, let alone set voice to them. Instead I reach over and ruffle his hair affectionately. "Don't worry, babe, I've got no intention of starting anything, even if I could. He's not for me. He's definitely not interested, and I've never been one for barking up the wrong trees."

He looks thoughtful and conflicted. "Matty, I just said to be careful, but thinking about it, he's so different with you. Maybe—"

I shake my head decisively. "Enough now. Come on, I'll take you over to see Charlie's money-maker. I'm sorry, that should have been money-taker."

He laughs, and by unspoken agreement we say no more about our mutually shitty love lives.

John

It's twilight and I stand outside, waiting for the others with a drink in my hand. I'm dressed in grey herringbone checked shorts with a white polo shirt, and I've just taken a sip of my scotch when a shadow detaches from the house and Matt joins me, coming to stand next to me and look out in the direction that I've just been staring blindly.

"You do this a lot," he murmurs.

"What?"

"Looking out to sea in this exact position."

I smile. "It's the best view around." I shrug, not wanting to give him the flippant answer at viewing what I've paid for. "I just like the sea, I guess, and not just here. I like it when the beach is windswept and raining just as much as I like the pretty postcard views. I always have done but it's not exactly productive."

He looks at me sideways. "What?"

"It isn't productive to daydream."

"*Productive?*" He says the word curiously.

I smile at him. "I tend to be a bit of a daydreamer. My father tried everything to cure me of it. In the end it was the discipline of boarding school that did it for me."

"When you were seven," he says slowly.

"Exactly. My father was right, I suppose. Daydreaming doesn't sign cheques, and I wouldn't be where I am today if I hadn't had that discipline installed in me."

He looks suddenly enlightened. "Is that why your desk faces away from the window? I noticed it the other day and meant to ask, because most people would be looking at that view."

I shake my head. "Not a good idea. I'm meant to be writing a book. I'd probably still be staring at the sea in a trance now if I was looking that way."

"But—" Whatever he was going to say is interrupted by Bram and Viv emerging and the taxi pulling up.

Four hours later I am officially pissed. In fact we're all very drunk. We've been systematically working our way round the bars of St Tropez, and now we're in a little waterside piano bar sitting in comfortable oversized wicker chairs and watching the people milling round.

I down my vodka and cranberry and stare out at the huge yachts moored up on the famous front. "Ever thought of having one of those?" I ask Bram, and he snorts.

"Fuck, no. I get seasick on a ferry." His Irish accent is strong and his eyes are slewed slightly, as I think are all of ours.

Matt laughs, grabbing my arm to get my attention. "Once in the early days we were on a ferry going over to France, and he threw up in Sid's hoody but forgot to tell him."

Viv giggles loudly. "Oh my God, I remember that. It was disgusting, and it totally ruined Sid's side parting."

Matt collapses into laughter, still holding my arm, and I join in, but I see Viv shoot a glance at the hand and I know that I'm going to be cross-questioned tonight at some point.

"Do you remember that weekend we had here and that Dutch woman?" she asks Matt.

"Oh my God, yes." He turns to me. "We were all really drunk and waiting for Mabe, I think, who'd left her bag in a bar. Anyway, Charlie was leaning against the gangway of this massive fucking yacht, and this little Dutch woman comes up to him and starts fucking haranguing him at the top of her voice about over-the-top consumerism because she thought that he owned the yacht."

"What did he do?"

Bram smirks. "He told her to go aboard if she wanted a real close-up look at consumerism, so she did and we scarpered."

Viv sighs. "The last we saw of her were two bouncers escorting her off while she tried to hit them with her hemp bag."

Bram and Matt break into peals of laughter while leaning on each other, and I smile affectionately at them because they look a bit like puppies at the moment with their lack of coordination. They become involved in perusing the menu for new cocktails to try, and I shake my head in disgust at the suggestion of a blow job. Matt laughs, cupping the back of my head and drawing me closer. "Can't miss out on a blow job, babe."

"I can if it comes in a glass with whipped cream," I say in disgust, sending him into more paroxysms of laughter and making me smile. The waiter comes over to take our order and Viv scoots closer so I mentally start the countdown. *One. Two. Three. Four -*

"What's going on with you two?" she hisses. *My God, I never even got to five.*

I turn to face her. "Nothing, would be what's going on."

She eyes me sharply. "Last I heard you bloody hated each other. Bram and I were half convinced that we'd find a bloodbath when we got here."

I raise my eyebrow. "Was it a long discussion?"

She smiles. "Bram got *very* involved in the descriptive element of what we'd find, but instead, here you are." She shoots a glance at Matt who is talking to Bram. "All chummy."

I shrug. "We're friends now. We had a long chat when he got here and cleared the air, and voila."

"He touches you a lot."

"That's just Matt. He does it to everyone."

She shakes her head vehemently. "No, he doesn't."

"Well, he always seems to be touching somebody when I see you all."

"That's just us, though, John. We're his family. He's not like that with anyone else. You have to *really* be in with Matty to get that closeness."

I feel a wave of warmth at the thought, and then immediately school my expression when her gaze sharpens. "John—" she begins, and then falters.

I smile. "Viv, are you asking me if Matt and I are fucking?"

"Ssh," she hisses, glancing at the other two, but they're in close conversation, looking at something on Bram's phone.

I laugh. "Well?"

She slumps slightly. "You just seem really close."

I throw my arm around her. "We are, or we've become so. I think he's great, but I'm straight, Viv." I'm saying what I know to be true, though for the first time in my life it sounds a bit hollow and unconvincing, but she accepts it, although her face is troubled.

"Matt likes you," she says slowly. "Please be careful with him, John."

I glance at the man smiling happily at his best friend. "Why?"

She shakes her head. "He's not as carefree as he seems. He's got some bad baggage and scars and I don't want to see him get hurt."

"I wouldn't hurt him. I don't think that I could," I protest, and Matt looks up and then grants me with a big smile before going back to Bram. Viv shakes her head doubtfully, so I press on, "I know about his parents. I know how bad that was."

She looks up, startled. "He told you about that?"

I nod, confused as she stares at Matt, something flitting across her face too quickly for me to see, and then she turns back to me. "Has he told you about Ben?"

I shake my head and open my mouth to ask who Ben is, but I'm interrupted by the waiter bringing our order. "One blowjob, sir," he says, placing the glass full of something disgusting in front of me.

I look up to see Bram and Matt wearing identical looks of glee on their faces, and I shake my head at them. "You're like bloody children." They collapse into laughter and then start reminiscing about something again.

When I look back at Viv she's staring at me. "For Christ's sake, Viv, take a picture and then you can look to your heart's content," I say crossly, but she just smiles and gestures at Bram and Matt.

"You don't mind this?"

"What—them?" I'm surprised by the question, but she nods. "No, why would I be?"

"Plenty of their partners haven't liked their closeness. It's caused problems in the past because they can't be without each other for very long."

"Viv, I'm not either of their partners, so that's a bit of a redundant statement." She raises her eyebrow at me and I feel the power. This is why I use it. I sigh. "No, of course I'm not bothered by it. I like Bram and they make each other happy. They're each other's family, and I know what they did for each other when they were kids. They saved each other, so I have no problem with them being close. I'd have more of a problem if Matty dumped him just to make someone else happy."

She stares at me, and her expression which had been troubled clears for some reason, and she smiles.

"Happy now?" I ask. She nods. "Thank fuck for that. Now, please drink this shit for me before they notice and make me do it." She throws her head back, laughing.

I STAND on my balcony in a pair of loose pyjama trousers, enjoying the heat on my body and listening to the lapping of the water in the pool and the breeze blowing in the trees. It's four in the morning and everyone else has gone to bed, but I can't sleep. The alcohol is still flooding through my veins and I feel loose and vibrantly alive at the same time.

My mind won't shut off, either, showing me snapshots of the night, and once again I feel the impression of Matt's hand on me burning like a phantom pain. I can't help thinking of that moment when I'd said to Viv that I was straight, because as more and more time passes and we get closer, the harder it is to dismiss the feelings that I'm having as friendship.

At first, I'd thought that it was just an echo of old teenage friend-

ships which create such deep attachments to people, enough sometimes to confuse vague hero worship with love.

He's funny and bright with a sharp intelligence which challenges
mine in a way that few do, and I'd thought that I just admired him,
but admiration doesn't make the skin heat under another's touch. It
doesn't make my voice thick when I feel him near. It doesn't switch
me on like a lightbulb.

I can't believe that I'm having these doubts. I'd thought them
restricted to my teenage years with that baggage of uncertainty, not
when I'm a grown man. I'd probably be totally freaked out if this was
the real world, but here, tucked away in our bubble, I feel dreamy and
cut off and free.

My thoughts are interrupted by a sound, a half groan, and I'm
instantly alert. It must be coming from Matt's room, as Bram and Viv
are at the back of the house and only we share this balcony. The noise
comes again like someone's in pain, and I'm instantly moving towards
his open balcony doors. He could be sick or have hurt himself. He'd
certainly had enough to drink tonight.

I fly to the open doors and then come to a jarring stop at the
threshold as the filmy curtains billow out in the night breeze, gifting
me a glimpse of Matt lit by the moonlight like he's on the stage.

He's lying naked facing the windows, but he doesn't see me as
he's patently too busy and definitely not injured. His legs are spread
open and his fist is working at his stiff cock furiously, the slick noises
loud in the stillness of the room.

I stand still like I've been turned to stone, unable to stop taking
everything in with a feverish desperation that I've never felt before.
The length of his cock wet and shining in the moonlight with the
head dark and wet. The strength of his grip as his fist shuttles up and
down, and the cords in his neck standing out as he throws his head
back and gives another of the throaty, deep moans that had drawn me
here to stand alone like some voyeur.

I tell myself to move and go back before he sees me and awkwardness ensues, but I'm rooted to the spot by his next action. He spreads

his legs wider, showing me the mounds of his balls drawn tight up against him and the shadowy cleft below, and then he lifts his other hand, spits on it and sucks for a second. When he withdraws his fingers they're glistening, and I watch in fascination as he lowers them down, caressing and tweaking his nipples before raising his knees and pushing two of the wet digits inside himself.

I gasp, but it's drowned out by the sound of him groaning harshly again, and that quickly I feel my dick spring up against my stomach, making me almost dizzy with the speed of my erection. I draw breath in through my nose, trying not to pant as his hand moves quicker on his cock and his fingers push in and out of his hole, the noises dirty and so very exciting.

I reach down against my will and palm my throbbing cock, feeling the wetness of pre-come already gathering there. I have never been this aroused or got hard so quickly, and the pulse in my cock sounds in my head as I reach under my pyjama trousers and give myself a long stroke.

My inner voice is screaming *abort, abort*. Being caught wanking over my friend wanking is something that the etiquette books that I was forced to read by my mother never covered. However, I can't stop, and my thoughts are blown when he suddenly lifts his head and sees me standing in the doorway. I freeze with my hand still on my dick and the moment seems to elongate and pulse as he stares at me through heavy-lidded eyes.

"John," he groans, and then as if against his control his motions become frantic, and he arches back against the bed, all the muscles in his arms and torso drawn tight in seeming agony as he shoots all over his torso, creamy liquid running down the funnels of his six-pack. "John," he says in a quieter, thick voice, lifting a hand glistening with his come towards me, but I still say nothing.

Instead I back away, breathing harshly, and race back to my bedroom like something is pursuing me. Slamming the doors and locking them behind me, I lean back against the wall panting heavily, my prick throbbing like a toothache. I can't believe that he saw me watching him. How can we talk normally ever again? I can't believe that I was turned on by it. Does that make me gay?

I can't find any answers because the pressure between my legs is too fierce, and ripping my trousers down I fist myself with a groan of relief, feeling the wetness running down my cock. It only takes a couple of strokes and then I come, calling out his name and ejaculating great gouts of semen onto the marble floor.

I fall onto the bed, my vision dark, and my last coherent thought before I succumb to sleep is to wonder what would have happened if I'd answered his call and gone to him. I'm amazed that I'm not more frightened of the answer to that question. I'm amazed to find that I wish I'd done it.

5

John

TWO WEEKS later I'm still no nearer answering those questions, and I've had no help from my housemate, who appears to have vanished from sight. He goes out in the morning and comes back very late at night and then zooms straight up to bed.

He's definitely giving me space, which with other people I'd be grateful for, but strangely not with him. I'd thought that I'd feel awkward around him. I mean, my God, he caught me with my hand down my pants watching him tug one off and staying for the money shot. I looked like a total creeper, but I still need to talk to him.

I sit in my study, wearing just my brown and white striped board shorts. My desk may be solidly pointing away from the view but I've circumvented it today by sitting on the sofa, so consequently I've been staring into space for an hour.

I feel utterly ridiculous, but I miss him. I miss our early mornings and late nights talking. No one makes me laugh like him and this last couple of weeks have been ... boring. I don't know how I stood being on my own all those previous summers that I spent here. It used to be the highest luxury to have that peace, but now it just seems like a silent prison.

Something snaps in me and I stand up, slipping on my white t-shirt which I'd left lying on the chair. I'm going out to the house and I'm going to take him out for lunch and then we're going to hash this thing out. After all, nothing really happened. A sudden image of his hand holding his wet dick with come spilling down it flashes into my head, and I feel a whole body flush sweep over me. Okay, something big did happen, but I need to talk about it with the other person concerned, damn him. I move into the hallway, kicking into my trainers and swiping my car keys.

Five minutes later, I pull up outside the villa and I look around with interest, as I haven't been here for a few weeks and already huge changes show. The outside is cleared of weeds and the exterior building work looks halfway completed, with the brickwork repointed and the new roof being worked on. I leave the car and follow the sound of loud voices, but I pick up my speed with my heart pounding when I catch the sounds of urgency.

A man comes shooting around the corner and bumps into me and I recognise Monsieur Dubois the carpenter, who is covered in blood.

"Jesus Christ," I say, grabbing him to prevent him landing on his arse. "Are you okay, sir?"

"I'm okay," he babbles in his rapid French, and then he seems to recognise me and clutches me to him. "It's not my blood, it's Mathieu's."

"*What?*" I growl and try to get free. "Where is he? Is he okay?"

"He's through there." He gestures to the pool area and then I'm gone running full tilt, a panic filling me unlike anything that I've ever felt. I tear round the corner and come to a shuddering halt as I see him sitting on the ground surrounded by a chattering group of work-men. He has a dirty towel clutched to his arm that is rapidly turning scarlet and another saturated towel lies next to him.

My stomach turns. "Jesus fucking Christ, what have you done now?" I growl.

He looks up, startled, and for a second I see relief and something else cross his face, and then he smiles lopsidedly. "A chisel slipped, and voila."

"Are you okay?" I reach him and part the cloth gingerly, relief filling me so quickly that I feel dizzy. He has an extremely deep cut running from his palm down his right arm that's leaking blood thickly, but it's not spurting out so he hasn't nicked an artery, and although he's pale, he's coherent.

I look at the towel in revulsion. "Who the fuck put this filthy thing on an open wound?" I grind out, glaring round at the chastised faces. "Where's the medicine kit?" I snap, and several jump and shuffle their feet.

"Johnny, it's fine," Matt soothes and I shoot him a fulminating glare that he trades for a confused, humorous one of his own.

"It's not okay. Has anyone called for an ambulance?"

"I don't need one." He struggles to his feet and then sways slightly. I exclaim and grab his arm until he steadies himself, and then I curl my hand around his skull, feeling the silkiness of his hair which is warm from the sun.

"Wait a minute," I mutter. "Get your feet steady. You've lost a fair bit of blood and that wound definitely needs stitches and *cleaning*," I say on a louder note, staring around at the sorry-looking men.

"Johnny, for Christ's sake," Matt mutters. "You're making me look a bit girly here. I've got an image to maintain."

"I'm sure you'll manage to keep that. Just keep cracking the jokes. They'll get the punchline when you lose your arm through catastrophic blood poisoning."

He breaks into laughter, leaning on me slightly. "John, your mother must have been overpowered by what a ray of sunshine and positivity you are."

"She was too concerned with what the world saw as the second coming, now shut up," I smirk, becoming suddenly aware of two things. One, I'm still hugging him close to me and two, the group of men are now giving us very strange looks. I subject them to a level stare, refusing to remove my arm, until they give very Gallic shrugs and start to move away, offering him pats and manly slaps of pride.

Finally, only one man is left—a tall, tanned, good-looking man who is holding an industrial-sized first aid bag. He removes the towel and stares hard at the cut. "You definitely need stiches, Mathieu," he offers in a rich, deep voice accented with French, and I recognise the project manager, who I think is called Christophe.

He holds onto Matt's arm a little longer than I think necessary, and when he looks at him I see a clear interest in his eyes which makes me bristle. "I'll take you to the hospital, my friend," he says decisively and Matt smiles at him, making me step forward, still holding his arm.

"I'll do it," I say brusquely.

"Oh no, Johnny," Matt protests. "That's too much trouble. Chris will take me."

Christophe raises one arrogant eyebrow at me almost challengingly, his face dark and amused.

"No trouble at all," I say, coldly smiling at him, and I see Matt do a double take looking between us, but then he winces and I forget my anger instantly. "Matty, let's get you in the car. That's a deep cut and you've lost a fair bit of blood." I turn to Christophe. "I'll take him and then I'm taking him home. I presume that you can manage without him for the day."

"*John,*" Matt mutters chidingly but Christophe just smirks, giving me an insulting half-bow.

"I am sure that we'll cope, but it will be boring without him."

I shake my head, bored of the conversation now, and steer Matt to the car listening with half an ear to his commentary over how he could cope on his own and wondering why that man wound me up so much.

I'd like to blame his attitude, but let's face it, I do arrogance on a whole different level to him. However, I think, no, I know, it's to do with the familiarity of his touch on Matt and the way that he looked at him. I hated it, and the thought occurs as to whether this is why Matt's been coming in so late. A feeling of rage spreads throughout me like a contagion, immediately followed by confusion as normal. I can't believe that these feelings are being stirred up in me for the first time ever, and by a man. I never saw that coming.

Matt settles into the car with a wince, holding his arm close to him. I exclaim and reach into the back for my navy sweatshirt. "Put this on it, Matt. It's cleaner."

"I can't use that. It's fucking Ralph Lauren."

"It may be, but it's also *clean*," I enunciate. "That towel looks like someone's wiped their feet or something worse on it."

He grimaces and takes the sweatshirt gratefully, and I reach over to get his seatbelt, but I still suddenly as he flinches away from me. "What the fuck?" I say softly. "What was that for?"

He shrugs, looking embarrassed. "Caught me by surprise," he mutters, but I know that's a lie. I open my mouth to say I don't know what, but then Christophe bangs his hand down on the bonnet and gestures to me to go.

"Arrogant twat," I mutter, putting one arm behind Matt's seat as I reverse. "I know what I'm fucking doing. I don't need bloody directions."

"He's not arrogant," Matt mutters. "And really, pot calling kettle, dear."

"I am not arrogant," I mutter, and he turns his warm brown eyes on me disbelievingly. "Okay, I may be arrogant, but I have a great deal of charm which buttresses the arrogance."

He laughs and then winces in pain. "Oh, Johnny, never change."

I wave mockingly at Christophe before accelerating away. "Is that where you've been for the last couple of weeks?" I mutter and he jerks.

"Where?"

"With him." I wave back at the man standing with his hand raised in farewell.

I can feel Matt's stare on the side of my face like a brand. "I've not been with anyone."

"You could be if you want to. He's interested."

"Well, I'm not," he says sharply and then sighs. "I'm not interested in him at all."

I feel a wave of relief spread through me and I sag slightly. "So where have you been?"

"Avoiding you," he says lightly, and I flinch.

"I knew it. I'm so sorry, Matt, but I heard you groan and thought that you'd hurt yourself, and then I got there and found—" I trail off.

He's silent for a second and then, as if the words are torn from him, he says, "Why did you stay, John? Why did you watch?"

I look straight ahead at the road. "I don't know," I say finally. "I don't know why I stayed, but I couldn't have moved if someone had forced me."

Silence falls between us for what feels like hours but is only minutes, and I welcome the sight of the hospital. "We're here," I say softly, stopping the car and finally looking at him. He's pale and dirty and obviously in pain but he stares back at me calmly, and there's something deep in his eyes that looks like hope before he shakes his head.

"We'll put it to one side, shall we?"

"And you'll come home at a good time and we'll talk again?" I say solemnly like a child.

"Home?" he queries, and then nods as if he agrees with the word. "Yes, I'll do that."

I open my door and I'm sure that I hear him say that he missed me, but when I turn back to him he's fiddling with his makeshift bandage, so I dismiss it and race around the car to help him out.

Matt

I jerk awake as we pull up to John's villa, or home as he called it earlier. He looks over at me and smiles lopsidedly. "You alright there, Matt?"

I rotate my head and wipe off the drool gathering beautifully on the shoulder of my t-shirt. "I'm fine," I mutter, and then go to unclip the seat belt and groan as the pain shoots straight up my arm before centering in the wound and starting a heavy throbbing.

"Careful," he chides, leaning over to release my seatbelt. I make a determined effort not to flinch like an idiot this time. I remember that he'd just suddenly been so close to me, and all I could see were those amazing blue eyes and his firm lips so close to me. My brain had short-circuited and I'd been on the edge of reaching out and kissing him and filling my hand with all those black curls which have slowly rioted over the weeks against his control. Luckily the fact that I was gushing blood all over an expensive Ralph Lauren sweatshirt and his E-Type prevented me from doing something so unutterably stupid.

He sighs and pushes his hand down my head, smoothing my hair back from my face which, now that I think about it, feels funny, all sort of numb. I stare at his concerned face. More and more I've noticed that he's a very tactile man who likes touching and being touched, but it's almost nervous, as if he's trained himself not to touch too often. It hurts my heart a bit because—

I shake my head, my thoughts trailing away like smoke, and focus to find him racing around the side of the car to open my door and help me out. "John, I've cut my arm, not sawn it off," I say irritably, feeling like some sort of Victorian maiden. He'll be covering up the legs on the tables next in case I have impure thoughts. I snort out a laugh and he looks at me curiously.

"Ookay." He elongates the word. "The hospital said to keep an eye on you because you said that some pain medications make you stupid. Apparently, if you were going to have a bit of a funny reaction to the painkillers it would hit you quite quickly. Luckily we're home now."

I laugh again. "Funny ha ha," and then I lapse into giggles at the look of puzzlement on his face. "There's that word again," I sigh lavishly, pointing at him until he relocates my finger so that I'm actually pointing at him. *Fuck.* "Home. I like being at home with you."

He looks at me in complete abject bewilderment, his brow furrowing, and I poke the line between those spectacular eyes. *God you're pretty,* I think, and then see the look of consternation on his face. "I said that out loud, didn't I?"

He nods, a grin tugging at his lips. "I am not *pretty,* Matthew. I am extremely good-looking with a brain the size of the Tower of London. That makes me handsome, not, I repeat, pretty."

"Hope other things are the size of the Tower of London," I laugh, and get up with a groan and then stand swinging idly back and forth on his door enjoying the breeze, while hoping that my mouth stops talking right about now. *A reaction to the painkillers,* I muse. *Right, at this point, really, could it get any stupider?*

He looks at me as I hum a song that's just come into my head and attempt to thread my good arm through his sweater. "Case proven for the painkiller reaction, I think." He shakes his head and takes the sweater off me. "That's back to front, babe." He throws it onto the back seat and pushes his shoulder under mine. "Come on," he growls, sending shivers down my spine.

I like that noise. It goes straight to my balls. He freezes. "Shit, I said it out loud again, didn't I?"

He shakes his head and closes his eyes. "Maybe we need to get some food down you, Matty? Mop up the painkillers."

I nuzzle into him. "Let's get some protein in me," I growl. "Let's have a liquid lunch. I promise that I'll swallow."

He closes his eyes in what looks like pain. "Fuck, the things that you say."

"It's not what I say, it's what I do." I'm starting to feel very weird now, so to take my mind off it I attempt a lascivious wink, but judging from the consternation on his face I don't think that I quite pull it off. "I'm very, *very* good at the things that I do, Johnny," I say proudly.

"Matt, you're actually shouting, did you know that?" he says nervously, still attempting to get me up the stairs. *Good luck with that,* I think distractedly, *because my legs don't appear to be working.*

"Oh my God," I shout in panic, and it must be loud because he nearly drops me. "My legs don't work. I can't walk."

"It's okay," he soothes. "The hospital said to let you sleep and the reaction will wear off. I've just got to make sure that I wake you up occasionally."

"To check that I haven't died," I say slowly and painstakingly. "You must *definitely* do that, Johnny. Hey, you know what?" He jerks to a stop again. "We should get in bed together, then you can keep a check on me." He closes his eyes and I go to nudge him and miss his arm by what feels like quite a lot. I smirk, or try to. My face is so numb now that I might be dribbling, for all the fuck I know. "My face feels funny, but my penis is still working," I reassure him.

"Oh my God," he groans.

I laugh. "I know, that's what they all say. 'Oh my God, Matty, that's so fucking *good.*'" I shout the last and I think that I end it on a bit of a howl because his shoulders are shaking with laughter. I nuzzle into him. "You smell really nice, babe, like blackberries and sunshine and hot skin. Sometimes I want to lick you," I say dreamily and his steps falter. My thoughts clear a little like clouds drawing back. "Oh, Johnny, is it all getting a bit too gay for you?"

He stops. "What?" He sounds fierce.

I gesture with my bad hand and hiss at the pain. "All this between us." He turns his head to stare at me and I desperately want to stop talking now, but it doesn't happen. "You've felt it, babe, I know it." I sigh sadly. "It's okay, Johnny, it's perfectly normal to be attracted to someone of the same sex. It doesn't mean that you're gay or bi or whatever, it just means that you find them attractive. Don't worry about it."

He stops abruptly. "What if I'm worried that I'm not more worried?" he mutters, and I pause, trying to make sense of his words, but my muzzy head won't allow it.

I shake my head finally. "I don't understand anything," I say disconsolately, and he laughs sharply.

"Nor do I, Matt, nor do I. Now let's get you upstairs."

"I like your shorts, Johnny. Sometimes I can see your penis."

"Oh Lord."

"That's a song," I say delightedly, throwing my head back and singing loudly, "Oh Lordy, trouble so hard."

"Moby," he says patiently.

"Is that the little bald one? I *love* his music. Let's sing some."

"There aren't many words in his songs," he mutters, staggering slightly as I list into him.

I pull to a stop, hit with a brilliant idea. "Let's make some up."

"Make what up?" He sounds wary.

"I'll start." I throw my head back. "Johnny is very wary of my cock, cock, cock when it's not covered in a sock, sock, sock."

"That is like some sort of horribly dirty Dr Seuss rhyme."

"Ssh!" I put my finger to my mouth. "Ouch, what happened there?"

"You poked yourself in the eye," he says patiently.

I hug him expansively while he makes silly, joking, chuckling noises, and I sing out the next line loudly. "I poked myself in the eye, but at least I won't catch a stye."

"Oh God, please make him stop."

"Has never been said in my bedroom *ever*," I say proudly, and smile at his loud laughter.

John

I manhandle my chatty patient into his bathroom and start the shower. He leans against the sink, looking at me with slitted eyes and attempting a smile which is really more wonky than I think he'd like. I eye him worriedly. Should I take him back to the hospital? He's wobbly and keeps poking his face. Then I remember the nurse saying that it might happen but not to worry too much. She didn't mention the sex talk, though.

I want to think about this later because a lot has come out in the last ten minutes, and if the drugs aren't to blame and he meant it, then it means that he's as attracted to me as I am coming to realise I am to him. I feel the panic unfurling in me again, but as normal it's mixed with this potent pull towards him that means I can't take my worries seriously.

I shake my head. Seriously, I have now devolved responsibility for making rational decisions to my cock for the first time in my life. I look down at my crotch and snort. *Good luck, Sergeant. Do your best.*

"What are you thinking, Johnny?" Matt slurs. Then his attention is drawn to the shower. "Gosh, is that water? I'm *so* thirsty."

I straighten up hurriedly. "Not for drinking, babe." The endearment slips out without conscious thought. "I'll get you a drink in a minute." I eye his dirty arms and legs and clothes that are covered in brick dust. "How about you have a shower and get that muck off you now? Then I'll make you something to eat and you can sleep." I think for a second. "I'll change your sheets as well. It'll be nicer for you to sleep on cool, fresh sheets."

"Are you sure that you're a lawyer?" he asks slowly. "You sound like a housekeeper." He sends me what he obviously thinks is a sexy look, but it's slightly spoiled by the fact that his eyes are crossed. "I like sexy housekeepers."

I snort. "Seen many, have you? The life that you jet setters lead."

He shrugs, huffing petulantly as he tries to get his good arm out of his sleeve. "Here, let me help you," I say calmly. I grab the neck of his t-shirt. "Bend forward."

He snorts. "I've heard that before."

I laugh before I think about it, which happens a lot with him. "Okay, Romeo, I'll pull this and you move back gently."

"Nudge, nudge, wink, wink," comes the muffled voice from the depths of his t-shirt, and I can't help smiling as I pull it gently until he comes into view, his hair a complete mess and his eyes screwed up like a little mole seeing daylight.

I kneel down to undo the laces on his work boots and look up at him. "Please don't say anything," I beg and he smiles lopsidedly, before it stills and he runs his fingers through my hair. For a second I lean into his touch and then, remembering that he's technically fuck-faced and I am sort of straight, I pull back, focusing instead on working his boots and socks off his feet. He even has nice feet, long and nicely arched with neat, square toenails. I shake my head. I'm even admiring his toenails. Fuck, my life gets stranger.

I pull to my feet. "Okay, take your shorts off." He squints at me and I hold up one finger warningly. "Underwear on, please. This is strictly a PG show."

He huffs, reaching down and undoing his cargo shorts with an unsteady hand. It takes three attempts and I'm just going to help, when he does it and the zipper separates with a sibilant hiss. I swallow hard as he pulls them off his hips, letting them fall to the floor cavalierly, and then I still because he is beautiful. Tanned sleek skin stretches tighter than a drum over lean muscles, and his grey Calvin boxers cling to a high, firm ass and show off the 'v' of his pelvic muscles with one long vein stretching down his lower torso and into the briefs.

I swallow hard and then curse myself for being a creeper, but I release the tension with a snort as he gets caught in the material of his shorts. I catch him as he lists sideways, trying to kick irritably at the offending material. "Easy, Bruce Lee," I soothe, putting my foot on the material so that he can lift his leg up, which he does so slowly it's as if I'm watching a film in slow-motion.

I steady him and then reach into the shower to test the tempera-ture. It's cool and should be nice and refreshing for him. I guide him in, where he slumps against the wall totally out of the reach of the spray. He leans there, his eyes half-closed, and I think that we're moving to the sleepy stage of the proceedings.

I look at him for a second and then, mind made up, I kick off my own shoes, throwing them to one side and stripping off my own t-shirt and shorts. Clad in only my boxers, I step into the shower and take hold of his shoulders, sliding my hands over his warm skin.

"Come on, babe." I indulge myself with the endearment, secure in the knowledge that he's barely paying attention now. "Let's get you washed up."

I pull him under the water, making sure to position his bandaged arm out of the spray, and the shock of the water seems to wake him up a bit because he opens his eyes, staring at me before smirking. "This reminds me of a porn film that I saw once."

"If this was porn," I say briskly, turning him so that the dirt runs off him and pouring soap into his good hand so that he can wash himself, "I would be called Dirk and you would be called Colt. We would have had a terribly poorly acted conversation before any action, and both of our dicks would be considerably bigger."

He laughs softly and looks down at where my boxers are clinging to me. "I'm not complaining, babe," he says archly, and I chuckle.

"Shut the fuck up. Turn around and lean back a bit. Let the water wet your hair." He does it docilely. "Okay, lean back on me." I reach for the shampoo and work it into his hair thoroughly, smelling the citrusy scent that always seems to cling to him. He leans back, and something about his lowered eyes and wet spiky eyelashes strikes me because he looks almost vulnerable, and a wave of protective feeling courses through me that startles me.

"Nobody has ever done this for me before," he mumbles, and sighs contentedly as I work my hand through the longish strands until they're thoroughly coated. I feel a sharp wave of happiness, but trying not to think too hard about it, I shield his eyes with my hand to avoid the shampoo stinging them and direct him under the spray. I pull him back out when it's all gone and reach for a towel so that he can wipe his eyes.

However, I still as he grabs my hand in his when I pass the towel to him. He is almost dropping with tiredness, but despite the cloudiness of the opiate that is still there in his eyes he looks searchingly at me. "Thank you, Johnny," he whispers. "I feel safe with you, you know?"

"I do," I say in a low voice, wrapping the towel tenderly round him and patting him dry. "I do with you."

It's the truth, and as I marshal the sleepy man into bed where he rolls over with a huge sigh, nuzzling into the pillow and falling asleep instantly, I wonder when I've ever felt that before. It feels new enough to know that I never have.

6

Matt

I COME awake in drifting increments, slowly surfacing until finally I become aware of the delicious scent of something sugary. I try to open my eyes, which seem as if they're stuck together, and wince at the pain that flashes across my temples.

"Headache?" a deep voice enquires, and my eyes snap open.

I'm blinded by the bright sunlight spilling into the room for a second, but then I focus on John, who is standing by the bed dressed simply in a pair of red-checked cotton pyjama shorts and holding, *oh my God yes*, a tray filled with things that smell delicious. I struggle up on my elbow, letting out a hiss as my arm registers its extreme soreness.

John puts the tray down on a side table and rushes to help me sit up. "Does it hurt much today?" he asks as I gingerly manipulate my arm.

I look at the offending limb consideringly. "It's sore. I suppose fifty stitches would account for that, but it doesn't hurt as much as it did in the night." John had woken me a few times on his many scheduled wake-up calls to check that I was still breathing.

"That's good. Are you hungry?"

"Fuck, yes," I sigh, and he laughs and puts the tray on my lap. On it is a plate piled high with toast and buttery mounds of scrambled eggs flecked through with tiny pink slivers of smoked salmon. Next to the plate is one of his deep blue and white cups holding milky hot chocolate. "My favourite breakfast," I sigh. "You are a god."

"Glad you've realised it," he says placidly, and ignoring my snort, he reaches for the cup of coffee on the tray and settles himself comfortably on the corner of the bed cross-legged.

I stuff my face happily, watching him consideringly while he's not looking. He looks startlingly at home on my bed relaxed and unshaven, drinking his coffee and chatting. *I could get used to this* comes the traitorous thought which I immediately ignore, instead taking a hefty mouthful of hot chocolate.

When I've finished, he moves the tray and takes from his pocket a vial of prescription medication along with a red cardboard packet. "Okay, this is your choice," he says briskly. "You can have either the painkillers from last night, which undoubtedly work on the pain but lead to you being almost outrageously outspoken, or plain old ibuprofen which will allow you to keep your secrets." He smirks. "And your dignity."

I stare at him in mystification. "What on earth are you ... oh!" Memory shoots straight through me with the speed of a train, and I slide back down into the bed, throwing my good arm over my face in mortification.

"Yes, oh," he snickers. "I now know that I smell of blackberries and sunshine and hot skin, that you cannot produce poetry to save your life, and that you have a very talented penis that has driven many, many men to paroxysms of ecstasy."

I remove my arm cautiously. He doesn't look angry, only amused, so I venture a comment. "Many, *many* men?"

"Yes, that was the message last night, Casanova."

I shoot him a quick glance because I'm sure that I also remember telling him how much I liked him, but his expression as he stares back at me is bland with nothing showing at all. John, when he wants to, has very sphinx-like qualities. "I think just ibuprofen," I say in a small voice, and he smirks.

"Good choice." He hands me a glass of orange juice and I swallow the tablets. When I'm done he takes the packet and stands up, stretching. Against my will my eyes flash down his muscled chest and that tight visible 'v' and the shape of his cock swinging loose behind his shorts. I swallow hard and when he looks up, I'm drinking my juice in a virtuous silence.

"I take it that you're not going to work today?" he says and I look up.

"Oh, no, I thought—"

"I'll rephrase the statement," he says clearly. "I take it that you're *not* going into work today?"

I slump like a chastised child, knowing that I'd be a liability on a building site today, and shake my head.

"Good," he says pleasantly, and I shoot him a warning glare which he ignores with a quirk of his lips. "So if you're free for the day, you could lie out by the pool and sleep some more, or—"

"Or what?" I ask, my disinclination to sit still rearing its head.

"Or we could go out for the day and I could show you some bits of the South of France that don't include building dust and plumbing." His tone is coolly amused, but underneath it I detect a hint of eagerness and a wariness that I'm going to rebuff the option. No chance of that. I wouldn't do that to him.

"I take the second option," I say firmly, and he smiles eagerly, looking like a young boy for a second.

"Great. We'll take it easy, though. I don't think that you're up to too much today. Have a shower and meet me downstairs. Make sure that you keep your arm dry. I've put a bin bag out for you to cover the bandage. Dress comfortably and coolly and bring your swimming shorts."

"Aye aye, Captain," I drawl, and he laughs.

"I like that. Make sure that you say it a lot today. You can intersperse it with comments like 'Oh, Johnny, you know so much. You must be very, very clever,' and 'Oh, Johnny, you do fill your shorts out nicely.'"

"How about 'Oh, Johnny, what a bossy jackass you are,'" I say sourly and he laughs, ruffling my hair.

"See you downstairs."

When I meander downstairs half an hour later I feel loads better. The shower has cleared away the lingering cobwebs, and the tablets have reduced the pain in my arm to a distant soreness. I'm wearing navy board shorts with an old navy and white striped t-shirt and my yellow Vans as per my orders, and I'm ready and eager to find out where we're going.

He appears round the door of his study, mobile clamped to his ears as he shoots quick-fire questions at whoever is on the other end of a legal problem. I slump a bit at the thought that our day might be over before it's begun and at the knowledge of how much I was actually looking forward to it, but he shakes his head at me, mouthing 'five minutes' before throwing me the car keys and motioning for me to wait in the car.

I drop a lopsided curtsy and he snorts with laughter before saying, "No, I'm not laughing at you, Conrad, don't be ridiculous. Focus on the problem at hand."

I roll my eyes and wander out to the car. Five minutes later he walks out. He's carrying a rucksack and wearing a navy polo shirt, burnt orange board shorts and old leather deck shoes. He looks cool and stylish as always. Even in pyjama shorts the man looks like a male supermodel.

He starts the engine with a throaty purr which we both pause to admire, our heads cocked to the side like puppies. "Ready?" he asks with a grin and I nod, feeling my own grin wide on my face as exhilaration fills me.

"Let's go."

We drive along the coast road with the top down and the wind in our hair, and I never once feel nervous despite the steep drop by the side of the road. He's an extremely competent driver who handles the car with relaxed ease. His hair falls into his face and he gestures to the glovebox. "My baseball cap's in there. Can you pass it to me?"

I open the glovebox and take out a faded red cap with a Grand Prix logo on it. I pass it to him, watching him slide it on and angle the brim. "That's better," he shouts, and I spare a thought to wish that I'd brought my own cap.

"You like cars?" I shout above the sound of the wind and Amy Winehouse's 'Back to Black' album which is playing on the stereo.

He shoots me a look and smiles, the lines at his eyes crinkling and lengthening. "I love them. I always have done. My grandfather had a collection of them when I was little, and he used to take me out in them sitting on his lap. Strictly illegal, of course, but it was a private estate."

I suddenly remember that his mother is the daughter of a lord which must be the grandfather that he's talking about, and the collection that he's talking about is actually a world-renowned classic car collection of about one hundred cars. With anyone else I would make a sarcastic comment, but he's just given me a glimpse into the private him and I won't do it. Something about John brings out a very protective side to me. I don't ever want to see him snubbed. The man may have an arrogant exterior, but I've come to realise that inside he's got a very soft underbelly.

"So what would be your dream car?" I shout and he grins, looking eager and animated. The next fifteen minutes pass in a very lively discussion of the pros and cons of most of the world's super cars, and he shows a very keen love of all things retro.

Finally, after a quick stop to buy coffee, we pull into a car park full of other cars and I look around curiously. "Where are we?"

"The old port of Cannes."

I look at the boat bobbing gently on the water that's painted bright white and red and festooned with bunting. "We're going on a ferry? I haven't been on one of those in a long while."

"Is that okay?" he asks, a line appearing in his forehead. "I know Bram gets seasick. Do you get it too?"

"John, he's my best friend. We're not co-joined. Relax, I'm fine."

He smiles again quickly and then reaches into the back to grab his rucksack. "I'll just go and get the tickets." He throws something onto my lap. "Here, take this. You'll need it today because it's going to be a scorcher."

I look down to find a cream-coloured Panama hat with a blue coloured ribbon on the brim. I pull it on, tilting the brim at a rakish angle. "How very Merchant Ivory of you," I smile, and he laughs loudly.

"It actually suits you. Bella bought it years ago for me. She always persisted in trying to dress me like I was just about to read the cricket scores."

I laugh but to my ears it sounds hollow, because while I'm feeling things about this man that I never have before for anyone else, he is still trying to get back with his ex-wife. *You're a fucking idiot, Matty,* I tell myself. *Pull back now or this is going to fucking hurt badly.* The trouble is that I've never been good at listening to my inner voice, as it usually wants to curtail any happiness and is heavily modelled on my father.

Therefore, instead of listening to the wise advice, I step out of the car smiling. I look at the water speckled with sunbeams and hear the cries of the gulls and the voluble French being spoken around me, and I fucking ignore that little bitch of a voice. Nothing ventured, nothing gained, and if all I gain is his friendship and a broken heart, then my life will always have been better for having had him in it.

When John comes back with the tickets we board the ferry with only a handful of other people, most of whom look like locals, maybe travelling over to visit family or the markets. We make our way up the steps to the top level and position ourselves at the side, leaning against the railing and watching the bustling dock until finally the clock tower strikes the hour and the boat backs out slowly and then sets off.

It's a beautiful morning and the sun is already hot and I turn my face up to it, enjoying the warmth and feeling the judder and sway of the boat. Opening my eyes, I see an old woman sitting on the bench opposite us, dressed in the customary black that the old women seem to wear a lot around here. She's smiling at me, so I smile back and we exchange a few remarks in French about the boat and the weather and my injury. Looking up, I see John looking at me with a smile on his face.

"What?" I ask.

He shakes his head. "Nothing. You're just always so at ease in yourself and with others. I rather envy you."

"*You*? But you're 'Mr Lord of All He Surveys,'" I splutter, and he smiles a little sadly.

"I'm confident enough in my work, I suppose, but in real life I tend to be a bit reticent with people that I don't know."

I stare at him. "I've not really seen many signs of that here."

He shrugs a little awkwardly and then hands me my coffee, and we turn to lean on the railings in a comfortable silence.

We pass villas gleaming white and pink and nestling into the green hills that frame Cannes, and sunbathers lying in brightly coloured rows on the sandy beaches. Yachts sail near us with their coloured sails jauntily swinging, and the spray from the water leaps up and cools our faces, leaving behind a salty residue on our skin.

Land nears and the ferry slows and I straighten. "Where's this?"

"This is the island of Sainte-Marguerite, part of the Lérins Islands which are a group of four islands. Two of them are uninhabited, and we get off at the next one, which is Saint-Honorat."

An announcement comes over the tannoy telling passengers to stay on for Saint-Honorat and the rest of the passengers promptly get off, chattering briskly, until we're alone.

"Perhaps they know something that we don't know," I murmur, tongue in cheek, and he smiles.

"There's not much on Saint-Honorat for the locals."

I open my mouth to ask why but the ferry begins to back out, and once we're on our way again he distracts me by pointing out the cliffs. "Sainte-Marguerite's fort on the island has deep dungeons which are dug into the sides of those rocks, and that's where the Man in the Iron Mask was imprisoned."

I'm amazed and turn to him curiously. "He was a real person? I thought he was a fictional character created by Alexandre Dumas."

"He was real. He was imprisoned here for ten or eleven years, seeing hardly anyone. Legend says that he was the half-brother of Louis XIV, but other people say that he could have actually been a woman."

"Woman or man, it would have been a lonely existence," I muse, staring at the lonely view that the prisoner would have had, all sea and sky and with only seagulls for company.

Hardly any time passes before the ferry approaches another island and I see a large stone building set back from the shore. "Saint-Honorat," John murmurs, and I shiver slightly at the feel of his breath in my ear.

He's standing close again and I can smell the scent of blackberries and bay mixed with his natural scent. It's heady and makes my head spin slightly. I'm confused by him a lot. If he was gay I wouldn't hesitate to say that he's attracted to me, but with him being straight and not naturally inclined to the gossipy closeness that I share with the boys in the band, I wonder whether he's just simply enjoying having a friend.

I clear my thoughts from my face and turn to face him. "So this is Saint-Honorat, your mystery destination. What's here?"

He laughs. "Not that much, I'm afraid. It's unoccupied, apart from a community of Cistercian monks."

"I know that I haven't been laid in a while, but you're not leaving me here."

He smiles. "Don't worry, your monkhood is delayed." He looks at the island drawing closer. "It's just a beautiful place, a bit desolate. I come here every time that I'm at the villa. It's one of my favourite places." He hesitates, looking surprised. "I haven't brought anyone here before."

I look at him, touched. "I'm sure that I'll love it," I say softly and he nods.

We disembark and then stand to watch the ferry manoeuvre out past the rocks, and when it's gone the silence descends on us like a cloak. We stand still for a second, and I look around curiously. The sun beats down on us and as far as I can see there's the sparkling turquoise sea, endless pine trees, and the bright coastline slumbering under the hot sun. I take a deep breath, inhaling the scent of pine and eucalyptus, and turn to John, who's watching me carefully.

"There's such a strong feeling of peace here," I say, something making me talk quietly. "Like we're the last two people on earth." He relaxes and nods, smiling widely, and I don't think that I'll ever forget the sight of him framed against the sea and sky.

John

I relax as soon as I see the look of wonder on Matt's face. I've never brought anyone here before because I never trusted that they'd get the place. It would be awful to walk around here with someone who felt the need to fill every second with mindless chatter, but luckily, Matt's not like that at all. For all his ease and charm with people and his humorous sarcasm, there's something in Matt that's at home with nature and the quiet, like me.

I point out the statue of the Virgin Mary that stands above us, her arms outstretched as if to welcome us. "Lérins Abbey is up there, about a five-minute walk away. I thought we'd go up there and then circle the island and maybe have a dip in the sea before lunch, and then catch the boat back."

He nods, pushing the Panama hat back on his forehead, showing his tanned clear features and deep brown eyes creased in a contented smile.

We wander up the path and come to the honey-coloured stone monastery where we push through some tall iron gates and find ourselves near the abbey shop. The quiet everywhere is palpable, and we talk in low voices as we go into the shop. The normal voices of some tourists sound almost overloud in the room after the quiet outside, and he and I potter about browsing while they talk in loud voices about wine and soap.

I choose some lavender oil and soap for Odell, who loves the stuff, and take them to the counter. Along the way I spot some rosemary honey and nab a bottle, holding it up to the woman on the till. "I love this. I try to buy some every time that I'm here." She smiles at me as Matt comes up behind me brandishing a bottle.

"What's this?" he asks her with a smile, and like most women she melts instantly.

"It is our herb liqueur, monsieur. It's famous in the area. Very—" She pauses and then smiles. "Very potent."

"I'll take it," he says instantly, and she smiles before embarking on a conversation with him about where he's from, smiling and laughing while I lean against the counter smiling wryly. If we went to the end of the earth it's almost guaranteed that there would be somebody there who would want to talk to Matt. He just exudes this natural scruffy warmth and people flock to him. I become aware that they're staring at me and I smile hastily.

"Ready?" Saying goodbye to the woman, we leave the shop and stand looking at the old fortified monastery and the sea. "Shall we walk?"

He nods and we roam the island talking about anything and everything, splashing in the clear warm water and watching fish judder and dart away. We plunge into shady areas that smell of lavender and a deeper herbal smell, and then back out into a sky lit by a sun that's almost white.

Finally we reach a little cove where the water is clear and the only sounds are that of birdsong and the wind in the trees that line the beach. "Here?" I ask him and he nods, looking around curiously.

"How about a dip in the water first and then we can eat the lunch that Odell prepared?"

"Is that what's in the bag?" I nod and he laughs. "Oh, Johnny, were you in the Scouts?"

"Dib dib dib," I say solemnly, and he bursts into peals of laughter.

"I bet you ran that bloody Scout pack."

I keep a straight face. "It's not my fault that the Scout Leader had his limitations." He bursts into laughter again before reaching up and stripping off his t-shirt, revealing his wide brown chest and torso tapering down to his navy board shorts. I'm struck dumb for a second at how very good-looking he is, his shoulders wide and his hips narrow, the bands of muscles stretching the skin tight on his body.

He looks up and catches me looking. "Just looking at your tattoos," I say quickly.

He looks down at the line of script running across the inside of his right bicep that reads '*Play it fucking loud.*'

"What does it mean?" I ask.

He smiles. "It's something Bob Dylan said once to his band when he was on stage and being heckled really badly. I liked the idea of using something beautiful in life to drown out the criticism."

He sounds a little raw so I quickly point to the outline of a heart on his hip. Half of the heart outline is made up of rainbow-coloured stars and the other half is made from the words 'love is love.' It's beautifully done. "When did you get that one?"

He twists to look at it. "A few years ago with Bram in Amsterdam. A friend of ours from school has a shop there and he did it."

"I'm surprised that Bram didn't want his name there," I say lightly as I strip off my polo shirt, leaving me in my burnt orange board shorts.

He snorts. "He did suggest that I have the words '*Bram O'Connell is the best man that I've ever met*' put there, but I managed to dissuade him."

"I don't think that's far from the truth, anyway," I muse. I stop him before he can move away and bend to grab a bin bag from my rucksack to wrap over his bandage. "No swimming today," I say sternly. "Salt water will hurt like a fucker if you get it in that cut. Just wading." He makes a grimace of distaste but doesn't argue, watching me tend to his cut in silence.

A few minutes later we stride towards the water eagerly, but he suddenly throws his arm round me, pulling me to a stop and ruffling my hair affectionately.

"It might have been true once that he's the best man I know," he says softly. "I don't think it's the case anymore."

Warmth flows through me and I open my mouth to ask a question but he's gone, wading into the cool water with a shout of happiness. We splash about happily for half an hour enjoying the water and looking at the many fish that swim around us, too used to never seeing anybody to view us as a threat. Finally we walk back to our clothes, and while he spreads out the towels I start unpacking the food.

"Jesus," he sighs happily. "If I wasn't gay I might marry Odell."

"Well, I packed it," I say, and I'm flabbergasted to hear the flirtatious note in my voice. For a long second he stares at me and the silence lengthens and thickens, but then something about my dumbstruck look must amuse him because he breaks out a wide, white smile.

"Enough flirting, Johnny," he says briskly. "Feed your man."

I shake my head at him and start passing him food. The walk and the swim and the sea air has made us hungry, so in no time at all we've demolished the bacon and shallot quiche with the sausage stuffed potato galette, and he finally declares a ceasefire after he's eaten one of her individual lemon tarts.

"God, that's lovely," he sighs. "I could eat that forever." He lies back on his towel with a great sigh of satisfaction.

"I really don't know why you aren't the size of a house," I muse, and he turns his head sideways.

"Too active, I guess. Same as you. I've noticed that you still use the gym every day at the villa and swim."

I nod. "I hate not having exercise."

Silence falls for a second, and I lie back next to him, feeling the sun beat down on my body and listening to the sound of the gulls wheeling around and the water hitting the rocks. Finally I stir. "Do you mind if I ask you something?" I ask quietly, and he rolls to his side, putting him very close to me and scrambling my brain for a second.

"You can ask me anything."

"*Anything*, really?"

"Anything," he says solemnly.

I hesitate and then go for it. "When did you realise that you were gay, and how did you really know?"

He stares at me for a long second, his eyes deep and warm. "Any particular reason that you're asking me that?" His voice is very deep and low.

I shrug awkwardly. "I just wanted to know."

He takes pity on me and moves to lie on his back, staring up at the intensely blue sky. "I don't remember a time when I didn't know that I was gay, really. It was just this natural gradual progression at a time when everything was up in the air anyway. I just realised that a man's body made me hard. I love women's bodies, they're so soft and fragile, but a man's body is what does it for me."

"Were you worried?"

He shoots a glance at me. "Of course I was, because I already had an inkling that it would sour things with my family. For a while I wished that a girl's body *would* do it for me, and I slept with a couple of girls, but it just didn't feel right and couldn't do much for me, so there was a sense of inevitability about it."

"Who was your first man?"

He smiles, gazing back in time, his eyes hazy. "Sam Phillips. He was the son of a neighbour of ours. He was the same age as me. We'd been friends for years and had sleepovers, but they became a lot less innocent when we were fifteen."

"Do you still see him?"

He shakes his head. "I lost contact with him when my dad threw me out. Last I heard he married a woman." He shrugs.

"I'm sorry," I say quickly, grabbing his hand. "I didn't mean to make you think of your dad."

He shakes his head, turning his hand in mine to clasp it more firmly. His is warm and dry and big with long fingers. There is no way to mistake that I'm holding hands with a man, but surprisingly I have zero desire to draw away, instead enjoying the warmth and sense of tactile closeness. Silence falls for a second as we lie staring at the sky and then I stir, remembering something that Viv said that's lain in the back of my head since.

"Can I ask you another question?"

He looks at me. "What, *more*?" I nod and he smiles. "Okay, ask away."

"Who's Ben?"

His smile instantly falls away and I immediately want to grab it back. His body stiffens for a second and I think that he's going to turn away, but instead he turns back to me, still keeping one hand in mine and resting his bandaged arm on his chest, and then he smiles slightly.

"Viv, I suppose?"

I nod. "She didn't tell me anything. Just asked if I knew about him."

"I wonder why she thought that you would know. I don't make a habit of talking about it."

I instantly shake my head. "Then don't, Matt. Leave it and forget that I asked."

"No, it's alright." He stares over my shoulder into the distance and then starts talking. "Ben was my first proper boyfriend. We met when we were sixteen."

He looks at me and I smile encouragingly. "What was he like?"

"Oh, funny and sweet and everything that I wanted at the time."

A shaft of pain runs through me at the thought of him feeling that way about someone and I jerk slightly, making him look at me curiously, but I gesture for him to carry on. "I was his first and we went out for a year."

"Was it difficult?"

He understands what I mean and shakes his head. "Not really. I got the usual abuse from narrow-minded twats, but you've got to remember that I was at school with all of the band, apart from Seth, and we all stuck together. Viv was probably the scariest."

I laugh and he smiles. "Ben was a friend of theirs as well. We were a tight group and then—" He hesitates and I wait patiently until he's taken a deep breath. He looks up at me determinedly. "Ben got hooked on drugs."

"Shit!" I exclaim, having a horrible feeling where this story is going.

He nods. "Yeah. He started off with the small stuff, but then gradually it got to be harder and harder shit. There was a group surrounding the band at the time that were wild and it was easy to get hold of shit. Sid was doing it, too, and to start with I was too concerned about him to notice Ben." I nod. Sid Hudson is the Beggar's Choice guitarist and Charlie's brother and had suffered a much-publicized overdose last year after years of being an addict. He sighs. "By the time that I did notice Ben, he was in too far to get out and he changed rapidly. He went from being everything that I wanted to everything that I hated. He stole from me, he was dirty and lied all the time, and then I found out that he was cheating on me, too."

"Oh, Matty," I sigh. "I'm so sorry."

"Anyway, it got worse and worse. The lads hated him by then because they knew that he was lying and stealing from me. I tried and tried to get him help, and then one night I found pictures of other men on his phone." He takes a deep breath. "There were text messages, too, and it was obvious that they weren't exactly boyfriend material." He sneaks a look at me. "They were customers paying him for a fuck." I gasp but he carries on stolidly. "It was also fairly obvious that he wasn't too bothered about his personal health." He pauses.

"Or mine, for that matter." He looks at me determinedly as if he wants me to know everything. "Barebacking can get you more money."

"Jesus!" I sit up and grab his shoulders. "Did he—" I hesitate. "Fuck, did he give you something?" My heart is racing.

He stares back at me. "Would it matter that much to you?"

"Of course it would," I say without thinking. "I'd hate to think that you were sick. Fucking hate it. But if you're asking whether it would make me treat you differently, then I'd hope that you'd fucking know me better than that."

He looks suddenly very young as he relaxes. "I know that," he says softly, "And don't worry, I dodged that bullet. I had a few weeks of horrendous worry, but I'm completely clean and I've been very safety-conscious ever since."

"What happened to Ben?" I ask cautiously, and his expression clouds.

"We argued very badly and I threw him out. I told him that I didn't want to see him again. He left and ... he died that night. Over-dosed in a squat down the road. I wasn't allowed to go to his funeral because his family blamed me."

"Oh, Matt," I say softly, drawing him up and close to my side without thinking. He rests there staring out to sea, and silence falls for a second while I stroke his hair back from his tanned face, enjoying the feel of the silky strands, and then he sighs.

"He was the first man I met that it felt like it was totally right. That I'd made the right choice when I alienated my family."

"*You* didn't alienate your family," I say furiously. "That was your wanker of a dad. And you did make the right choice."

His face cracks open in a sad smile. "Did I? I've never found another bloke who's made me feel like that."

"You will," I say firmly, ignoring the fact that the thought of him being happy with someone bothers me a great deal more than I'd like.

We sit quietly for a while after this, and then by unspoken consent we gather our stuff together and make our way to the ferry.

On board and out on the water he stares contemplatively out to sea and then sighs and rests his head on my shoulder suddenly. I jerk but then grab his shoulder to keep him there when he makes a move to sit up again, so he relaxes and stares back at the island.

After a second he sighs but it's not an unhappy sigh, more a release of tension. I look at him curiously and his face is totally clear of the distress it held earlier.

"You okay?" I murmur and he nods instantly, making me relax.

"I am," he says clearly. "I really am. Talking about it in that place it felt, I don't know—" He pauses but I don't rush to fill in the silence, giving him time to order his thoughts. "It felt cathartic and right, like I was finally laying it to bed and leaving his memory there on that lonely island."

I rub his head gently, feeling the silkiness of his hair. "That's good, Matty, right?"

"It is," he says quietly and then grabs my hand. "Look," he gasps, and I look down at the sea in time to see a disruption in the water and then a grey, sleek shape breaks the surface and the passengers cry out in pleasure at the pod of dolphins that swim next to us. We watch them as if they've been sent to lighten our mood, and at no point does he release my hand.

An hour later we drive up to the villa, quiet but strangely content. I feel relaxed and easy down to my bones, the way that a day of sun and sea always leaves me. The top is up on the car now and it feels intimate in here.

"Thank you," he says suddenly, reaching out to lay a hand on my thigh. It's meant as a friendly gesture but something fires in my blood suddenly, and before I can help it I gasp, feeling a dizzy rush as my cock hardens unmistakably.

"Johnny," he says in a low voice. "Oh my God, Johnny." His hand moves, and I can't help but give out a low moan as it travels up towards my cock and I push back in my seat to allow it. Instead, he gives a sharp gasp and his hand falls away. "Who the fuck is that?"

My attention drawn in again, I see a figure sitting on the steps of the villa beside a couple of suitcases. I look at him as I draw up beside him. He looks vaguely familiar and I rack my brain as Matt lowers his window and the man rests his hands on the side of the car. "Matty, babe," he says in a low voice full of intimacy.

"Ed," Matt says slowly, and it suddenly comes to me where I've seen him. This is Matt's ex-boyfriend.

7

John

ED LEANS against the car familiarly as we both get out and I resist the urge to shove his fingers off the paintwork. He's a very good-looking man with sleek blond hair, bright green eyes and a slender build. He looks like he could be a model, and I dimly remember Charlie telling me that he'd signed on with one of the big modelling agencies before I came out to France.

He certainly looks trendy and very expensive in his skinny beige chino shorts and red and white gingham-checked shirt, and I suddenly become aware of how very untidy I look. Hair dried every which way by the wind, stubble that's very nearly a beard, skin coated in a thin layer of salt, and the beginnings of a sunburn on my nose.

However, when I look at Matt, he's no better. In fact, his hair is the wildest that I've ever seen, collapsing over his face in a sun-streaked mess. I snort out a laugh, making Ed lean back from where he'd leant forward to embrace Matt and look at me almost hostilely. "What are you laughing at?" he asks sharply.

I don't even deign to acknowledge that question, ignoring him completely and making him huff indignantly, a fact that doesn't seem to escape Matt, who has a half-smile curling his lips when he looks at me. "What *are* you laughing at, Johnny?"

Ed looks sharply at him when he hears his warm tone, but I just laugh and gesture to his hair. "It's a bit—"

"Wild?" he smirks.

"It passed wild about an hour ago," I confide, and he grins.

"Oh my God, is my hair terrible?" he asks in a faux-shrill voice, and when I nod slowly he laughs. "It's your fault, anyway, for giving me that fucking Panama hat and taking me on a boat. I now have unmoveable hat hair."

Ed gives me a reprimanding look which makes me want to laugh. "Well I, for one, think that your hair looks great," he says smoothly, and then leans forward, saying in a low voice, "Makes it look like you've just pulled out and rolled off." He sighs, giving him a lecherous look. "I remember those times, babe."

"Ed, what are you doing?" Matt asks in a low voice, shooting me a quick glance, but his next question is in a firmer tone. "What are you doing *here*?"

Ed takes his arm familiarly, saying something into his ear in a low voice. I feel my fingers clench involuntarily, and Matt shoots me a quick glance full of an emotion that I can't identify.

Ed shakes his arm. "Are you listening to me?" he demands. Matt turns back to him slowly. "I'm here because I realised that I made a mistake, babe."

"A mistake?" Matt echoes in a low voice.

"Yes, I missed you so much, and I knew as soon as I put the phone down that it was the wrong move, but you'd gone when I came looking for you, and I didn't know where to find you."

"How did you find me?" I can't read anything in Matt's voice.

"Oh, I asked Lucy, Seth's girlfriend, and she told me. Really, the band are a bit unfriendly without you there. Bram mistook me for a pizza delivery man and we had the most confusing conversation, and then he shut the door in my face."

Matt's lip quirks. "That's terrible."

Ed leans into him, throwing his arm around Matt's lean waist, and I remember dozens of parties where I'd seen them together like this, back when he hated me and hardly gave me the time of day, when he used that cool voice to speak to me.

I'd always thought that they made a good-looking couple, both of them tall and blond, and I realise with a start that they were together for a year. The fact that Matt hasn't mentioned him at all had led me to believe that the ex-boyfriend was a nothing in his life, but this man has shared a lot with him.

Suddenly all the closeness that I've felt with him seems like posturing on my part. I'd fancied that he was attracted to me and I'd allowed myself to get closer. I'd allowed myself to toy with the idea of doing God knows what, like I'd be doing him a favour or an honour by changing my life, and I feel very stupid because why would he want that?

Why would he want a man who doesn't know the first thing about his sexuality now? I'm almost the fumbling virgin in this scenario, and I know that many men never want that level of ignorance in their bed. Ed knows what to do and doesn't need to think about everything before he does it, and they have a long history together.

I feel my cheeks flush with embarrassment at what an idiot I've been, and then come back to myself to overhear their conversation.

"No, you can't stay here," Matt is saying sharply, and I notice that while I've been in a daze he's moved away from Ed slightly, his arms folded.

"For Christ's sake, Matt, I won't be taking up much room. I mean, I'll be sleeping in your room, so he hardly needs to air a bed or whatever people do."

"No," Matt says firmly. "You can't stay here, and it was wrong of you to make that decision for yourself without asking. You were wrong in thinking that."

I break in, suddenly wanting this awkward-as-fuck conversation to be over so that I can retreat upstairs and gather my armour around me so that I don't feel like such a fool. "You can stay here," I say in a flat voice, and Matt jerks round to me.

"John, *what?*"

"It's fine," I say with my cool professional smile in full bloom. "Any friend of yours, et cetera. Ed is very welcome to stay here."

I can feel Matt burning a hole in my face staring at me and positively vibrating with some message that his body is trying to convey, but I don't catch his eye. I give Ed my cold smile, and self-centred as he is, something about it must give him pause for thought because he steps back slightly. "I'm going for a shower," I say coldly. "I'll leave Ed to bring his bags in. Matt, watch your arm if you help him."

Matt

I watch John walk coolly into the house and up the stairs, my mouth hanging open slightly. *What the fuck just happened?* Twenty minutes ago we were the closest that we've ever been. I'd told him things that I hesitate to tell anyone and he'd looked after me. For the first time I'd felt heard and that I mattered.

I narrow my eyes, because also, what about that moment in the car? I know that I didn't imagine that stiff cock. Well, I have imagined it many times, but not this time. He felt it. I know that he did, so why the change?

I turn slowly to look at Ed who is whistling unconcernedly and pulling his cases towards me, probably with the intention that I take them upstairs for him as per every other fucking trip I've ever taken with him, like I'm some sort of combination butler/daddy.

He suddenly seems to notice the bandage on my arm. "What have you *done,* Matt?"

I pull away from the display of concern which would have been nicer if he'd noticed when he first saw me, rather than metaphorically pissing on me at John's expense. Even John's throwaway concern just now means more. "I had an accident at Charlie's villa. A chisel slipped."

He pouts. "Matt, for fuck's sake, why do you put yourself out for these people? Charlie won't think any better of you for doing this, and you should have been networking in an air-conditioned office rather than on a building site miles away from anyone important."

This is a topic that I've heard enough of over the last few months, and I grit my teeth. "Why are you here?"

He looks at me, surprised. "I *told* you. I'm here to get you back. I'm not leaving until I do."

"Well, you'd better prepare John, then, because I don't think that he was anticipating a rerun of 'The Man Who Came to Dinner' when he issued his invitation."

"*What?*"

I shake my head. John would have got the old film reference immediately. That's one thing I've learnt while being here, and it's the difference between being with someone who has something between his ears, as opposed to somebody with just something between his legs.

"I finished with you," I say through clenched teeth.

He waves his hand cavalierly. "Well, you've done that before, Matty." I open my mouth to shout at him not to call me Matty, but close it as he carries blithely on. "Let's face it, Matt, we're fireworks and flash. We've always fought, it's just the way that we are."

"Yes, but that's not a good thing, Ed. It's not something to strive for. I don't want a relationship based on fireworks and flash, because when they're over they just leave a mess and a nasty smell."

He stares at me. "What has got into you? I thought you'd be glad to see me." His face falls and he pouts. I used to find it adorable, but now I just find it very tiring after weeks of being with an actual grown-up. "Come on, I know that it's not over, Matt, it's never over. You and I, we're going somewhere, you always said that." His eyes look glassy suddenly. "Unless you really don't want me anymore?"

Unbidden, I feel a sense of pity creep up on me. After all, we did have a fairly good year together, and surely it's partly my fault for the way that we'd ended. If I'd let him know how I felt when he behaved badly, if I'd set proper boundaries, perhaps he'd have been better. I don't want him back, but I feel sorry for him now.

He stares at me, reading my expression intently like he always did, but for the first time I see something controlling and manipulative in it, where before I just saw someone who cared for me. Perhaps that was the real problem. I saw what I wanted to see.

"Matt," he says in a wheedling tone. "Just let me stay here for a few days. Give me a chance to show you how it should have been."

"Ed," I sigh. "You can stay, but—"

"Great," he interrupts, sending his hand in a warm caress over my groin that just leaves me cold. "I'll be upstairs. This is a fantastic place, but a bit out in the middle of fucking nowhere." And then he's gone before I can finish my sentence.

"We're not *ever* getting back together." I finish my sentence anyway, but the words just echo emptily in the hallway.

An hour later I approach John's bedroom door, which is firmly closed in a very clear message. I wipe my hands down my shorts, suddenly nervous, because it's occurred to me in that time that maybe he wasn't put out by Ed's arrival. Maybe he's relieved that he's here. Maybe he's bored of me and has just been sociable, and I redden at the thought that I've let myself get physically closer to him every day thinking that it was reciprocated, when in reality he was probably just being the polite host.

He probably grew up with a large etiquette book. Maybe there was a piece about gay men making fools of themselves over you. I imagine it saying '*Under no circumstances acknowledge the overtures. Instead treat him in a friendly, welcoming manner, and eventually he will go away. Your life can then go back to normal with your perfect wardrobe and your perfect, beautiful wife whose hair is never a mess, and who always knows what fork to use at dinner and never makes remarks about talented penises and wanting to lick you.'*

Okay, maybe I should stop now. I take a deep breath and then rap on the door.

Hearing him shout to come in, I wipe my hand again quickly and then let myself in, making sure to shut the door firmly behind me. I'd lock it, too, if it wouldn't probably panic John. I know Ed, and if he thinks that I'm attracted to John he will make the situation a billion times more awkward than it's going to be.

I take a second to quickly look around the room and inhale subtly the scent of his blackberry and bay cologne that he buys from Jo Malone. It permeates the room. As befits the master suite, it's a big room with whitewashed walls and a grey flagstone floor. There's a flat screen TV on the wall, and through one door I can see a gleaming bathroom, and through another what looks like a dressing room. His bed is huge with a grey suede headboard and made up with white linen and a grey and sky blue-checked throw, and it faces the light oak French windows which are open, letting in a cool breeze and showing the lights of Cannes twinkling like stars.

I glance at where he's sitting cross-legged with his laptop in front of him and a legal pad on the bed beside him full of his slashing bold handwriting. He's wearing his black-framed reading glasses that make him look like a really hot professor. I swallow hard because every time that I interrupt him when he's wearing them and he looks up at me, his blue eyes far away behind the frames, I want to fuck him really hard until the only thing that he can see and feel is me.

I come back with a start to find him examining me curiously and I swallow hard, thinking horrible thoughts about tax returns until my incipient boner goes down.

"Are you alright?" he asks, his voice rich as usual, but still somehow cool.

I want to shout at him to be normal with me, but I equally don't want him looking at me like I'm an imbecilic twat so I settle for, "Fine. You?"

He nods coolly. "I had some work to do after the phone call this morning, so I thought that I'd get on with it. I hope I'm not being rude, but I thought that you'd like some time alone with him."

"Why?" I ask baldly, and he blinks.

"Well, reunions and such. You don't need three people for that."

I refrain from informing him that over the years I've had some very memorable reunions with three people involved. Instead I say, "Well, our reunion consisted of me putting him in the room that Viv stayed in, fending off his extreme handiness, and then coping with the massive fit of the sulks which usually happens when he doesn't get what he wants."

He'd been fiddling with his pen, looking as if he wasn't really listening, but at that his head shoots up. "I thought that he'd be sleeping in with you."

I shake my head. "John, I've done many things that I wish I hadn't, and sleeping with the exes ranks up there along with role-play in sexual situations."

His lips curl at the edges. "Not a fan?"

"No, it makes me profoundly uncomfortable, like I want to hide in a cupboard." He throws his head back, letting out his rare, deep, uninhibited laugh. I love to hear it because it gives me such a feeling of accomplishment when I make him laugh, to the extent that I'm sure some days I'm perilously close to doing jazz hands.

He sobers and fiddles with his pen again, and my eyes sharpen as I look at him because I suddenly realise that he's nervous. John's usually so self-possessed and can sit in an almost preternatural still-ness when he's concentrating on something. I gesture to the bed. "Can I?"

He stares at me, his bright blue eyes piercing. "You've never asked before."

"I've never felt like you were pissed off with me before."

He jerks. "I'm not pissed off with you."

"It feels like it, especially now that you've holed yourself up in the bedroom to avoid us."

"Not you," he says abruptly, and then looks like he wants to slap himself.

"Ah, Ed, then. Not a fan?" I say wryly.

He shrugs and says nothing, but I wait him out and eventually he cracks. "So, that's Ed, then?"

I catch his eye and bite my lip, and he grimaces at me until I laugh out loud. "Say what you think."

He looks at me seriously and my laughter dies. "You were together for a long time."

I shrug, lying back on the bed and staring at the ceiling. "A year."

"He doesn't seem very *you*."

I turn my head to stare at him. "Why?"

He seems to be weighing his words. "Well you're very easygoing and warm, and he's very ... very high maintenance by the look of him."

"He is, but to be fair, I knew that. He never hid it. I just fell into the relationship, I suppose. I wanted it to be something that it was never going to be, and that's my fault, because he patently could never give me what I wanted."

"What's that?"

I sigh and he looks at me intently, giving me his whole attention the way that he always does when I speak. "To come first, I suppose. All my life I've been the one to look after people. I give them what they need, I am what they want, but then afterwards there just always seems to be something more important for them to have. Ed would never want the real me. He wants what I became for him—the worldly man with rock star friends. The man who was lighthearted and had money. He wouldn't have stayed around very long for the real me—the serious me that likes the quiet as much as the parties, that likes looking after people, that likes books and cooking and just sitting on a beach looking out to sea."

"Then he's an idiot, Matt. They were all idiots," he whispers fiercely, and I look at him with a start as he nods. "He had something that most people look for and he couldn't see it. That's *his* idiocy, not yours."

I snort at his customary autocratic tone that suggests that what he states is the absolute truth, and then I say softly, "I don't always want to see and be seen at the best parties, because I've done that for too many years. I want something real and true." I pause and shoot him a sideways look. "I want a real partner, not a boyfriend who brings home a twenty-two-year-old twink to make up a threesome for my birthday present."

"What the *fuck*?"

I look at him and start laughing helplessly. "I just wanted the latest Jeremy Clarkson biography," I gasp out, and he starts laughing, and soon we're in fits on the bed rolling around.

The sound of the door interrupts us mid-howl and we both fall silent, staring at the elegant figure of Ed. He's leaning on the door staring at us beadily, and I sigh inside at that look. I've seen it too many times in the past when he'd make a huge scene at someone paying me too much attention. It had led to us being ejected from a couple of parties to my eternal embarrassment, but I hadn't paid attention to the warning signs and persisted in believing that it meant that he cared. He did, I suppose, but only in the way that a dog cares about pissing up a lamppost.

"What's going on here?" he says coolly. "There's a lot of hilarity. Don't tell me that Matty's found another straight man to convert."

Bastard, I think, seeing John flinch. I'm not having a scene in here, not when I've just got him laughing again. "Ah, alas," I say lightly, getting to my feet and giving John a hearty slap on his shoulder. "This one is irredeemably straight, Ed. He's straighter than Peter Stringfellow, aren't you, Johnny?"

He stares up at me for a second and I think that I'm the only one that sees the hesitation in his eyes, but then he sits up and nods. "I am."

I shrug as if that didn't send a shaft of pain through me, and waving goodnight I stroll out of the bedroom, no wiser, really, than when I entered.

John

A week later I sit in my study, listening to the sound of 'John, Johnny!' echoing through the house. I shudder. I don't even feel safe in my study anymore. I'd thought about locking the door, but he'd only have come through the patio doors instead the way that he did yesterday, coming up behind me while I was staring into space and making me jump.

"John!" the yell sounds again, and I grit my teeth finally and shout out, "In here."

Matt had taken the cowardly way out and gone back to work a couple of days ago, telling Ed when he complained that if he didn't like it then he could leave. I'm not sure whether he honestly expected it to work, but it hadn't. Instead his standoffishness seems to be regarded by Ed as some weird form of foreplay, and instead of leaving he has since ensconced himself outside on the patio, oiling himself up with suntan oil and wearing the skimpiest pair of trunks that I've ever seen.

However, that's infinitely better than his original outfit, which had been nothing, and had totally scandalised Odell who'd threatened to leave. I'd had harsh words with him about the nakedness and his using Odell like she was some sort of slave, shouting for drinks and food whenever he felt like it. Ever since then he's been sulky with me, which has actually suited me because I'd really be happy if he never spoke to me again.

If he was anyone else I'd have asked him to leave, but his connection with Matt means that I can't. Matt may have decried his relationship, but he'd still let him stay, and I realised that he never actually said that he didn't want him back.

So I've left him here and had to watch him fawn over Matt and manipulate him. At first when I'd met him I'd dismissed him as a not very bright pretty boy, but after watching him last night with Matt I'd changed my opinion and upped my dislike because what he is, is a very manipulative, opportunistic man.

I'd watched him play Matt, only just remembering to close my mouth which had dropped open in amazement as he told sad stories about his childhood, which I'd be prepared to bet were lies. He'd laid himself seemingly bare, while at the same time admiring my Rolex and managing to convey the idea that his pain would be eased by having one.

He didn't do it that brashly, of course. It was actually a very subtle, masterly performance and I'd be willing to bet that it had taken Matt in many times, because that is his big weak spot. He's too kind and generous and it makes me furious to think of someone taking advantage of this.

I'd sat there last night and felt a wave of protectiveness roll through me that had rendered me speechless with the realisation that I wanted to keep that soft underbelly of his safe from scars. I wanted him to continue to be the warm, caring man that he is without getting hurt.

The strength of that feeling, that desire to stand in front of him and take the blows that such kindness draws, astounds me. I'd always looked after Bella and God help anyone who had hurt her, but this white-hot feeling of possession and protection is like nothing that I've ever felt before.

I come back to the present with a jerk to find Ed in my doorway, leaning poised against the wall. "Johnny, do you know when Matt will be back?"

"My name is John, not Johnny," I say coolly.

He affects surprise. "Matt calls you Johnny, so I thought it was okay."

"Matt's a friend."

His eyes light up with malice and I know that what comes next is going to hurt. "I think it's so nice that the two of you have become friends," he says gently. "I would never have seen that coming." He waits for me to ask why, but I just stare at him with a raised eyebrow that unluckily doesn't deter him. "I mean, when we knew you in London he couldn't stand you."

I'm ashamed to say that I don't stop the flinch, and his eyes sparkle with enjoyment. "I'm sorry. I hope that I'm not speaking out of turn. I got the feeling that you didn't really like him much, anyway." He pauses. "But Matt, well, he had a really passionate dislike of you. I've never seen him like that before, because normally he likes everyone." A smile plays across his lips. "Well, everyone except you. He used to go on about how arrogant you were, how you thought you were God's gift to mankind, when in actuality you were just some poor schmuck whose wife had left him."

I swallow hard because I feel bruised by this. I don't know why, because I've always known that he didn't like me, but somehow to have it actually confirmed hurts like a bitch and makes me wonder whether he really does like me now, or if he's just too polite to be antagonistic to someone who's housing him.

I don't let my feelings show, however, because better men have tried to hurt me and never succeeded. "I'm so glad that you came in to see me," I say coldly and he looks slightly worried. "Yes, I'm very happy, because what I really needed today was some bimbo twink with a pert backside and a flabby, underused brain to come in and give me the benefit of his sadly lacking wisdom and view of the world. Are you available for the rest of the year, Ed? Because my life would be sadly lacking if I didn't have you following me around gifting me with your very important views on how tight one's trousers should be this year, and whether pink shorts are ever really acceptable in the fashion calendar."

He glares at me poisonously and opens his mouth to fire God

knows what inanities back at me, but a deep voice comes from behind him, making him jump. "What's going on in here?"

Ed spins around, holding his hand to his muscled chest. "Oh, babe, you made me jump. I swear we should attach a bell to you. You move so quietly, like a big tawny cat."

Matt rolls his eyes. "Or a six-foot man moving normally and a model who needs to listen." I smile and his eyes meet mine in perfect accord, but then his expression clouds with worry as he must see something in my face that bothers him. "I say again, Ed, what's going on in here?"

"Just chatter," I say smoothly as Ed flounders slightly. "And chatter that probably should stop, as I have a deadline to finish this book and it won't write itself."

Matt gives me a very intent look and then nods, grabbing Ed by the elbow. "Leave Johnny alone, Ed. I've told you that he's busy."

He shuts the door behind him and I slump in my chair, letting out a slow breath, only now aware of how tightly I was holding myself.

Dinner that night is excruciatingly painful. Odell has outdone herself with Moules Marinières and homemade bread and a custard tart for dessert, but all three of us pick at our food, hardly touching it. Unfortunately, the same can't be said for the alcohol, as we've gone through four bottles of wine already.

Ed's face is flushed and his eyes glittery while he elaborates on how the possession of a new car might improve his sad life. Matt hardly makes any pretence of listening, instead staring into space, his face distracted and pensive. I'm still smarting over the conversation in the study to the extent that I can't look Matt in the face, a fact that I know he's noticed, as for the first half hour he shot me increasingly worried looks.

Finally Ed gives up and shoves his plate away with a petulant huff. "Fucking hell, it's boring here," he gripes. "I don't know how you've stood it here this long, Matt. You must have been dying of boredom."

Matt's head shoots up. "Don't be so fucking rude," he chides, his voice harsh. Then his expression softens and he looks at me affectionately. "It's actually been the best couple of months that I've ever had," he says softly, and I raise my glass mockingly.

"Yes, a few weeks of being covered in every dirt known to man, a very bad injury, and an allergic reaction to medication. I should really market this place out."

Matt throws his head back laughing, and then his face softens. "Don't forget Saint-Honorat."

I smile, but Ed lets out a rude snort. "Whatever!" Then his head comes up, excitement on his face. "I've just had a good idea."

"Not a statement that you've ever made before, I expect," I say pleasantly, and he glares before returning to his idea.

"Let's go out."

"Go out where?" Matt asks warily.

"Into Cannes," he says excitedly. "There's a fantastic gay club there. I've been a few times when I've been on modelling shoots." He grabs Matt's hand, caressing it slowly. "Come on, Matt," he pleads. "You used to be such a live wire. I can't stand to see the way that you are now."

Matt smiles and removes his hand. "And how's that?"

"Oh, all boring. I thought that we'd be in Cannes or St Tropez every night when we made up, but we haven't gone out once. I brought so many good clubbing clothes with me because I miss the way that we were out every night. Do you remember Ibiza? I had to have a week off work when we got back, just to recover." He caresses Matt's hair. "Come on, babe, take me out."

Matt shoots an imploring look at me. "Ed, we're guests of John and I'm not going out and leaving him here, and besides, I think a gay club is about the last place that he'd want to go."

I stare hard at Ed's hand in Matt's hair, stroking through it and probably feeling the silkiness of the strands the way that I had when I'd stoked his hair on the beach. Suddenly I feel a wave of possessive anger go through me as he smirks at me, obviously thinking that I won't go. "You know what," I drawl. "It sounds good, let's do it."

Ed looks astonished and pissed off which is not a good look on him, but Matt just stares at me. Then something passes over his face, a look of first astonishment and then an almost feral anticipation that makes my pulse speed up and my dick stir. For a second our gazes meet and hold and the silence thickens. He licks his lips and my heart jumps—it fucking jumps. Still holding my gaze almost challengingly, he gives a sensual smile that twists his lips. "Okay, Johnny, you're on. Let's see what the night brings."

8

John

HALF AN HOUR later after getting changed, I come down the stairs to find Matt waiting in the foyer. He's changed, too. He's pulled his golden hair back in a low bun and looks exceptionally good in black skinny jeans and a black v-neck t-shirt that hangs low, showing off his tanned chest. I look at him worriedly. "Do I look okay?" I whisper, not wanting Ed to hear and take the piss.

He looks me up and down slowly, his eyes darkening. It's the first time that he's ever done it, and although I'm wearing dark jeans, a navy button-down shirt with the sleeves rolled up, and navy Vans, I still feel naked.

"You look—" He stops and clears his throat. "You look amazing."

I tug on my shirt nervously. "I don't want to stand out. I've never been to a gay club before."

He smiles. "Well, I'm disappointed that you didn't pack your pink leather chaps, but I'm sure the gay people of Cannes will get over their devastation."

I shove him playfully. "Oh, fuck off!"

His smile slides off his face and he looks serious. "I get the feeling that you were goaded into this, so if you want to back out I'll make your excuses."

I feel suddenly let down. "I'm going to be in your way, aren't I? I won't come."

"Stop," he says, grabbing my arm and pulling me closer. I swallow hard as he talks in a low, intimate tone. "I want you to come. There's nobody else that I would rather go with, but I need to know that you *want* to go, as opposed to having some sort of pissing competition with Ed."

"I would very much win that," I confide. "I think the only thing that he can beat me on are the salaries of the supermodels. I'm afraid that my knowledge of useless facts is a little limited."

He looks at me almost fondly. "You never fail to surprise me."

"In what way?"

He shrugs. "It's been a funny few months, but you don't approach anything the way that other people do." He pauses, shooting me a sharp look. "What did Ed say to you in your study this afternoon? I know that I walked into something, and you've seemed bothered all evening."

I shake my head. "He can't bother me."

"Johnny," he says in a gentle voice. "You are the cleverest man that I know and very worldly, but you are also straightforward, direct, and honest, and expect other people to be the same. Someone like Ed isn't any of those things, and he has a horrible way of identifying people's weaknesses and digging the knife in. Now, what did he say?"

I shrug, affecting disinterest. "About how much you hated me. Nothing that I didn't know already, but very detailed."

He curses, shoving his hand through his hair and upsetting the bun so that strands fall around his face. "Bastard! What a fucking bastard! Well, he's gone tomorrow. I didn't want to throw him out and upset you, but he's fucking gone."

"How the hell would him going upset *me*?"

"Well, you issued the invitation to him and I didn't want to usurp you in your own home. Plus, I'm not going to be pleasant, and embarrassingly I didn't want you to see me when I get nasty."

"*Really?*" I ask in disbelief. "You're going to be horrible to that gold digger? How did you not think that I would want to reserve front row seats?" He stares at me and I nod firmly. "I might even invest in one of those foam pointy finger things and wave it in the air, and I'll definitely eat popcorn."

"Really?"

"Okay, you've got me, I hate popcorn."

"How can you hate popcorn?" he asks wonderingly.

"It's flavoured, airy cardboard."

"It is not." He stops and shakes his head at the turn of conversation. "Why are you pleased that he's going?" he asks, coming closer. His voice has gone deep suddenly, and the air seems to thicken around me.

I swallow hard and he watches my Adam's apple rise and fall, a hungry look on his face. "I don't think that you should get back together with him."

"Don't think, or don't *want* me to get back together with him?" The question has an abrupt edge to it as if it's been on the edge of his tongue for a while.

I stare at him, feeling unnerved. If I say this, I am stepping out onto a bridge with no chance of going backward but equally no knowledge of what lies ahead, but the words come out anyway. "I don't want you to get back together with him."

"Why?"

He stares at me uncompromisingly, all pretence of lightness gone now. I pause and then open my mouth, but shut it again as a door slams upstairs and we hear Ed making his way down the hall.

He grabs my arm and hauls me close, speaking quickly and intensely. "No playing around, now. We *will* revisit this conversation, but I want you to listen to me now. I may have disliked you on first sight, John, but I didn't *know* you. Anything that Ed said can be taken with a pinch of salt and with the knowledge that this was everything to do with me and not you. You did *nothing* wrong at all. You are a fine man who makes my life better for being in it, and that just makes me an idiot for not recognising it at first. But I'm glad that I came here and got to know you, because knowing you has been the most unexpected and confusing pleasure of my life."

I swallow hard, unable to say anything, and he looks me in the face, checking that I've understood him, so I nod. Appearing content, he drops my arm and turns just in time to see Ed coming down the stairs. He looks good in a red polo shirt with the sleeves rolled up to the tops of his arms, skinny jeans that look like they might cut his circulation off, and his hair swept up in a quiff, but as normal there's a petulant expression on his face. "Matty, I broke the strap on my watch. Can I borrow yours?"

Matt looks down at his Breitling Skyracer watch reluctantly. "Will I get it back?"

Ed looks sharply at him. "For fuck's sake, when have I ever not returned something that I borrowed from you?" Matt looks as if he wants to list a few times, but Ed continues. "I just want to borrow a watch, for Christ's sake."

Matt looks hesitant and I push away from the wall. "I've got a spare. You can borrow that." I head upstairs and retrieve the watch before walking back downstairs to find them in the middle of what looks like a very intense conversation. Ed is puce in the face with rage but Matt just looks bored and edgy.

"Here," I say quickly, and Matt exclaims at the watch.

"Jesus, that's a Tag Heuer, John. You shouldn't lend that out."

"It's nothing," I shrug. "I'd rather loan that than the one you're wearing. Bram bought it for you, didn't he?"

He nods gratefully and Ed huffs. "Oh, Bram, then. Well, we must all bow down if he bought it. I'm just surprised that it's not in a fucking display case."

I shake my head in disgust. "That's his best friend. What sort of person would he be if he didn't value something that someone went to the trouble of buying and engraving for him?" The watch has the S.E. Hinton quote engraved on it, '*If you have one good friend, you're more than lucky.*' Bram has its twin with the same engraving, and I know that Matt treasures it. He gives me a grateful look and I shake my head at his obvious worry. "It doesn't matter, don't worry about it."

Ed looks at me, his face still flushed from the alcohol that he drank earlier and a dangerous glint in his eyes. "It must be nice to have such a *very* good friend like John, Matty. One who knows you *so* well. But does he know that you like having a dildo inserted when you're having a blow job, or that you liked licking your come off me when you'd blown your load?"

Matt groans, but I laugh. "And *that's* the sum of your knowledge of him after a year, is it? I'll make a note of those observations but it'll be a small note, maybe a Post-it."

Ed swells up and opens his mouth but Matt forestalls him. "The taxi's here," he says curtly. "Shut up, for God's sake."

Ed storms out, slamming the front door hard, and Matt sighs. "Remember the foam finger," I say softly, and he drags one hand down his face.

"Don't give it to me, for God's sake, or I might end up inserting it somewhere."

"I think that sounds like something *you* might enjoy more after that little revelation."

"Oh, fuck off," he laughs, pushing me out of the door.

We pull up outside the club which already has a long line of people waiting outside, but Ed waltzes past them to talk to the bouncer on the door who promptly smiles and lifts the red rope by the door to let us through.

Ed gives me a triumphant look. "Perks of the modelling jobs," he says smugly. "I'm not sure what use a lawyer is here."

I stare at him seriously. "I'm sure that when my job requires me to get people into nightclubs I'll have to adapt, but for now I'll try and restrain my natural jealousy."

Matt snorts, but when Ed gives him an indignant look his face softens. "I'm glad that your job's going well. I always knew that you'd make a good model," he says kindly.

Ed looks at him beadily. "I'm sure it seems exotic to you, Matt. I mean, you're a bag carrier for Bram, not a star in your own right."

Matt rolls his eyes. "I'm wounded," he says, patently lying.

"You see, that was the real problem," Ed retorts. "You never had any real ambition. I mean, your company does well, but if you'd just used your connections you could really have been something."

"I didn't want to use my connections," Matt says wearily, and it's obvious that this is a well-worn argument. "Because those connections are my friends and family."

"Oh please, they'd dump you in a heartbeat if you stopped being useful. I told you that often enough."

"That's enough," I say sharply. "He's done exceptionally well for himself. The business is very successful, and those connections that you're on about would do anything for him. Can you say the same?" I look at him in disgust.

"Can we not do this here?" Matt says loudly and gestures to the double doors where the thump of a heavy beat can be heard.

Ed stalks past us, opening the doors and letting out a wave of sound, and Matt seemingly shakes off his mood and catches my arm. "Ready to go through the wardrobe, babe?"

"Is that a euphemism for coming out of the closet?"

He snorts. "No, it's a reference to Narnia."

I smirk. "I know, although if we were being realistic and you were Mr Tumnus in this scenario then you shouldn't be wearing anything on your bottom half." He laughs loudly and then I frown. "Equally, that would make me a schoolgirl called Lucy."

"Disturbing, but not as disturbing as the story looks to an adult." He shakes his head mockingly and puts out his hand. "Come on, Lucy. You're going to go with a half-naked, trouserless stranger to his home where he will give you food and drink and then play you a tune on his fiddle."

I put my hands over my ears. "Oh my God, stop ruining that book for me." We both start laughing uncontrollably while Ed holds the door open, tapping his feet.

"Come on before Mona Lisa over there self-combusts," he says, and draws me through the door.

I look around curiously. I don't know what I expected, maybe just another nightclub, but there's definitely a different atmosphere to this one. It actually looks a little shabby, and it's either been a while since they decorated or they've gone for retro 1980's. However, the atmosphere is frantic and lively with the dance floor packed with same-sex couples who are grinding against each other, and as I look around I see a lot of people who are in the advanced stages of foreplay. It makes my blood thrum through my body as if anything is possible here.

Matt pushes me towards the bar lit up by neon pink and green lights. "What do you want to drink?" he shouts in my ear and I lean into him.

"Beer, please."

He nods and while he's turned away I look around for Ed, who seems to have disappeared, and then I see him grinding away on the dance floor with a young dark-haired man. I nudge Matt and point and he shrugs dismissively before handing me a beer. I clutch it, hastily averting my eyes from a couple of men next to us who appear to be trying to eat each other's faces.

Matt laughs and glances around. "Is it what you thought?" he asks, leaning sideways to talk into my ear and sending a shiver down my spine. His eyes darken, and he puts his hand on my back and draws me nearer to him so that I can smell the warm citrus smell of his Miller Harris aftershave. It makes me dizzy so that my thoughts spin and whir before I remember what he asked me.

"It's got a good atmosphere." I shrug. "I like the music."

For a second it's like he doesn't hear me, his attention seemingly centred on the slow movement of his hand on my back, and then he jerks and looks up and I swallow at how dark his eyes have gone.

Then he smiles in what looks like wonder. "You're amazing, do you know that?"

"Why?"

"Because you take everything as it is. You don't demand that it be something else and you don't freak out. You look at it every which way and then just shrug and get on with it."

"Is that what you see when you look at me?" I lean closer to talk and he shivers when my breath blows on his ear. He turns his head slowly.

"I see a lot when I look at you," he says slowly. I swallow hard, feeling my blood pulse round my body as if it's a new feeling, but before I can ask what he means we're jostled by the snogging couple who have lost their balance after moving onto almost obscene groping.

Matt laughs and accepts their apologies and holds his hand out to me. "Come and dance."

Riton's 'Rinse & Repeat' has just started playing and the heavy beat sounds through my body. "I'm sure that you think you're setting me a challenge," I say darkly. "Like I'm some starchy lawyer who needs help to let his hair down. I *can* dance, you know. I used to love clubbing, but work got in the way."

He smiles at me. "Johnny, I have learnt never to come at you with preconceived notions of how you'll react, because I'd be wrong every time."

"That's good, though?" I shout. "That's good, right?" He shakes his head and draws me into the centre of the dance floor where people are writhing and moving to the beat. When he finds his spot we immediately start to move, and I wouldn't be human if I didn't enjoy the look of surprise on his face when I let my body move sinuously.

"Fucking hell, Johnny," he shouts.

I laugh. "Told you I could dance," I shout back.

He laughs and we dance for ages, stopping only to get shots

which we down hastily before throwing ourselves back on the dance floor.

It happens quickly. One minute I'm laughing at some move that he's pulled which is cheesy to the extreme, and then I feel the warmth of another body against me and a hand pulls me back into a long muscled body and what feels like a very hard cock.

I jerk away and Matt's humorous expression changes in an instant and he moves forward and shoves the bloke back. The stranger is very good-looking in an arrogant fashion and holds his hands up in a gesture of apology, but Matt isn't appeased. "Fuck off," he mouths, and I grab his arm.

"Matt, it's fine," I soothe. "No harm done. Come on, let's dance."

Still glaring back at the offender, he lifts his hand and in a very deliberate gesture he wraps it around the base of my skull, caressing my hair and pulling me to him until we're resting our heads together. "No fucking way," he growls. "He's not fucking touching you."

I raise my hands, curling them round his, and meet his eyes, the pulse of the music echoing in every centimetre of my body. I thought that I would hesitate when I finally made my decision, but the most remarkable thing is how naturally my next words come out. "He won't," I say baldly. "Only you can do that."

He shudders and closes his eyes for a second, but when they open again he stares at me and something that feels very much like a promise is exchanged. When he moves back his eyes are clear again but there's a heat there that I've not seen before, and I can't help but feel the excitement run through me, as well as a feeling of reckless-ness that I was never allowed to have as a child.

Nothing more is said with words, but our bodies tell a different story because now he's dancing very close to me and touching me all the time. They're innocent touches at first, like a lingering touch to my arm to show me something on the dance floor, his hands carding through my hair or him grabbing my shoulders and pulling me towards him when he wants to tell me something.

However, when the slow, dirty beat of 'Angel' by Massive Attack comes on and slows everything down, the situation changes and he lifts his hands deliberately, fastening them on my hips and drawing me to him until one leg is between mine. Our hips meet and then we start to grind together.

I shudder wildly and his hands move tightly on my hipbones like he's thinking of doing more but is restraining himself, and I realise that he's holding back because this is new to me and he doesn't want to freak me out.

This angers me and I haul him closer. "Don't do that," I growl. "Treat me like you would another man, Matty. I don't need special circumstances. I might be new to this, but I'm not some Victorian maiden that needs treating with kid gloves."

His head jerks back and he pulls me to him with his hand on the back of my neck, long fingers spread wide, but before anything can happen I'm shoved sharply from the back. I whirl around, my fist clenched, but then groan when I see Ed, his face flushed and eyes sparkling with anger.

"I knew it," he shouts. "I fucking *knew* it."

"Not here," Matt says wearily, and grabbing him by the arm he pushes him off the dance floor, looking back to me and gesturing for me to follow. I consider not doing that because I fucking hate scenes, but I hate the idea of him doing this on his own more, so I follow him off the dance floor.

As I near the edge, a man appears who is tall and good-looking with dark red hair. He grabs my arm lightly. "Are you with anyone?"

I gesture to Matt. "Yes, him, why?" I say automatically, no thought to another answer.

"Shame," he says, looking me up and down. *Jesus, it's a bit like being a cow at a fucking cattle market in here.* He leans nearer. "If the evening goes wrong, come and find me."

I look at him properly for the first time and analyse my feelings. If I'm gay now, or bisexual, then surely I should have some reaction to him, because he's movie star gorgeous. But I have no reaction at all, whereas I only have to look at Matt to have so many feelings rush through me that I sometimes feel that I can't contain them. I shelve that thought for later perusal and smile politely at him. "Thanks for the offer, but I think I'm good."

He laughs. "I have a feeling that you're really not, but his gain is my loss." I hear a shout of 'John,' and looking up I see Matt glaring at the man and me. The man promptly smiles and melts away back onto the dance floor and I rejoin Matt, who is still holding onto Ed in a loose grip. I follow him until he guides us to one of the booths that line the dance floor, where he gives the attendant some money and she promptly unlocks the door.

As the door shuts I breathe a sigh of relief as the noise level lowers a little bit, but not for long. "Who was that?" he growls, and I look at him in amazement. I have never seen him angry in all the time that I've known him, and as I've always ended up watching him at whatever event we were at, I can say that conclusively. I didn't even see him angry when Ed kissed another bloke at a party. Now, however, he's fizzing with it.

"What is the *matter* with you?" I ask.

He reins in his anger with seeming difficulty. "Nothing. I just don't like seeing some man with his fucking hands on you."

"He was just talking," I soothe, but Ed steps forward, poking Matt in the chest. My fists curl but I take a deep breath and step back, letting Matt handle this.

"You never once behaved like this with me," Ed shouts, enraged.

Matt sighs, his anger dialled down almost immediately. "I'm sorry," he says thickly.

"What for?"

"I'm sorry that we wasted our time together. I'm sorry—" He pauses.

"No, tell me, Matt, what are you sorry for?" Ed asks dangerously.

"I'm sorry that I didn't love you," he says in a low voice. He looks up. "You're worth more than an emotionally unavailable partner."

"So you didn't love me and that's why you never got jealous?"

Matt shakes his head sadly, and Ed's eyes fire with rage to the extent that I move closer. "Does that mean that you love *him* now?"

He points at me dismissively and Matt's head shoots up. He looks at me and something passes over his face too quickly to work out what it is, but Ed laughs and Matt turns back to him. "What?" he asks hoarsely and something seems to have knocked him off-balance.

"I should have known, that's all. You're always after the challenge, Matt, and I know how much you like converting the straight ones."

"What? *No.*" Matt looks poleaxed and shoots me a desperate look as I step back involuntarily. "Johnny, that's not true, listen to me."

"You should worry, *Johnny*," Ed sneers, putting a horrible emphasis on my name. "You don't mean anything to him, so don't get serious because all you straight boys are just a stand-in for the original one." Matt gasps, looking winded, and Ed smiles coldly. "Oh, are we still not mentioning that? Does *Johnny* not know about Ben?"

"I do know about him," I say sharply, and surprise flickers over his face before he sneers.

"Oh, I'm sure that you know some of the story, John, but maybe not all. Did Matt mention that Ben was straight before him? That it was letting Matt fuck him that sent him over the edge, that—"

"That is fucking enough," I say icily, moving in front of Matt who is pale and shaking. "You shut your fucking mouth. Matt is not responsible for that."

"Oh, really, and you'd know that how? How on earth would you know how he felt?"

"I do know," I shout, my temper snapping like a piece of worn elastic. "Of course I fucking know. I was straight before I met him, and if Ben felt anything like I'm feeling now, then I'd fucking bet my house that he was happier and more alive than he had ever fucking felt before."

Silence falls like a thunderclap and for a minute the only noise is all of our elevated breaths and the thump of the music, and then Matt says 'Johnny' in a broken voice and I turn instantly to him, wanting to protect him, to soothe him, only to jostle forward as Ed pushes me.

Matt shouts out, but I turn on Ed, and with a hand around his throat I push him against the wall. "You only get one chance at that," I growl. "If you fucking touch me again I will hurt you, do you understand me?"

I let go abruptly and he falls back against the wall. He looks up at me. "That's so touching, Johnny, how you stick up for him, but watch your step. He goes for the dark-haired boys, and you're the spitting image of Ben."

Matt pushes between us as I can't help but flinch. His face is pale but all his spark is back. "He's about as similar to Ben as you are to Donald Trump, you fucking cretin. The only similarity between the two of them is hair colour and the fact that they both have dicks. You know nothing, because on his worst days, Ben was never a fucking bitch like you. Now fuck off and get away from me and make sure that you never come near me again, because any goodwill I had towards you is gone now. It vanished when you decided to try and eviscerate him." He points at me and then leans forward and shouts, "Now fuck off!"

"What the fuck, Matt? Where should I go?" Ed shouts in obvious amazement but Matt is already turning back to me, his expression stony.

"I'll send your stuff on, so either check into a hotel or fuck off home," he throws over his shoulder and then shrugs. "Either way, I don't care anymore."

Ed glares at the two of us and then shoves off the wall and out of the booth. He slams the door closed behind him with a heavy thump and silence descends between us.

Matt turns to me hesitantly, a look of dread on his face. "Johnny," he says hoarsely. "Please don't listen to him."

I stare at him, at the messy hair and beautiful face with the tired, warm eyes, and I realise that nobody has ever felt more to me. Suddenly all my doubts and hesitations and worries over such a drastic change in my life fall to ashes, and before I can even think anymore I pull him to me and seal my lips to his, tasting spearmint and the faint tang of beer.

For a second he stands stock-still as if stunned, and then a groan rumbles up in his chest and he grabs my shoulders hard and pushes me back against the wall, crowding in against me so that we're standing chest to chest, sharing our panted breaths. The grinding beat of the Massive Attack track echoes in the room, seeming to reverberate through my body.

"Be sure," he rumbles. "Be very sure."

However, instead of speaking I just grab his head and pull his lips back to mine, and then there is no more thought, just a hot red darkness around us. He kisses me, opening my mouth and forcing his tongue in to tangle with mine, and even if I wanted to I couldn't have pretended that there is anything but a man kissing me now.

I feel his stubble against my cheeks and the warm softness of his lips. I feel the weight of him against me which is so much more than the light, fragile feeling of a woman. I feel the height of him and the width of those broad shoulders under my hands, and I'm so fucking turned on that all I can do is moan harshly and press against him, deepening the kiss and tangling my hands in his silky hair, keeping his face against mine, his lips locked to mine.

"Johnny," he gasps, tearing away. "Oh God, I want you so fucking much," and he finally allows his hips to sink against mine, and for the first time in my life I feel another man's cock hard against my own. The feeling is indescribable, all heat and pressure and hardness rather than the softness and yielding of a woman's body.

I groan out something unintelligible and throw my head back, moaning as he licks down my throat. He fastens his lips around my Adam's apple and sucks gently, wringing more desperate sounds from me, and all the time his hips writhe sinuously against me and the feel of his hard cock sends sparks down my spine.

"Matt," I moan, fumbling to pull off his t-shirt, wanting only to feel his silky skin against mine. "I need. Fuck, I *need*."

"I know, babe," he pants, his lips partly open as he draws in desperate gulps of air. "I know. Let me take care of you." He looks around the booth. "Shit, I didn't want this to happen somewhere like this for your first time. Let's go home."

"No." It's a desperate groan and I pull him by the t-shirt, my hand going underneath and feeling the hard silk of his ribs. "Don't you fucking stop. God, Matty, I fucking hurt."

I try to grind against him and he pants, his eyes dazed and unfocused. I grab his arse and cry out in pleasure as his cock is back against me where I need it most, giving me sublime pleasure to the extent that I can feel pre-come painting my boxers.

Suddenly there's a gap and air between us, and I slit open my eyes and make an inarticulate protest. "No, babe," he whispers. "Trust me, I'm going to look after you. Do you trust me?" I nod weakly and roll my head back against the wall as his nimble fingers pull down my zip and reach into my boxers to pull out my cock.

We stare down at his large calloused hand on my dick, and nothing has ever looked so hot. "Look at me," he pants, and I manage to force my eyes open. "Fuck, John, you're the hottest thing that I've ever seen. Do you want this?"

"I want it all," I groan. "Don't hold back."

He moans, closing his eyes for a second, and while he's distracted I reach for the buttons on his fly. "Wait," he moans, and I push him slightly, making him look at me.

"Matty, it's me, and if I'm in, then I'm in all the way. I'm not letting you hold back for fear of offending me. I want you so fucking much that you can't offend me. I trust you. You won't do anything that I can't take."

I fumble open his boxer briefs, finally feeling the warmth of his cock, and for a second I pause, staring down in disbelief. I, John Harrington, have another man's dick in my hand. I wait for the doubt and shame that everyone goes on about to hit me but it doesn't, and all I can really think about is how hot this is, and how I have never been as turned on in my life as I am right now in some seedy back booth in a club.

The skin on his dick feels sleek and silky and it's hard as a pipe with an angry purple head that's leaking pre-come. He's longer than I am but I think I might be wider. I give it an experimental squeeze and then my head shoots up as he gives the most sinful grunt, pushing into my hand and panting through his open mouth. "It feels so good, Johnny," he whispers. "God, so good."

I decide to treat his cock the way that I like, as surely I can't go wrong with that, so I take it in a firm hold and stroke it from root to tip, twisting on the top and feeling the wide wetness of the flared crown against my fingers.

He gives out a choked groan and then suddenly he's all decisive motion, pushing me back against the wall, stripping off our shirts and fumbling between us, all signs of hesitation gone. I feel air on my cock and then he lifts his hand up to mine. "Spit," he says in a gravelly voice and I instantly do as I'm told, and then all thought vanishes and my head goes back and smacks against the wall as he grabs both of our cocks in his large hand and starts to rub and thrust against me.

The feeling is strange but so fucking good that I can't stand it. The silkiness of the skin and the wetness of our pre-come lubricate the slide, and the fucking insane pressure against me feels desperate. Looking down, I see the angry red head of my cock against his, appearing and disappearing from his fist.

I grab his arse and bring him in closer, needing more and more, and he kisses me again, open-mouthed, until finally we're making jerky out-of-control movements, panting into each other's mouths as we rut furiously against each other.

If someone came in now they would see everything. Me pinned to the wall by this big man, both of us helpless in our need, and the thought sends a spark down my spine and I feel my balls draw up tight. "Matt," I cry out. "Fuck, I'm going to—"

"Yes," he groans, speeding up his movements and making a low groaning noise with each whip of his narrow hips.

"Matt," I shout out and my cock erupts, gouts of come exploding out of me with more force than I've ever felt before. It splatters up my torso and chest, draining out of me in creamy ribbons, and I give a choked moan as he leans forward and with one swipe of his tongue licks one of the streams that have hit my nipple.

He moans low in his throat and suddenly he stiffens and wetness spurts over me, flying over his fist and landing amongst my pubic hair in glistening streams, and incredibly I feel another spurt of come shoot out of me, weaker this time, but enough to make him groan.

Spent, he collapses against me and I lift my arms, pulling him closer, needing to feel him against me. We rest there as gradually our breaths slow and the silence of the room seems to close in around us. Finally his muscles tighten preparatory to him moving away, and I restrain my instinctive desire to pull him back where he belongs. *Where he belongs?*

He reaches into the pocket of his jeans with one hand, and finding a hanky, he dries his hand which is still full of come, and then he comes to me and without a word he cleans my dick tenderly, and then my chest. His head is bent and he's totally focused, the way that I've seen him so many times over the last couple of months when he's been bent over a book or a newspaper, or listening to music with a dreamy look on his face.

Finally done, he chucks the hanky into a bin and then tucks me back in and zips me up. He does the same for himself, and still he's silent.

"Matt?" I finally whisper, suddenly afraid to the depths of me that he's regretting this. His head shoots up and worry creases his forehead. *My God, is he regretting this?* "Was it not good?" I finally whisper, hating how pathetic I sound.

He stares at me, so patently flabbergasted that I want to smile and I relax a little. "Not *good?*" he echoes. "Jesus, John, I've never felt like that or come like that, *ever*. I've had a lot of hook ups and nothing ever felt like that."

I flinch a little at the thought of how many experienced men he's been with, who knew what to do and probably put me to shame. "No, Johnny," he says firmly. "Don't think that."

"How do you know what I'm thinking?"

He smiles. "I know you. I don't know how or when it happened, but I know you better than I know myself, and despite their experience those men never made me feel an ounce of what you did." He sighs heavily, looking worried. "But my experience in situations like this is telling me that I should never have let it go that far."

I jerk. "You didn't want it?"

"Don't be ridiculous," he says sharply. "I couldn't have stopped if Demis Roussos walked in."

"*Demis Roussos*? Where on earth did that come from?"

"That caftan," he shudders, smiling, and then looks up at me. "I wanted to do this properly, Johnny. Your first time with a man shouldn't have been like this, all seedy. I wanted to make it good for you."

"It *was* good," I say harshly, reaching a hand for him and feeling immediate relief at the feel of him against me again. I feel safe like this, more able to talk. I cup his face, making him look at me. "I'm not saying that I have all the answers."

He gives a small smile. "Bet you hated saying that."

I consider it for a second and then nod. "It doesn't happen a great deal, obviously, but in this case it has." He snorts out a laugh which dies as I stroke his cheekbones, feeling the brush of his scruff against my hand, so alien and yet so strangely familiar. "I don't know where this is going. I don't know what's going to happen, but for the first time in my life, I don't care." He looks at me solemnly and I repeat firmly. "I. Don't. Care. What I care about is being with you and seeing where we go."

Some weight seems to lift off him but I keep talking, needing him to get this. "The only thing that I don't want is you treating me like I'm fragile. Don't treat me like a novice or as if I'm weak. Treat me as an equal and trust me to be able to speak up if I'm not comfortable with anything. It's the same way that I totally trust you to take care of me, and that's not an easy thing for me to say, Matt, because I don't trust easily."

He leans into me and rests his head against mine, staring deep into my eyes, and I watch his doubts visibly drain away, for now, anyway. Finally he runs one long finger down my nose ending up at my lips, where I surprise myself by kissing his fingers lightly and almost romantically. He stares at me, rubbing his fingers gently over the grooves on my lips. "Let's go home," he whispers. "I've had enough of this place. I just want to be together now."

I nod, unable to say any more, because I want that too. I want that more than I'm comfortable with.

9

John

I WAKE up the next morning lying face down amongst my sheets, face shoved half under the pillow like normal. For a second I stretch, thinking nothing and just enjoying the feel of my muscles loosening and the warmth of the sunshine pouring through the open French windows as the curtains move lazily in the breeze.

I feel loose and content and utterly unwilling to move, which is sufficiently unlike myself to actually focus my mind, and then suddenly memory pours back in and my eyes shoot open. Twisting my head, I see his broad, muscled, tanned back first as he's lying sprawled on the mattress, the white sheet sitting low enough over his arse to display the dimples above his cheeks. His face is turned towards me, his eyes closed and his hair a mess over the pillows. He has a relaxed, contented look on his unconscious face and I stare at him, wondering for a second what I should be feeling right now.

I would expect to feel panic welling up at the thought of what we did last night, at the way that my life has just dramatically changed. I would have thought that I'd be concerned over what everyone will think of me, but it's the total lack of these feelings which utterly surprises me and I lie looking at his tanned face, the full lips now pursed slightly. When I examine what I actually feel, I realise that I feel ... happy and energised.

I don't actually care what anyone thinks of me, anyway, so people changing their opinions about me because of my sexuality actually just renders them imbeciles and undeserving of friendship, so that doesn't bother me and I feel no panic. I just feel warm and peaceful lying here next to him, and when I inhale and smell his warm citrus scent on my sheets, I feel proud that such a gorgeous man wants me. Is that odd? Who the fuck knows and actually cares, because that's what I feel and that's all that should bother me.

I feel connected to him in a way that I haven't felt with any other person and I want to be with him and see where this goes, so that's what I'm going to do. For the first time in my life I'm going to switch off the ever-active part of my brain that calculates every move that I make, and I'm going to take a leaf out of this man's book and live for now.

My lip quirks and I reach out and lay one hand on his back, feeling the sleek heat of his skin and the muscles lying dormant underneath. A sudden mental snapshot flashes into my head of me pushing my hands under his shirt and feeling those muscles moving as he rutted against me, and just that quickly I'm rock-hard.

I suppose the sheer heat of last night's encounter might be switching my worries off as well, because nothing that I've ever done, and I've done a lot, has ever made me feel an ounce of that passion. I'd felt like I would have come out from my skin if I didn't get to come, and *all* of that had been tied up for the first time in the identity of my partner.

I roll over and stare at the ceiling, feeling the breeze blow over my naked chest, and consider that more thoroughly. Before, in any sexual encounters, I've always been concerned that my partner enjoyed it, but that was probably more a matter of pride than any real feeling for the person. Even with Bella, there had always been something slightly perfunctory about our sex life. It was an itch that I needed to scratch. But last night had been as different from that as bread is to chocolate, because if the other sex was bland, then being with Matt had been rich and a feast for all my senses.

I smile slightly. Even my thought processes have become florid and over the top, because we haven't even had full sex yet. Last night we'd come home sitting in the back seat of the taxi close together and he'd left his hand on my thigh, tethering me to him for the whole journey, but by the time that we'd got home I'd been expecting actual sex and a massive rehash of everything, and it had made me jittery.

Then, as always, Matt had seemed to read my mind, and instead he'd guided me to the shower, stripped us both, and then showered with me, his arms around me cleaning me and washing my hair. He'd towelled us off and then led me to my bed, and without my having to ask he'd slid in next to me and drawn me close, and I'd fallen asleep like that, lying held tight against hair-roughened strength rather than silky delicate fragility. I'd slept better than at any other time in my life.

I jump when a finger traces down my forehead and I twist to see him now awake, his warm brown eyes very alert. "That's a thoughtful wrinkle," he says slowly with no tone in his voice at all. "You look like you're thinking hard and maybe regretting things?" His eyes are watchful and guarded.

I twist to face him, lying on my side with the sheet pooling under my hip, and his eyes betray him. They flick down, tracing my torso and the curls of my thatch of pubic hair that are showing, and for a second they flash fire and want and need before he shutters them like he's packing his house up for the winter.

However, it gives me the confidence to do what I want to do, and without thinking I slide over and throw my arm over his back, pulling myself close to him and kicking the sheet aside so that I can feel all of him against me. He rolls slightly onto his side, and the warmth of his skin is my first impression, followed by the tensile hairy length of his legs now pushed against mine, and the crispier wiry hairs on his groin along with the weight of his cock, half-hard and lying against my thigh.

He breathes in sharply and then rolls fully onto his side and wraps his arms around me so that we're face to face. It's almost unbearably intimate because he can see everything that I'm thinking, and his eyes rove over my face intently. Before, I would have shied away from this, but now with this man I let him look his fill before I lean forward the few centimetres needed and touch my lips to his.

For a second he seems held immobile by surprise, and all his muscles lock up as if he'd expected me to be out of the door and running by now. But in the next second he moans low in his throat and his arms band tightly around me and he deepens the kiss, pulling my tongue into his mouth and sucking it, humming in his throat as I groan and press against him.

We kiss lazily for what seems like forever with no sense of urgency, until eventually he draws back. His pupils are blown, making his eyes look almost black in the sunlight, and I can feel the weight and heat of his cock now fully erect and pressing against my stomach as he must feel mine against him. However, instead of carrying things on he pushes back, and I make a lazy, inarticulate sound of protest.

He smiles in a muddled sort of way and pushes my hair back from my forehead almost tenderly. "We have to talk," he says hoarsely and I groan, rolling onto my back.

"*Really?*"

"Yes, really." He's stern now, and I focus on him. "I need to know where you are with this, John. This is a big thing."

I smirk. "It really is."

He groans and half smiles but then Captain Serious appears again and I take a moment to wonder when *I* became the lighthearted person in any scenario, and then I focus again on him as he speaks. "Don't make jokes now—how do you feel?" He swallows. "Do you regret it?"

His hair is a crazy bedhead and I run my fingers through it, smiling affectionately and enjoying the sensation of the sun-warmed silky strands against my palm. "I feel ... good. I've been lying here examining my feelings for a while." I stop. "You look relieved at my analysing?"

"I am," he says simply. "You shouldn't do this on a whim, babe. It should be thought out."

"Why?"

"Because it changes everything, the way that people regard you, your own self-image. It's a path with many pitfalls."

I put my fingers over his lips to stop him talking. "This is me, Matt. Of course I think about things. I doubt that will ever stop, but the conclusion that I came to is that I feel—" I hesitate. "I feel *happy*." His face lightens and yet possesses a hint of consternation, so I carry on quickly. "I feel happy and I don't feel all that confused. I want more, but at the same time I also feel out of my depth, because I don't know anything about this. I don't know what to do and I hate feeling like that. I want to be good at it and please you, but I don't know how to do that. I don't have the inbuilt knowledge that you do that comes from years of being gay. Apart from that crazy mix of feelings, I can't give you any more at the moment. Will the confusion and worry come later? Maybe. I don't know, but I need to know more. I want to carry on with this because I've never felt like this before. I just don't want to disappoint you."

He stares at me, thoughts running over his face too quickly to read, until suddenly his face clears and he smiles slightly, making me want to kiss those full lips so I do, lingering gently and licking their firm texture and feeling his early morning stubble rough against my cheek. "Everything feels brand-new," I say slowly. "It's like I'm a new person."

"Johnny, in a way you are, but you're still you, and once again you amaze me because I just can't second-guess you." He caresses my cheekbones, cupping them in his wide calloused hands tenderly, and once again I feel that shock of recognition that this is a man touching me without any doubt. He talks in a low, soft voice, and the deepness of his voice and the slight early morning raspy catch hit me in the chest and balls. "I thought that you'd be torturing yourself about how your partners at work will look at you, maybe feeling guilty and ashamed. Maybe wishing we'd all had less to drink?"

"Jesus, that's a lot of thoughts and emotions for first thing in the morning, even for me. I'm quite a simple bloke. I normally just want to have a shower and a cup of coffee."

He shakes his head knowingly. "Not simple at all. You're a very complicated, clever man whose thought processes I think will always start at full gear in the morning." I shrug and he smiles. "Instead you're just so *you*. Not really overcomplicating this. You're examining all the angles and dealing with it and ready for problems along the way, like a lawyer, I suppose." He smiles. "It is very typical, however, to find you struggling against the knowledge that you don't know everything about everything."

I snort and pull myself closer, accepting his open arms and nestling my head into his neck where I can smell his warm citrus scent strongly. "I do know most things. I'll just have to get a book on it and read up on it."

"What, like the 'Dummy's Guide to Homosexuality'?" he drawls and then laughs as I pinch him.

"Laugh away, but my way is always a good way." I reach for my tablet by the side of the bed. "I'll have a look on Amazon now."

He laughs out loud and grabs my arm and I'm struck by the strength there. When a woman tries to pull you it's usually joking and playful, so to have someone in my bed who could actually manhandle me about is different, and I have to admit surprisingly erotic.

He pulls me close. "I don't know what thought just crossed your mind, but that's a very interesting expression. How about rather than looking at a book you see me as your consultant?" The smirk is evident in his voice. "A very, very experienced and *able* consultant."

I snort. "Shall I hire you? Do you charge by the hour?"

He laughs out loud. "That is so wrong and yet I'm finding it very hot. We're obviously made for each other." I laugh, but he stiffens as if surprised at his words and rushes into speech. "I don't mean *together* forever, obviously. I mean we're mates." His smile twists slightly. "Mates who fuck each other at the moment."

I stare at him. I've never really seen him flustered before, and something inside me flinches at his words and I don't know why. Surely I can't view him as anything permanent, can I? We're blokes, so surely it doesn't have to be a huge, big deal if we just fuck? I mean, there is obviously a big attraction between us, but you don't make life partners from just attraction. There have to be mutual goals and respect as there had been with Bella, and I'm abruptly reminded that my goal three months ago was to get her back. Surely I haven't changed that much?

I ignore the twisting sensation in my stomach, because Matt obviously doesn't see this as the start of a permanent relationship, and I shouldn't, either. I have my target set. My chest feels a bit hollow and I rub it absently before I realise that I've been quiet for too long and he's waiting for an answer.

"Yes, that sounds good," I murmur, and although he relaxes instantly there's still something tight about his body. I frown at him, wondering what he's thinking, until he strokes my hair back gently, staring into my eyes.

"Let's spend the day together," he says softly. "Let's go out, the two of us, and leave big decisions far away for the day. While we can, let's just be together and leave everything else alone."

I stare at him for a second, seeing worry at the back of his warm eyes. "Let's do that," I say softly.

Matt

Two hours later we stand in a very expensive art gallery in the hilltop town of Vence. We've wandered the picturesque market town munching on crepes and tried different artisanal French beers at a small wine bar, but now we're standing in front of a gigantic canvas full of splashes of paint and broad slashing brushstrokes all in yellows and oranges and greens.

John stands in front of it, his head cocked to one side, looking a bit like the way my mum's old parrot used to look at you when you were eating peanuts. I snort out a laugh involuntarily, and both he and the gallery assistant turn to look at me in consternation. They've been standing here for the last half an hour in a passionate conversation about abstract impressionism and blah blah blah, and I'd drifted into my own thoughts, and now here we are.

I wonder what to say, but instead opt for a helpless smile which I like to think is charming. The assistant obviously views me as a complete Neanderthal and turns back to the hard sell, but John's lips quirk slightly as he stares at me for a moment too long, enough to make me wonder what he's thinking. Another second or two passes and then he gives me a very enigmatic shrug.

"I'm going to have a wander," I say softly.

He's instantly the well-mannered gentleman. "I'm sorry, Matt. This is rude."

"No, it isn't. You're enjoying yourself, and I love art galleries, so I'm happy to potter about."

He draws closer and away from the assistant. "Art galleries but not *this* piece of art?"

I smirk slightly and lower my voice so that only he can hear me. "I don't mind modern art, but that looks like something that somebody regurgitated on the pavement. I can't even begin to imagine where I'd hang it."

He breaks into a howl of laughter, making the assistant and a few people in this hushed environment stop and stare at him, but I ignore them, staring at the way that the laughter lights up his face, turning a taciturn man into someone who looks warm and totally approachable.

Becoming aware that I'm staring and he's now looking quizzically at me, I feel myself flush slightly. "I'll be around," I murmur, waving my fingers about and he grins, squeezing my arm before turning back to the assistant.

Dismissed, I take the opportunity to wander as far away as I can from the man who is totally rattling my thought processes at the moment. I end up alongside a set of silk patterned screens and I closet myself amongst them, staring blindly at them while I try to think properly.

Last night in that booth had felt unlike anything that I've ever felt before. I must have had hundreds of encounters in back rooms in clubs, but I've never felt so in the moment with someone. Every breath that he took and every groan that he gave made me hotter than I've ever felt.

Damn! I blow out a breath, trying to think of something unpleasant to scare away my incipient hard-on. I think of that fucking awful picture and sigh with relief. Job done.

I stare at the colours of the screens and the purples and rich reds of the embroidery, and I give myself a good talking-to. I have never made a habit of imputing real emotional feelings into what is just good sex, and I'm not going to start now. Yes, last night had felt amazing and I hope to have a lot more with him, but I cannot forget that this is a man who three months ago was determined to get his ex-wife back and was resolutely straight.

I've done this dance with a few straight men before and it always ends the same way, with them tangoing back into heterosexuality without a backward glance. Not to mention that I would never stand in the way of him being happy, and no matter how horrible his ex sounds, I would like him to be happy.

But what if this isn't just a toe dipped in the water? What if he decides that he wants a man instead? The thoughts shimmer into my head like a bright temptation, but I shove them aside because this is still no excuse to get involved. How shitty would it be of me to tie him to me with the chains of friendship and being the first man that he's been with? That would make me a despicable person and it would only lead to disaster, because in my experience relationships should be about a mutual desire to be together, to put each other first.

I sigh, because therein lies my very real problem. I have never in my life been in a relationship where the other person chose me fully and decided to put us as a couple first. Every relationship that I've ever had I've had to push to get what I want, and the other person has still prioritised other things over us.

I'm not being needy. I don't wish to have my partner want to be with me twenty-four hours a day and to have no thought beyond me. That idea makes me shudder in horror. I just want to *matter*. I want my feelings to matter, because what I want more than anything is to find that one person who I can do the same for. I want to look after them and be with them, but in a safe and easy way.

I grimace, because that's not going to be John. Maybe at another time in his life it would have worked with him, but he has so many loose ends and unclear paths to take that it's just not going to happen now. I sigh, because the thought hurts more than it should.

"That's a big sigh. Seen anything you like?"

I jump, and turn to find him standing close with one eyebrow quirked queryingly. *Fuck, I love it when he does that. Makes me want to lick him all over.* Trying to marshal my thoughts and with the worry that my feelings are written all over my face, I look back at the closest screen and stare at it blindly. "I like this one." I search for words. "It's very powerful."

"*Really?*" His voice is incredulous enough to make me take a real look at what I've actually *not* been looking at for the last twenty minutes. Instantly I feel myself redden, because what looked like a beautiful collection of colours on a screen is actually erotic art, with a man being taken up the arse by a three-armed and two-headed man.

"Erm—" I hesitate and cock my head to one side, aware that he's doing the same. Silence reigns for a second before I say casually, "I think I might have dated him a few years ago. It's the hands I remember most."

He bursts out laughing really hard. "Really? I'll come up short, then."

I look up, about to make a dirty pun, but the words die in my throat as I see a tiny bit of real worry in his eyes. He honestly does think that I'll find him lacking because I'll have to show him stuff that he doesn't know. I wish he knew how fucking hot I really feel about being his first, but as Ben was the last one that I could say that about I don't feel able to tell him, especially not with Ed's words still ringing in my ears from last night.

"You'll never come up short, Johnny," I settle for saying, and instantly that vulnerability that he only seems to let me see is gone and he blinks.

"Going to buy it, then? Put it in your Red Room of Pain."

"Oh, shut up." I shove him with my shoulder. "Fuck off and buy your pavement pizza."

He bursts out laughing, throwing his arm over my shoulder and hugging me to him. "I know where we can go to look at real art."

Half an hour later I stand outside a simple whitewashed building with a cross. I look at John enquiringly and he smiles. "It's the Chapel of the Rosary, otherwise known as the Matisse Chapel. He helped to design the building, the stained glass windows, even the priests' vestments, and he decorated it."

"I somehow don't think that you mean he put a roller over the walls," I say wryly, and he laughs.

"No, come and look."

I follow him into the building, watching the broad set of his shoulders in his sky blue shirt and feeling the sacred hush of a religious building wrap around me, and then I look up and gasp because it's the most beautiful building that I've ever been in. It's simple to the point of being stark with its plain white walls, but they serve to emphasise the colour flooding through the stained glass windows. Blues, greens, and sharp lemons swirl through the glass laying lazy, vibrant stripes across the tiled floors, and although the designs are simple they seem almost miraculous in the plain rooms.

John touches my arm and I jump, so absorbed am I in the colours, and he smiles gently and turns me to face the other walls which are full of elegant spare black drawings. They're exceptional, but I'm drawn most to a huge picture of what must be Mary with Jesus as a baby. It's simple but full of a real feeling of great love and devotion that brings a lump to my throat.

I stare at it, wondering why it touches me, and I think that it must be because it reminds me of my mum. When I was little she'd been the main focus of my life. Beautiful with a warm laugh, she'd lavished love on me, and I only have to smell the scent of 'Beautiful' by Estée Lauder when walking through department stores to be taken back to sitting on her lap, wrapped in her love while she read to me or tended to my cuts and bruises.

It wasn't my dad that had nearly broken me, it was her, because I have never been able to reconcile that woman with the one that stood silent and stone-faced as my dad laid blows on me and threw me out. It was the one defining betrayal of my life, and everything that came later just seemed to reaffirm her choice.

A warm arm wraps around my shoulder and I look sideways at John, who is staring at the drawing meditatively. I would almost see it as shared artistic appreciation if I didn't know suddenly and irrefutably that he knows what I'm feeling and is offering his own comfort. I feel a surge of warmth run though me and I reach up and squeeze his hand in appreciation.

We remain there for a while wandering the chapel, speaking in low-voiced murmurs and in the language of the slight weight of a hand to the back or fingers brushing a hip bone, and by the time we leave and go to find a restaurant I feel centred and as if a weight has lifted slightly.

10

John

IT'S dark when I pull through the gates and onto the driveway. We'd sat late in a little restaurant in the square, people-watching and stuffing ourselves with a delicious cassoulet and drinking an earthy red wine.

The drive back had been largely quiet as we listened to the 'Attack and Release' album by The Black Keys and kept to our own thoughts, but it wasn't tense or awkward. It isn't with us. I've found that I'm as comfortable with him in silence as I am when he's chattering and joking.

It's still very hot when we get out of the car. The sky is a deep, dark velvet blue spattered with stars like one of the stained glass windows that we'd seen earlier. He veers to the side rather than walking up the steps to the front door, and I follow him until he reaches the swimming pool. The water is totally still and reflects the stars so that for a second it looks like a piece of the sky has fallen to the earth. The air is headily perfumed with the scent of jasmine and the sweet smell from the orange tree that grows near the pool, and I take a deep breath.

"It's gorgeous, isn't it?" he whispers, looking out at the multi-coloured lights of Cannes, and I stare out too, welcoming the slight breeze that blows over us bringing the faint tang of the sea. "I am very hot, though," he says almost casually and I go to agree with him, but my words stutter and die away in my throat as I watch him undoing the buttons on his chambray-coloured short-sleeved shirt one by one, his long fingers looking elegant and dexterous.

"What—" I clear my throat and he grins knowingly. "What are you doing?"

"Well, Johnny, I'm taking my shirt off." He matches his actions to his words and the shirt flutters to the ground, and then his fingers move to the fastening of his cargo shorts.

"Don't tell me, let me guess what you're doing now," I drawl mockingly and he grins, his smile white and wide in the moonlight.

"That's your expensive education and the fancy letters after your name showing right there," he laughs and I smile, charmed as ever by him, before gulping hard.

"That's right, and my time at Eton tells me that you are actually getting bloody naked," I croak as his Vans hit the patio, followed by his shorts and red striped boxer briefs, and as a final gesture he takes off the band that had been holding his hair back in a ponytail so that his hair falls loose around his shoulders.

He stands there confidently for a second, letting me stare at him without showing any signs of embarrassment. He's so confident in his body that I almost envy him. "I am naked because I am going for a swim," he says happily. Then he laughs loudly, clutching his side. "Oh, Johnny, you look like an outraged Victorian chaperone. You just need a pearl necklace to clutch." He waggles his eyebrows lecherously. "I can definitely help you out with that."

"Oh my God," I groan. "Stop!"

He laughs again and then gestures to me. "Come on then, chop chop."

"What?" I ask slowly.

"Get naked, Johnny." He comes to me and starts to unbutton my shirt, stopping occasionally to slide his warm calloused fingers over the skin that he exposes until I swear that I can feel my heartbeat echoing in my ears.

When he's done he slides it off my shoulders and moves on to the buttons of my shorts. His fingers move slowly, and I groan at the feel of them moving against me until my cock is rising and pressing impudently against his hand. He palms my erection with just the right insane amount of pressure, and I grunt, which sounds loud in the still night air.

"Johnny," he whispers, sounding almost stunned as my shorts and boxers drop to the floor and I hastily kick off my Converse. "God, you're beautiful."

"Not beautiful," I remind him and he nods, a smile playing around his full lips.

"Okay, I forgot. God, you are smart and clever." He pauses and then smiles wickedly. "And you have the most *intelligent* cock." He dances out of the way as I go to punch him, before turning and diving neatly into the pool. He surfaces, shaking his hair back and running his hands down his face. "Fucking hell, it's lovely in here, Johnny, so cool. Come on, get your ass in here."

I obey and dive in, surfacing next to him. The water feels amazing, sliding silkily against my skin and my cock. He laughs loudly, throwing his head back before throwing himself onto me, his weight borne by the water, and I gulp as his wet body slides against mine. However, he spins away and a second later slaps a massive wave of water into my face.

I splutter, wiping the water off my face, and gaze at him intimidatingly. "Oh, you're going to suffer for that," I say darkly and lunge after him.

For the next hour we play and muck around, splashing and ducking each other while the huge harvest moon hangs full and yellow in the sky and bats skim the sky above us. Finally we surface together in the shallow end, clutching onto the side while we catch our breaths back. The white shape of an owl swoops low over the pool, but apart from that the night is still with not a sound apart from our breathing, and it feels almost unbearably intimate.

"Johnny," he whispers, and I turn to find him standing close. "Johnny," he whispers again, and takes my mouth in a lush, warm kiss. I open my mouth and moan under my breath as his tongue slides inside and tangles against mine.

He lets go of the side, standing up in the water as it streams off his muscled torso, and then his hands come up and he takes my jaw in his palms, pushing my face to one side so that he can go deeper, his breaths striking the side of my face.

For a while we kiss, not touching apart from where our mouths connect, and incoherent murmurs of pleasure drift around us. I can feel the water lapping around me and it feels cool against my heated skin, and the push and pull of the water as we move swirls around my erect cock in an amazing tugging sensation.

I'm so hard it hurts and I can't believe that it's from just a kiss. For a second I wonder whether it's affecting Matt like this. I mean, he's done so much that a few simple kisses can't have the same effect on him as they're doing to me. Then he groans deep in his throat and his hard muscled arms band around me dragging me against him, and I grunt as our bodies collide in the water and I feel the force of his cock, hard and throbbing against me. I feel the heat and hair-roughened surfaces of his body against mine and it's like nothing that I've ever felt before. I have no comparison for this act because it's totally new, like I'm on a different planet.

The kisses pick up pace as our hands start to wander. I send mine over his shoulders, feeling the tensile strength of him under all that sleek wet skin, the play of his muscles, his biceps bulging as he grabs my arms and drags me closer against him. The movement is strong enough that I know I'll be bruised tomorrow, and even that sends an erotic thrill through me, because before I've always had to temper my strength for fear of hurting the woman. Now I don't fear it and I give into the darker side of myself that I've always known was under there, the desire to grapple and push and thrust without the fear of hurting someone, because I know that he will like it. I feel as connected to his wants and needs in this moment as if we are psychically linked.

As we kiss I stroke my hands hard down his chest, feeling the wiriness of the sparse hairs against my palm. He groans and grabs my hipbones, pulling me into the cradle of his pelvis and making me gasp loudly, throwing my head back and overtaken by the feel of the sleek hardness of his cock thrusting against mine, rubbing and rutting and driving me mad.

"Matt," I gasp, as he kisses a chain of biting, stinging kisses down my throat culminating at the Adam's apple where he licks and sucks, panting out harsh gasps of air.

"Matty, please." I don't know what I'm asking for, maybe just the same as we'd done last night, rutting against each other until we came, but at the sound of my voice he pulls away, holding me at arm's length and staring at my face in the moonlight. It's light enough for me to see how wrecked he looks, his eyes heavy-lidded and his lips full and glistening.

"Johnny." His voice is low and rough and hits me in my balls, and without thinking I reach below and touch my cock, shuttling my hand down the length and feeling how hot it is. He watches the movements of my arm, the biceps bulging and relaxing, and for a second he seems to forget what he was saying. "Johnny, that's so fucking hot." He pauses and then looks me full in the eyes. "I want you to fuck me."

"*What?*" My movements stop in surprise. "Really?"

He smiles. "Yes, really. I want it so much, but we don't have to do anything that you don't want to do."

"I thought—" I swallow hard. "I thought that you'd want to fuck me."

He groans. "I do, but not now. You're not ready for that yet." He pauses. "Do you want to? Do you want to fuck me?"

At his words my hips involuntarily thrust forward as I fuck into nothing. "God, yes!" I gasp, so turned on at the thought of being inside him, taking him and fucking into him, that I can feel the pre-come building on my shaft.

He winds himself around me in a desperate, tight hug, burrowing his face in my neck. "Let's get out of the water, baby."

I blink at the endearment which sounds so strangely right coming from him that I want to hear it all the time, especially when it's said in that low husky voice that seems like it's been made for, and by, me. I take his hand and let him lead me from the pool, but the heat in me flags a little because this suddenly seems very real. I'm about to fuck a man.

He senses my thoughts as normal and pauses on the steps, looking at me intently. "Be very sure, John, because this is a very real step. Once we've gone past this there's no going back. You'll have fucked a man. Are you ready for that?" He pauses. "I need you to be ready, babe, but there is *no* pressure. If you back out I won't feel hurt or angry. I will understand, and if you don't want to do anything again we will go back inside and never speak of it again, and I will always be your friend. If fucking me is too much and you still want me then we can do other things. I mean, I could drop to my knees and make your eyes cross in seconds, but this is all your choice."

I stare at him, at the body where moonbeams cling to the dips and swells of his muscles, at that face with the high cheekbones and sleepy eyes, and the sun-streaked hair which is almost white in the moonlight. A burst of clarity hits me like a thunderbolt as I realise that there *is* no going back from this, because my feelings for him are so intense and wanting. Suddenly my decision is made and I stride through the water to him, taking his shoulders and pulling him into me and kissing him so hard that our teeth clash and my lips feel bruised.

He doesn't shriek like a woman might. Instead he groans and pushes against me hard, grabbing my arse cheeks and rutting against me, and suddenly heat rushes right back in like a conflagration and the only thing that I can feel is the urgency and the need to put my dick inside him.

He pulls back and grabs my hand, pulling me to the double lounger. "Here," he says low. "In the night under that moon. I want to remember you fucking me here in the heat of a French night."

He lowers himself to sit, putting him at my waist height, and I know what he's going to do even before he grabs my hips, pulling me toward his face, and the hot, wet warmth of his mouth envelops my cock. I shout out, uncaring of who might hear me. "Matty, oh *fuck*, Matt, so bloody good," I groan as he takes me down quickly until I feel the back of his throat and the ripples and tugs like the tide as his throat works.

I twist my shaking hands through his hair, holding him against me and feeling his hands lower to my arse cheeks to grip and guide me. For an eon all I can feel are the tormenting movements of his lips, and all I can hear are the sounds of his grunts and moans and the wet slurping noises as if it's the soundtrack of our night.

The feeling grows in intensity until I pull away from him, wrenching myself from his mouth with a reluctant groan to stand over him panting as I grab the base of my cock to stop myself from coming. "So close," I gasp. "Don't want to come like this."

He smiles and pulls me down against him for another kiss and then bends low and grabs his shorts, reaching in to pull out two packets. He holds them up and I see a condom and what I think is a lube sachet. He opens the lube packet, and I'm relieved to see that his hands are shaking as much as mine.

He pours some of the liquid onto his fingers until they glisten in the moonlight and then lies back against the lounger, finding a cushion and bunching it under his hips so that as his legs part I can see everything. I lean closer, staring ravenously at the hard length of his cock visibly pulsing against his belly button, and down to the mounds of his balls drawn tight. His legs part wider and I gasp as he spreads them fully, arching up as if presenting himself to me, and I look avidly at the dark line of his taint leading to the shadowy pucker between his cheeks.

"Jesus Christ, Johnny, how you look at me," he groans suddenly, grabbing the base of his cock. "It makes me feel wild."

He lifts up his fingers in a silent question. "Do it," I say hoarsely. "Let me see," and then I groan as he reaches down and inserts one long finger slowly inside himself. My mouth tastes coppery and my breath is thick as I watch it slowly being sucked inside. It's the most erotic thing that I've ever seen, and he throws his head back panting as he inserts another, and suddenly I don't want to be a bystander anymore. I want to be a participant.

I grab his fingers and pull them away, and he looks startled and almost as if he thinks that I've changed my mind. "When I'm drawing up deeds, I do the work, not the client."

His body relaxes and then he snorts. "Did you just compare me to a dry, dusty document?" He pauses. "Or a client? Because babe, that's dirty and hot."

I slap his hip. "Shut up and let me prep you." I pause, thinking hard, and then say slowly and reluctantly, "You'll have to tell me how to do it, though."

Matt laughs. "Bet you fucking hated saying those words, babe," he says mockingly.

I stare at him, at his gorgeous face full of heat and humour, and suddenly the air thickens. "Not you," I say in a thick voice. "I don't mind you showing me anything."

We stare at each other for a long second, and then something fierce and soft passes over his face, making me almost want to turn away because nobody has ever looked at me like that. Then it vanishes and he draws me down into another kiss, and suddenly the heat that had ebbed through our conversation roars back, only bigger like a tsunami, and then we're kissing with deep, open-mouthed kisses fighting to get closer and closer.

Finally we separate, sharing our panting breaths between our mouths so close together, and I swallow hard as he squirts the viscous fluid onto my fingers, watching me closely all the time. I wriggle them slightly. It's thicker than I expected. I swallow hard and reach down.

I cup his balls gently, rolling them in my hands, and he arches up, groaning as if he's been electrocuted. I reach down and kiss him, forcing my tongue into his mouth as I trace back, pressing firmly on his taint and hearing and feeling his groan in my mouth. Then I can't wait any longer and I press my finger against the tight pucker. I pause there. "I don't want to hurt you," I say hoarsely, and he cups the back of my skull tenderly.

"Don't force it in. Do it gently, but John, you won't hurt me. Do it." Before I can think anymore I press my finger, wriggling it slightly against the pucker until it vanishes inside, and I gasp.

"Oh, Matt, it's so fucking tight."

"Yes," he pants, his teeth bared. "All the way in now." I push smoothly, eased by the lube until I'm knuckle-deep. The walls feel blisteringly hot and spongy, and the whole thing is so hot and dirty and real that I almost can't bear it.

"Another one," he gasps, and obeying him, I push the second finger in. *Jesus, it's tight, and this is only two fingers. What's it going to be like with my dick in there?* I press the heel of my other hand against my neglected erection which is pulsing hard at the thought.

Matt is panting and groaning, his head arched back, mouth open and eyes unseeing, and before he can tell me I slide the third digit in. "Yes! Now scissor them," he groans. "You're opening me up and getting me ready."

I do as he says, becoming more confident every second as he writhes against me riding my fingers, and I feel his passage opening. I curl them slightly and stop open-mouthed as his whole body goes rigid in a tight arc towards the moon, a choked scream on his lips. "Right fucking there," he shouts, and I realise that I must have pegged his prostate. I've heard of this, and for a second I almost feel envious of how it obviously feels. I imagine him doing this to me and now it seems not only possible but eminently desirable.

He wriggles his hips away until my fingers fall free and for a second he lies still, eyes tightly closed and his engorged dick held in a restraining grip. He's clearly fighting for control, and I feel proud that I did this to him. Then his eyes open. "So good," he says hoarsely, pulling me into a deep kiss. He pulls back. "You need to fuck me now. I'm so bloody close."

I nod feverishly, coming up on my knees between his spread legs as he rips open the condom packet and then quickly slides a condom onto me. He dribbles more lube onto his hand and then it's my turn to groan as his hand grabs me firmly, stroking and caressing as he spreads the lube over me until my sheathed cock looks almost wet.

Then he lies back. "How do you want me?" he asks low. "On my hands and knees or—?"

"Like this," I say quickly, my voice so thick it's almost unrecognisable. "I want to see your face."

Something like relief and happiness crosses his face and then he lies back gracefully, his whole body a study in the moonlight as he pushes the cushion farther under his hips to make himself more accessible. "Are you sure?" he asks slowly.

"Shut up," I whisper, falling down against him, feeling the hair on his legs as he wraps them slowly round me, enclosing me as I lean up on one arm grabbing my dick and positioning it against his hole. "Stop trying to second-guess me. I need to be inside you."

He whispers my name and pulls my head forward, setting my lips against his as the tip of my cock slides into his hole slightly. We kiss as I slide forward in small movements, trying to be gentle, but it's so tight that it's like a velvet boa constrictor around my dick. For a second I pause as I come up against the tight muscle that guards the entrance, but I push steadily and then there's a pop, and he throws his head back gasping as I feel the muscle suddenly give way and I slide all the way home.

"Wait," he pants out, putting a restraining hand on my thigh. "Give me a second."

"Am I hurting you?" I gasp, and he shakes his head frantically.

"It just feels so full. Fuck, Johnny, you're big."

Incredibly, I find my mouth quirking. "Bet you say that to all the boys." He huffs out a laugh, which feels fucking incredible while I'm inside him. We lie together joined, and soon I'm kissing him deeply and wetly until he moans.

"Okay, I'm okay. You need to fuck me, John, because I'm really fucking close already."

I don't even stop to think what to do now. Instinct from somewhere deep inside me tells me to pull out until I nearly leave his body and then tunnel back in. He moans loudly and I throw my head back, gasping for breath. "Fuck, Matt, you're so tight and hot. I've never felt anything like this. It's fucking unbelievable."

He grabs my hips tightly, pushing himself against me until I'm up to my root in him and I feel my balls bang against his ass. "Yes," he hisses. "Fuck me so hard, Johnny. Do me."

I hover over him, my muscles burning and sweat dripping onto my arms as I look down and see my cock appear and disappear inside him, and the feeling and visual is so fucking good that need and want burn under my skin. Then I'm hammering into him, hearing him grunt and moan, his hands sliding against the slick skin of my back and his heels drumming on my arse.

I lean back and change the angle and he gives that frantic shout again. "Yes, there, baby, right there. Oh, fuck, do it again." I rotate my hips, rubbing against the spongy knot that I can feel inside his passage, and suddenly we're both on the edge, climax shimmering on the horizon.

"Matt," I groan low, my voice wrecked. "I can't wait."

"Johnny," he shouts out. "Fuck, I'm coming," and as I watch his cock pulses, white spurts arcing out and covering his chest and landing against me, blisteringly hot as they hit me. I watch his prick throb wetly into the empty air as he empties himself, and the visual is so hot and fucking dirty that I feel the pulse of electricity shoot down the base of my spine and into my balls. I cry out, riding him helplessly as I shoot into the condom, filling it with spurt after spurt until

I'm empty and I sag against him as everything falls quiet apart from the frantic rhythm of our breaths.

Eventually I feel myself soften and I grab the base of the condom as I start to slip out of him, tying it up quickly and slinging it into a nearby bin. Then his hands are on me again, drawing me close to him, his arms and legs circling me while my hand plays with his hair.

"Was it good?" he asks in a low voice.

I nestle closer. "If it had been any better, I'd be dead. Jesus, Matty, is it always like that? Because I don't know why the whole world isn't gay if that's the case."

He stiffens slightly. "No, it's not always like that," he says in a low voice.

We lie there for a while, a sated jumble of arms and legs with spunk and sweat gluing us together, until suddenly he chuckles. "What?" I ask.

"I'm just not a very fit gay mentor. I meant to do this in a bed the way I intended last night, and instead so far I've humped you against a wall and made you fuck me on a sun lounger."

"You're right, you're not exactly the Obi-Wan Kenobi of the gay world."

"And yet the force is strong with this one," he says in a dramatic voice.

"Nice Star Wars reference but don't get cocky, kid," I reply in my best Han Solo impression, and he laughs loudly.

"I can't help it, I have got a very nice lightsaber," he manages to get out before subsiding into a fit of the giggles.

"Bragging, you are," I say, which makes him laugh harder until we're practically holding each other up. We lie clutching each other completely naked on a sun lounger, stuck to each other and probably the cushion in the middle of the night. I have never felt so happy.

11

One Month Later

John

A MONTH later I'm on the treadmill in my gym. The television is on and showing Sky News, but I can't concentrate on that. Instead I'm staring out of the large window that looks out onto the pool. I'm running and thinking, and I've been doing that for the last hour.

The last month has been amazingly strange. Amazing because I've never felt so close to one person—wanting to know everything about them, wanting to be with them. Strange because it's a man.

We've done a lot of things together. I took him kayaking in Antibes and kitesurfing, and in return he took me cliff diving. We ate out nearly every night and when we returned home we came together in my room, passion burning hot, needing to touch and grip and thrust.

The sex is like nothing that I've ever experienced before. It's primal and urgent, but also tender and caring with moments of hilarity. It leaves me bewildered because everything in me says that this is something *more*, something outside of each other's experiences before, but Matt resolutely insists that this is just casual sex and something to while away the time. A space for me to experiment and find out what I like, and then we'll go back to real life and be friends.

This utterly confuses me, but what do I know? He's always been gay and this is my first proper experience outside the adolescent fumblings at boarding school, so I bow to his superior knowledge. I suppose a tiny part of me is also glad to hear him say that, because if this is nothing then I don't have to think too hard about anything. I can just be me for the first time in my life.

It's been a revelation in another way, in that I'd always thought that if I got intensely involved with someone then my thought processes and work ethic would stutter. Part of me has always felt that no matter how hard a worker I am or how many billable hours that I generate, they don't matter, because inside me is still the daydreamer waiting to get free.

With Matt, however, it's not proven true. When we're together at night I'm with him and totally absorbed in him, but during the day while he's at work I'm energised and more focused than I've ever been. The writing has flowed smoothly and I've written more productively than ever, to the extent that I'll be finished way before my deadline. I only have the summary to complete, and then it's the boring, nitpicking work of footnotes and glossary.

The sound of the door opening distracts me from my thoughts as the object of them appears. He's dressed in orange shorts and a grey t-shirt and he looks clean and polished, totally unlike any other day. I stop the treadmill, allowing it to wind down as I grin at him. "How's it looking?"

He smiles widely. "It looks great. Everything's finished outside so Charlie can bring Mabe out for their anniversary and she'll see it properly. The only things left to do are the interior decoration, choosing the kitchen and bathrooms, and they can decide between the two of them on what the terrace should look like. Charlie's really pleased, and the contractors will be as well, because he's giving them an early completion bonus."

"Have you brought him back with you?"

He shakes his head. "No, he's got an interview scheduled for this evening, so he said to say hello and he'll give you a ring tomorrow." He stares at me where I stand on the treadmill. "You look hot."

I look down at the sweat running down my naked torso. "I've been running for an hour. You'd be hot, too."

He smiles and then strides over to me, reaching up to trace a hand over my torso and tracking a bead of sweat as it rolls down. "No, I mean you look *hot*." His voice is low and focused and as I catch his meaning my cock stirs unmistakably against my loose athletic shorts, trained as it is now to respond to his cues. He catches it, of course he does, and his face turns lusty, his eyelids lowered and heavy with need.

"You don't mind the sweat?" I ask, my voice low. Bella had always hated it, not even allowing me to kiss her until I'd showered. Even after sex she'd jump straight up to shower. Matt, however, is—as normal—the exception to the rule as, holding my gaze, he leans forward and licks a broad swathe up my chest before stopping at my nipples. He draws one into his mouth, suckling with a sharp edge of his teeth, something that we'd discovered lights me up like the national grid. I grunt as a lightning bolt of pleasure sweeps down my spine centering in my cock, the head of which is now showing above the elastic waistband of my shorts.

I stare down at him from the treadmill, at the messy blond waves of his hair, the tanned lean strength of his body and the big hands with their long fingers that have explored every inch of my body, and suddenly an image of what I want to do to him comes into my head, making me moan involuntarily.

He sucks harder and I know that if I leave it any longer he'll be on me and in the driving seat, so I gather the strength and grab his hair lightly, lifting his face up to see him. I breathe in sharply because he looks gone, red flags across his cheekbones, mouth red and wet. He opens his eyes and looks at me enquiringly. "Not me," I say in a thick voice. "You."

He catches my meaning and hesitation crosses his face. We've done a lot together over this month in the goal of exploring my limits, and it turns out that I have very few with this man. We've watched porn and wanked each other off, played with toys, and I've fucked him many times. I can't get enough of him and I've enjoyed every second, but one of Matt's limits seems to be his hesitation in making me do anything that might scare me off. He seems to have classed blow jobs in this category.

He's given them to me, that talented mouth sending me mad and thrashing, but although I've sucked and licked him before, I've always finished him off with my hand when he pushed me off. Part of me had been grateful, as the idea of sucking a cock and having someone come in my mouth had made me nervous, and I know that he realised that.

Now, however, it's all that I can think about. I push him back, stepping down off the treadmill so that we're once again the same height. I lift up his t-shirt and strip it off quickly, displaying the broad width of his chiselled torso. I pause to caress this, pinching his nipples sharply so that he chokes out a gasp and his hips punch the air. I quickly undo his shorts, letting them fall to his feet as he kicks off his shoes, and then my busy fingers are sliding his briefs down, caressing the defined 'v' of his pelvic muscles and sliding my hands round to grip his firm, tight arse.

Then, all clothing gone, I stand back, looking him over deliberately. He stands proudly, his shoulders back, arms hanging at his side, and legs spread slightly. I look at the dusky mound of his sack drawn up tight under his cock which stands proudly against his stomach, throbbing visibly. He's cut, unlike myself, and the mushroomed head is an angry purple colour with a drop of pre-come glistening on the slit already.

My mouth waters and I grab his hand, gesturing to the treadmill.

"Lie on there," I say hoarsely and he raises one eyebrow and smirks, but then lies back gracefully, his body arching beautifully under my avid stare.

"Spread your legs," I command, and he does so as his cock jumps and thuds against his stomach in anticipation. The treadmill puts him at an almost perfect angle for what I have planned, but it just needs a little adjustment, so I reach over and raise the incline.

The machinery whirs and raises him at an angle so that his head is slightly higher than his lower body, like he's lounging on a sunbed. Perfect—now he can see everything. I've discovered with him that the visuals can make me hot enough to come without any contact, and I want him to have the same pleasure.

Holding his eyes, I lower myself slowly to my knees between his spread legs and view my bounty, taking my time. His chest rises and falls sharply and I hear him start to pant as I reach forward and start to kiss his chest, swirling my tongue around the muscles until I reach the copper discs of his nipples. I pause there to lick and suckle, feeling the whorled flesh under my tongue and relishing the taste of clean sweat and something that's just him. I move from his nipples, biting gently down on his chest and sucking hard, raising marks on his skin and making him writhe against me.

He groans harshly and I feel his hands come up to grab my skull, holding me to him as his body seeks more. His fingers slide in my hair, a sensual touching. He seems to love my hair, showing a keen appreciation for the slight curl to it when I haven't brushed it down. Today, however, I remove his hands, making a chiding noise as he groans and closes his eyes tightly in frustration and grips the sides of the treadmill.

"No touching," I murmur and make my way down his strong torso, coming close but then veering away from the angry length of his cock.

"Johnny," he groans. "*Please.*"

"Not yet." I kiss down his lower abdomen, licking and biting the muscles under the taut skin, and trail the broad part of my tongue down the blond hair of his happy trail and then farther down until I reach his groin. I nestle my face into the space where his thigh meets his groin, inhaling the scent of him here where it's fuller and darker and makes my fucking mouth water.

I lift my fingers as I nuzzle the blond curls in his crotch and cup his balls gently, rolling them in my hands until he pants and groans feverishly. "Johnny, please," he chokes out and then gives a grunt as I take one of his balls into my mouth, licking and sucking it gently.

"Fuck!" he shouts loudly, his head rolling from side to side. "That's so fucking good, Johnny. I love it." His voice trails off to an inarticulate groan as I pay equal attention to the other ball. When he's writhing uncontrollably, I pause and look at him and swallow hard because he looks utterly debauched. His torso is drenched in sweat, dark marks lie on his skin showing proudly where I have bitten him, and his cock is sloppy with pre-come welling out of the slit.

It makes my mouth water, and before I can second-guess myself I lean over him and take the broad flanged head into my mouth, sucking gently and tasting the bitter tang of his pre-come. I let it wash over my taste buds. It's salty and bitter but oddly arousing, and I let go and start to experiment, sending my tongue down the length of his shaft and bathing it in wetness as he chokes and pants.

There's something so powerful about doing this that I didn't expect. To have a powerful, strong man like Matt writhing and moaning and utterly at my command is highly erotic, to the extent that I can feel pre-come beading wetly in my shorts. I take him into my mouth again, sucking him back down my throat until I gag and he mumbles, snatches of words floating out. "Take it easy. Don't hurt yourself. Fuck, so *good*. Johnny, oh my God, Johnny."

Retreating slightly until I'm no longer in danger of gagging, I find a comfortable length and grab the base of his cock and start to jack the rest of him. I think back to when he's blown me before and what felt good, and I suck hard, taking him in like I would an iced lollipop on a hot day, sending my tongue over the mushroomed head to wriggle into the slit and then underneath to the spot that always makes me writhe and scream.

His moans and groans grow in volume, and I thank God for the soundproofing that prevents Odell from hearing. He's lain still until now, his body tight with tension, and I think it's so that I can get my bearings, but now almost involuntarily his hips start to move, thrusting into my mouth until he stills with a concerned murmur.

I take my mouth off him, holding tight to the base of his cock. "Don't worry," I say thickly, my throat hoarse. "You won't hurt me. I can stop you going too far, so relax and let go."

And he does. Grabbing my head, his fingers dig into my hair and he starts to thrust against me, fucking my mouth with grunts and panting cries as I suck hard now and twist my hand around his cock at the same time.

Suddenly the noise and the thought of what we must look like is too much and I lower my free hand and rip my shorts down to my thighs, impatiently fisting my cock and giving a groan around his prick. He lifts his head, his face blissfully fucked-out. "Yes, Johnny, touch yourself. Fuck your fist."

I suck harder and his cock suddenly seems to lengthen and swell bigger. The taste of the pre-come grows stronger, and even before he announces it I know that he's about to come.

"Johnny," he pleads, grabbing my head and trying to pull me off, but I suck harder, fisting myself faster, and suddenly his whole body tightens and arches and he gives out a heavy, choked grunt and his cock jerks in my mouth, sending pulse after pulse of come down my throat. I swallow greedily, and the eroticism of a man, of Matt, coming in my mouth, sets me off and I groan a garbled noise around his cock, still swallowing as I unload into my hand and over the floor.

I release his cock with a wet pop, knowing that he'll be sensitive now, and tenderly bathe it, licking away gently the stray drops that have landed on his stomach. "Johnny, Jesus Christ," he whispers, and I obey the tugging of his hands as he rolls off the treadmill to lie on the floor and pulls me down to him. I nestle into his side, feeling the chill of the air-conditioning wash across my heated skin and feeling his hands tenderly run through my hair as he pets me like a lion with its mate.

Then I swallow and make an inarticulate sound as I finally taste the residue of his come at the back of my throat. He laughs at me loudly, his eyes clear and shining and affectionate as I reach up for my water bottle and swig gratefully from it. "Jesus, no one tells you that it burns," I grouse as he laughs helplessly. "No, really, it's burning my throat and it tastes funky."

He brushes my hair back off my forehead. "You'll get used to it. In a few years you'll almost be able to tell what the man you're with ate for dinner."

I stare at him, feeling like I've been slapped. How can he mention me and other men so obliviously when the thought of him with anyone else makes my fist close?

Oblivious, he carries on talking as he stares at the ceiling. "Pineapple's a big show. You can always tell when a man's eaten pineapple because it actually makes spunk taste sweeter." He laughs easily as I stare at him, images flashing through my head and making my head and chest hurt.

I rub my chest absently and say the first thing that comes into my mind, anything to stop him casually discussing him swallowing other men's spunk. "So you're finished at the villa now?"

He stops laughing abruptly and looks almost startled. "I guess so, yes."

"And you'll be going home soon?"

He swallows hard, his expression still enigmatic. "Yes, I suppose I will. I've got a job to get back to."

The casualness starts an ember of anger brewing in my gut. I gesture between us. "And us, what will happen when we're both back in London?"

He doesn't seem to want to look at me now, awkwardness written all over him, and my heart sinks. "Well, I suppose that will depend on you."

My heart speeds up, happiness casting an elusive fairy wing over the organ. "What about me?"

He shrugs. "Well, if you still want to hook up, I'm game. It's been a good month." The last is said almost wistfully, but I don't pay attention to that as my happiness falls away.

"Hook up?" The question is sharper than I'd like, and it's in my courtroom voice so his head shoots up.

"Yes, hook up. If you feel like a fuck and you've got no one to hand, you can always ring me."

"And that's it?"

He shrugs, and it's clumsy for someone who's usually so graceful. "That's all it can be, I think, mate." I want to shout at him not to call me mate because it's so dismissive, but my throat has closed up and he carries on remorselessly. "I mean, you don't know whether you're gay or bisexual, and what about your wife?"

"Ex-wife, and what about her?" My words are cold now, the way that I am when I close down to someone. I used to do it at home all the time. I haven't done it with him since before we became us, and he looks at me questioningly.

"Well, three months ago you were trying to get back together with her." He shrugs almost apologetically. "You've got a lot of problems to sort out, John, a lot of decisions to be made. I can't tie myself to you. It wouldn't be fair."

I swallow hard. Of course he doesn't want my problems. "I understand," I finally say coldly. "Who would want to be with anyone with so much baggage?" I get to my feet, ignoring his hands which are trying to drag me back to him, as I walk over to my towel and start to wipe off the spunk that's cooled on me now and is tacky. *A bit like the ending to this,* I think slowly. *Tacky and cool.*

"Johnny." He comes towards me, his hands outstretched and a look of worry and almost hope in his warm brown eyes. "I didn't mean ... Baby, did you want—"

The doorbell rings shrilly, interrupting his stuttering words, and both our heads jerk to look towards the front of the house. "Who can that be?" I'm amazed at how cool and disinterested my voice sounds now, like I'm far away.

"John," he says urgently. "Don't answer that, please. Just listen to me."

The doorbell rings again, and for good measure someone raps urgently on it. Fending off his outstretched hand I open the gym door and move down the hall, glad to be away from him for the first time in three months. I feel stupid and foolish and sad. So sad.

I fling open the door but then stand and stare in astonishment. "*Bella!*"

She stands outside on the porch, dressed in a purple flowered sundress, looking coolly fashionable and surrounded by suitcases, garment bags, and a big vanity case. A taxi is parked on the drive and the driver is muttering under his breath and pulling more bags out.

"What are you doing here?" I ask dumbly.

She waves her hand casually. "I missed you, darling, and I sat there in Daddy's house yesterday and I thought about you being in France too and why we were apart, and it was simple, really." I stare at her, completely lost for words, and she tuts. "Pay the driver, will you, darling."

I turn dutifully away, taking my wallet out of my pocket and paying the man, who gives me a pitying look. I pace back up the steps to where she's examining her face in her compact mirror. "Bella," I say patiently. "You still haven't told me why you're here."

She looks at me calmly, confidence and self-belief written all over her. It was this that had drawn me to her the first time that I'd met her at a house party in the country. She'd been so utterly sure of herself, so contained. She'd never really needed me. I was always just an accessory to her, like a nice tennis bracelet. 'This is my Cartier watch. This is my husband. He's a lawyer and a member of the aristocracy.'

I'm suddenly aware that I'm staring at her open-mouthed, and she must take my silence for encouragement because she comes near to me, grabbing my arm with one hand and sending the other hand up to brush my hair back. I remember Matt doing that five minutes

THE SUMMER OF US   167

ago and jerk back, but she's talking again. "You wanted to make another go of things, darling, so here I am. We can have the rest of the summer together and then go back to London as a proper couple again. We can even get married again if you want to. I know you said that if we renewed our vows again we'd do it in Italy, so let's do it."

I want to shout out that this was before she fucking divorced me, but the words don't come as I hear a muffled gasp from behind me and Matt steps out of the hall and into the sunlight of the porch. He's dressed impeccably again, looking cool and calm and not like he's just been blown on a treadmill, and I jerk at the realisation that my ex-wife is talking reconciliation to me while I still have the taste of another man's come in my mouth.

"And who's this?" Bella asks, staring sharply at me.

I stare back, struck dumb for a second, and Matt intervenes. "I'm Matthew Dalton," he says, taking her hand gracefully. "A friend of John's. He let me stay here for a few weeks while I completed a project in the area."

She smiles up at him, obviously admiring his looks. Bella has always liked good-looking men and Matt looks beautiful at the moment, all sun-bloomed skin and tousled hair, his lips full and his eyes warm. However, I can see beyond that. He keeps biting at his lips, which is why they look full, and his long lean body is stiff with tension. He keeps shooting me sidelong looks that look almost imploring, but I can't deal with that at the moment. I feel almost numb, like I'm watching everything happen from behind a sheet of glass. The sounds are muffled and the words indistinct.

Bella's smile dims as she digests his words. "You're staying *here?*"

He looks uneasy. "Yes."

"But John never lets anyone stay here."

"He's a friend," I say wearily, recognising the sign of temper brewing in the tightness of her lips. Bella is totally spoilt. Her father gave her everything that she ever wanted and I continued the trend through apathy, and the result is that when her plans are thwarted she can get nasty.

She turns back to me. "If we're reconciling then we're going to need peace and privacy, sweetie. That's obviously not going to happen now."

Matt flinches and I open my mouth to tell her not to be rude and to tell her that we're not reconciling, but thoughts of half an hour ago flash back with horrible clarity. The raw feeling in my chest and the almost tentative stirrings of happiness, followed by his casual dismissal and the fact that he could obviously not give two shits about me being with someone else. The way that he'd made it clear that my problems are my own and not something that he wants to help me deal with. That's almost the worst of it, because I want to help him with his problems. I want to help him maybe contact his mother again and be there for him, but my problem of sexual identity is just too much for him.

I feel a scalding embarrassment in my chest, making my eyes feel hot and achy at the thought that I've obviously read way too much into what for him was just a summer dalliance, and I hate that that makes me sound like some sort of Jane Austen heroine. It's emasculating and the sole reason that I don't do deep emotions. They hurt.

I turn to him, looking at him as he stares back at me and Bella warbles on about reconciliation. I look at his warm eyes and scruffy, beautiful face, and even though it hurts so much, I let him go. I suppose in reality he's already done that himself, and I don't beg.

I turn back to Bella. "Matt's going today, anyway," I say coldly. "His work here is done. Isn't that true, Matt?"

He stares back at me, looking like he wants to throw up. "John, is it possible that I could have a quick word?" he asks urgently.

I shake my head instantly and he flinches, and out of the corner of my eye I see Bella's gaze sharpen. I can't do this and really, I don't want to. I want it over. "No need. You've finished here, haven't you?" I say tersely, and just like that the worry and concern fly away, his face once more smoothing back into the cold mask with which he'd always greeted me in London.

"Yes," he says clearly. "I'm done here."

12

THREE DAYS Later

Matt

I THROW my pen onto the counter in Bram's kitchen irritably and slam his diary shut. "You're double-booked," I say crossly, staring at the offending book. "Fucking typical of Craig. That idiot couldn't organise a fucking piss up in a brewery. He couldn't get laid in a brothel."

"Okay." Bram's Irish voice is calm. "You've established that your replacement assistant would have a hard time having fun anywhere, but how exactly has he caused the end of *my* world?"

I shoot him a glare, sending the diary spinning across the counter crossly. "Look at September 28th."

He flips open the book, his brow furrowed, and then he focuses on the entry before rubbing his nose. "So this double booking of a haircut and a suit measurement in a month's time is the *terrible* error that you're talking about?"

I huff. "You might not think that it's important, but in a month's time you won't be saying that."

"No, no," he hurriedly agrees, a smirk hovering on his lips. "We should really cancel Craig's next job with NATO and let them know that they can either have a tailored suit or a proper haircut, but never at the same time." He puts his hand to his cheek in mock horror. "The shame!"

"Oh, shut up," I sneer, heading over to the fridge and removing two bottles of beer. Tossing one to him, I wander into his lounge with him on my heels like a cocker spaniel. I throw myself down onto the sofa and look up to find him staring. "What?" I ask sharply.

"Matty, much as I love Budweiser, there is definitely a time when it's not appropriate." He looks at his watch. "Say, ten o'clock in the morning."

"Lots of people drink at this time," I say defensively.

"Hmm, yes, alcoholics or people living in Australia because of the time difference." He takes the bottle off me before I can open it, and I protest inaudibly as he sticks it on the table. Then he settles into the sofa opposite me and looks at me beadily.

"*What?*" I groan. "Why are you looking at me like that?"

His lips quirk. "Like what?"

"Like we're on Mastermind."

"I know what your specialist subject would be." I look at him and he smiles triumphantly. "A gay man with a broken heart."

I sneer. "That's so cheesy."

"Thank you," he says gravely. He raises one eyebrow. "Come on. Spill it."

I raise my own eyebrow, something about the gesture reminding me of when John does it with that arrogant tilt of his head that says he's waiting for the right answer. I remember sucking him off a few days ago when he'd done it to me over a crossword puzzle. The image sends alternate waves of heat to my groin and pain to my heart. I rub my chest absently and see that Bram's focus has now intensified.

"Oh my God," he says slowly. "I was totally joking, but I'm right, aren't I? I'm getting very good at spotting emotional distress."

"Please don't use those words," I groan. "You sound like a fucking social worker."

He leans back on the sofa. "I'm prepared to wait all day, you know, and don't worry, I'm not booked for a haircut or a suit fitting."

My lip twitches and then I sigh. "I thought my sex life was like the first rule of 'Fight Club' in that we don't talk about it."

He pshaws. "That's your rule, not mine." His brow creases in confusion. "I never really understood that."

I shrug. "I just never thought that you wanted to hear the grisly details. I'm quite a private person compared to you, Bram. After all—"

"No. Not *that*," he dismisses with an airy wave of his hand. "It's just that if the first rule of 'Fight Club' is not to talk about it, then where did all those extra members come from? I mean, where did they hear about it?" I stare at him in astonishment and he flushes. "Sorry, sorry, you have emotional distress. It's not the time for esoteric discussions."

"That's about as far from an esoteric discussion as I am from marrying Prince Harry."

"That would be excellent, though." He smiles. "You could be Prince Matty and have loads of corgis and wear a crown, and he is quite an attractive ginger."

"Bram," I say patiently, waiting for one of his flights of fancy to finish. "Can I go home now?"

His gaze sharpens. "No, you fucking can't. I want to talk to you." He stares at me hard in concentration. "So you've had your heart broken, but who did it?" I throw my head back, letting Miss Marple do his thing, and he chatters on. "Is it that broodily handsome project manager Christophe?" I raise my head and stare at him. "Okay, not him," he says hurriedly. "How about Bernard the plumber? He had the most spectacular moustache. Imagine that tickling your inner thighs."

"Oh my God, he's sixty," I groan and he looks at me reprovingly.

"Don't be ageist, Matty," he says piously. "There's many a good tune played on an old fiddle." I shake my head in disgust. "Okay, not him, so barring you going straight for the first time in a long time that only leaves ..." His gaze sharpens. "John."

I can't help the flinch at the sound of his name, and Bram's gaze manages to sharpen and soften at the same time. "Oh my God, Matty," he says softly. "John, really?"

I nod and he comes over to the side of me, dragging me into a hug. I lay my head against his shoulder as we stare ahead. "I knew there was something," he muses. "When we came over there for the weekend the sparks were visible, but I never dreamt for a minute that he'd go that way."

"I don't want to talk about it," I say quietly. "This is private business, Bram. I don't want you telling anyone."

He looks hurt. "Matt, when have I ever told anyone your private business?"

I stare at him in astonishment. "You tell the boys everything. You have weaker lips than Pete Burns."

"Not if you say that it's private," he says indignantly, and I nod because that's true, so he relaxes. Then he stiffens, shooting me a glare. "What did he do?" he asks sharply, his customary easygoing nature gone in a flash. "Was he just playing on your side of the fence like some of those assholes that you've been with before?"

I stare at him, incapable of speaking for a minute, because it's blindingly clear to me now that John wasn't playing. I'd behaved as though he was just experimenting with me, and it was only when we stood in the gym together that last day that I'd known suddenly and clearly that this wasn't a game for him. I'd realised it too late.

My silence has wound Bram up even more. "Fucking bastard. Did he take the piss out of you? Did he hurt you? Did he drive a car through the window of a car dealership?"

"Bram!" I can't help laughing. "Stop watching 'Queer as Folk' for advice on gay people's problems."

He huffs. "Charlie Hunnam played a very attractive character."

I nod my head. "Yes, he was a very attractive *character*."

He throws his arm back around me. "Matty, I'm very comfortable with my self-image and I'm always prepared to admit when someone is handsome, but just not as handsome as me." Laughing, I shove him, but it's half-hearted and I cave because talking to Bram is actually like talking to myself.

"He didn't do anything," I admit, and sigh. "Bram, I think that I was the one to screw up this time. I just never saw it."

He looks at me queryingly and I find himself telling him everything. When I've finished he reaches over and retrieves the bottles of beer, opening them cavalierly on his very expensive coffee table. He gives me mine with a solemn gesture. "I think it *is* time for beer."

I snort and take an unhappy swallow. "What do you think?" I ask softly.

He sighs, and I prepare for the sympathy that he always gives me. "Matty, you're a fucking twat."

I nod and then jerk. "*What?*"

He nods. "You really are, babe. Your problem is that you treat all your men like they're just waiting to leave." He holds his hand up to stem my protest. "You do, Matt, and it pisses me off. Granted, some of them," he pauses. "Okay, a *lot* of them were just passing through, but some of them weren't and you never saw it. Instead you focused on the unattainable or the feckless ones because your heart was never engaged. If you didn't care, then it wouldn't hurt when they rejected you."

He looks at me solemnly. "All men aren't like Ben or your dad, you know. There are some good ones about, and God, I just want to see you pick one. Someone who would treat you right. Someone who would love you properly because they recognise that you're fucking awesome." I smile at him with tears in my eyes but he looks sad. "I think John *is* a good bloke. I've always liked him because there's something very forthright about him, something honest and bolstering." He looks at me. "I don't think that he'd start something like that, make such a big change to his life, if he hadn't thought it through. He strikes me as the sort of man who has to have good reasons to do anything. I don't think that he's a jump in and see kind of bloke."

I nod, closing my eyes and rubbing the cool bottle across my hot eyes. "I know that," I groan. "I just don't know why I didn't remember it."

"Because you're in love with him."

I jerk the bottle away and look at him with wide eyes. "I'm not in love with him. I didn't let myself."

He shakes his head pityingly. "Babe, love isn't something that obeys your instructions and comes neatly packaged. It's a wee bit wild and wilful. You don't *let* yourself love, you just *love*." He stares at me challengingly and I slump.

I groan. "Fuck, I do love him," I say sadly.

"Why?"

I close my eyes, making it easier to have a conversation like this. "Because he's fucking gorgeous. He's fiercely intelligent, but he's also kind and honest and funny, and there's something about him that feels like—" I pause.

"What?"

"Coming home. When I see him I feel happy and I feel it in my chest and stomach, this lift."

"Babe, that's love."

I nod. "And I fucked it up. Fuck, I'm such a twat."

"Maybe it's not too late. From what you said he might feel the same."

"Bram, you didn't see him at the end. He was shut down and cold, so cold, and *she* was there. I can't compete with that."

"Compete with fucking what? Have you met her? She's so cold she could freeze a fucking snowman."

"But she's his wife and he wants her back. He let her in and threw me out."

"*Ex*-wife. I do wish you'd remember that, and he wanted her back *past tense*. To be honest, I think, and so does Charlie, that a lot of that was hurt pride. She was a challenge that he'd failed at, not a lost love. Also, not to be pedantic here, but he didn't have much choice other than to let you leave when you'd just told him that you weren't interested in his piffling little sexual identity problems, encouraged him to have other men, and said to just call you for a quick fuck if his balls were full."

"Oh my God," I groan. "I know. I'm such a fucking idiot. He can do so much better than me."

"Fuck off. He couldn't do any better. You're the best man that I know, Matt, and you always will be, and you're fucking gorgeous. Any man would be lucky to hit that." I laugh and he smiles. "He'd be a twat to let you go. I don't think that John's a twat, and I really do think that he has strong feelings."

"Not anymore," I say sadly. "Anyway, it would just be another relationship where I'm fighting to prove how worthwhile I am, and I'd be competing with men *and* women with this one. Bram, he has the chance of a family and children if he isn't with me. He won't be talked about behind his back as if being taken up the arse makes you weak. He won't have prejudice directed at him if he even holds hands with a man. He won't be spat at in the street. Jesus, gay people are being murdered."

"I know," he says passionately. "And you're right. The world isn't fair, but wouldn't you rather be facing that world head-on, hand in hand with someone that will support you and love you and take care of you?"

"I would, but Bram, I just want someone for once to fight for the right to stand beside me. Nobody has *ever* done that for me, and I really need it. I need to know that I'm worth fighting for, because I would always fight for the one that I'm with. I don't want to be someone that's chucked to the side and binned because there's something more important on the horizon."

He stares at me. "I'm not getting through to you at all."

I smile sadly. "It must be strange being on the other side of this equation." I sit up, mind made up suddenly. "You know what, I don't even want to be in London at the moment. I think I might pack up the car and get away for the weekend."

"Matty, please think about what I've said. Maybe when you get back you could see him."

"Maybe." I wave and head on out, knowing exactly where I need to go.

John

I'm sitting in the early morning sunshine staring at the pool numbly when I hear the sound of Bella shouting my name in a very shrill voice, and I give a deep sigh. Jesus, I really don't need to talk to her this morning about which fashion designer should design her new wedding dress. I just want to sit quietly, let the world go by and not think. Similar to what I've been doing for the last three days.

My wishes are ignored as I hear the clicking of high heels behind me and then Bella slides into the seat opposite me, prompting a flash of irritation because that's Matt's chair. The irritation fades as quickly as it came because this isn't Bella's fault. I don't know what the matter is with me. I'm not hungry, I can't sleep, and I just miss him.

I start as I become aware that she's talking and has stopped, obviously waiting for an answer. "I'm sorry," I say quickly. "How rude. What did you say?"

She shakes her head. "Is it the book, John?"

"Is what the book?"

"Is that what's making you so distracted?"

"No, I'm sorry. I finished the book a few days ago. I guess I'm just in a quiet mood," I finally say lamely.

She sniffs delicately. "Darling, there's quietness and then there's catatonia." I snort and she smiles coolly. "Is there someone else?"

I jerk. "*What?* What gives you that idea?"

"You're distracted, you don't seem to see me, and you haven't made any sort of sexual advance to me since I've been here. We're not even sleeping in the same bed because you've stuck me over the other side of the house, for God's sake." She pauses. "*Is* there someone else?"

I have a sudden image of telling her that yes, there is. That he's six foot and gorgeous. For a second I actually contemplate having a chat with her and telling her everything, and that maybe we could become friends, but then I realise that I actually don't want to be friends with her because I don't like her very much.

I don't owe her any loyalty because she's given me none. She's avaricious and grasping, egotistical to the extreme, and petulant and spoilt. She never loved me and I certainly never loved her. I've never loved anyone the way that I love—

My thoughts stutter to a stop. *Oh shit!* I sit back in consternation as Bella continues to talk, but her words are indistinct and there's a ringing in my ears. Fuck, I love him. I love Matt, my Matty. I love everything about him, his eyes, his smile, the wild mess of his hair, and his warmth and kindness that draw me like a magnet. I love the warm citrus smell of him and lying together wrapped around each other, feeling safe and at peace.

I become aware that Bella has stopped talking and is now staring at me, and that I really should have scheduled this epiphany better, say, not in front of my ex-wife and way before I shoved my real love out of the house in a fit of petulance, making him think that I wanted this woman who has never cared an inch for me.

For a second my stomach twists as I imagine how hurt he was, and then reality rears its ugly head in that he never wanted me for good, anyway. He'll probably settle in the end for some proudly out gay man. They'll marry and live happily ever after. I clench my fist at the image, and then a thought whispers insidiously in my head. *What if he felt the same way?* I know that he cared. I always saw that, because he wouldn't have treated me so well if he hadn't cared, but what if it was more?

Suddenly I know that I have to see him. I have to tell him how I feel and ask him the same. I can't be anything but forthright, because that's me. I don't play games and I meet things head-on. He may not want me in the end, but I have to take the chance and tell him how I feel.

I brush the worry of rejection aside for now and find that I've got to my feet, abruptly if Bella's wide eyes are anything to go by. Jesus, my body nowadays operates outside my control, rather like my life.

"I'm sorry," I say to Bella abruptly. "You have to go."

"*What?*" The screech hurts my ears.

"Yes, I'm sorry, but you have to leave because I have to go."

"Go where?"

"I have to find someone and make things right." I'm babbling now, helping her to her feet while she looks at me as if she's contemplating measuring me for a straightjacket. If this is madness, though, I don't want to be sane because I feel alive for the first time.

"John, have you lost your mind?"

"Yes, probably, darling."

"There is someone, then?"

I stop. "I'm so sorry, Bella," I say gently. "There is, and I'm in love with them, and I need to know if they love me back."

She glares at me, but as it's mostly comprised of chagrin and pride I don't take it to heart. She must see something in me that says how resolved I am because she steps back, regaining her customary cool, and I relax because she's fine with this. I think that I'd actually be peeved if I gave a shit and thought that she did the same.

"Well, darling, I hope that you'll be very happy. Obviously this isn't going to interfere with my getting the house?"

"Obviously," I say wryly, thanking God that I'm paying her a lump sum and won't have to see her again.

"Well, then, I suppose the civilised thing to do would be for the three of us to meet for lunch and talk civilly."

I suppress a smile at the thought. "You're right."

"I'm always right, John," she says chilly. "Now what's her name?"

"Ah, now that's the thing!"

FIVE HOURS later I stand outside Bram's front door and bang on it. I don't hear anything, so I bang again loudly for good measure, and then I hear footsteps and what sounds like muffled cursing. The door jerks open and his irritated face appears. "What the hell?" His words trail off. "*John!*"

"I'm sorry to interrupt you," I say stiffly, as he stands back to let me in. "I just wondered whether you've seen Matt?"

When I turn back, all of the irritation has drained from his face and he's looking at me with what looks like a strange mixture of astonishment, hope, and caution. This surprises me, because although he's always been friendly enough to me, it's obviously not family friendly the way that he is with Matt—oh!

"You know, don't you?" I say baldly.

"I know many things, John. What do you need from me in particular?" he replies cautiously.

"Cut the crap. Has he been here?" I ask, and his smile dims.

"Yeah, he was here this morning." He pauses and my heart thumps. "Throwing things around and swearing."

"*Matty* threw things," I say in consternation and he examines me intently for a second, his head on one side as if he's reading my mind.

"Yes, *Matty*. Why are you here, John?"

I slump down on a chair. "I just need to find him and talk to him."

"So go and do it."

I hesitate. "I don't actually know his address."

He tuts. "You young people nowadays. You fuck a man a few times and don't get his details."

My head shoots up, a flush on my cheeks. "I *knew* he'd tell you."

He looks uneasy. "Don't judge him, *please,* John. I'm his best friend, the only one that he talks to like that. Don't be angry, because he wouldn't tell anyone else your business."

"I'm not *angry*," I say impatiently. "And I could give two fucks who knows, anyway." His face lightens slightly but I'm talking again. "You're his brother, not his friend, and I love that he has someone like that who cares so much for him. I'd never be bothered by it, because it's great." For a second he stares at me and some of the unease leaves his face and he looks at me kindly. I hesitate and carry on. "It's just ... it's not like that, you know, just fucking. You don't understand."

"What is it like, then?" he asks, and I suddenly realise that I'm talking to Matt's gatekeeper. He won't give me Matt's address until he knows that I'm going to do right by Matt. I should be angry, but I'm actually oddly charmed by this tight-knit unit of two.

"I'm not baring my feelings to you until I've spoken to Matt first," I say clearly. "He deserves to hear it first."

His gaze sharpens. "You have feelings, then?" His tone sharpens. "Hear what? Have you come to give him a wedding invitation, because so help me—"

"No, no," I say hurriedly. "I'm not getting married. I asked Bella to leave. Please, Bram, I just need—" I falter.

"What?"

"I need to see him and hold him."

He softens suddenly, and for the first time he gifts me with his wide, warm, open smile that he gives to very few people. "That's good, John," he says softly. "You don't know how happy I am to hear that. Matt's a diamond. He deserves far more than he ever asks for, and he's the most loyal, most wonderful person."

"I know," I say calmly, and he examines my face.

"You really do know, don't you?" he says almost wonderingly, and then visibly comes to a decision. "I'm not giving you his home address." I open my mouth to argue and he shakes his head. "There's no point, because he's not there anyway."

"Where is he?" I ask fiercely. "Is he with anyone?"

"No, no," he says hurriedly. "Jesus, calm down, John, he's in Cornwall."

"Polzeath?" I recall, and he nods and rattles off the address, which I enter into my phone.

I thank him and get up but he stares at me, running his eyes down me. "Erm, don't you need to get changed or something, John? Because this is Cornwall we're talking about, not the Caribbean."

I look down at myself. I'm still wearing the khaki shorts that I had on this morning. When I'd left I'd simply grabbed my passport and wallet and glasses, thrown on a white t-shirt, and kicked my feet into my trainers.

"Did you just walk straight out of your house and get on a plane?" he asks, and I nod.

"I just had to get here and see him."

He smiles and claps me on the back. "Mate, that's fucking awesome. When you go big, you go big." He wanders over to a cupboard in the hall, and reaching in, he draws out an Oliver Spencer khaki bomber jacket. "Here," he says, smiling. "Don't want you freezing before the big meet."

"I'll give it back next time that I see you."

He shakes his head and draws me into a hug, slapping me on the back. "No need. You're family now, Johnny."

13

John

FIVE AND A HALF hours later I drive up a steep hill and pull up on a narrow road outside a small Victorian semi-detached house. Painted cream, it sits on a lane containing two other similar properties and one big Victorian bay-windowed house, and all of them look down on the wide golden stretch of Polzeath Beach.

I get out of the car and stretch, inhaling the salty brine of the cold air and gratefully feeling it wake me up. The village is charming even on an overcast windy day like today, with a little central street containing just a few shops and bars surrounded by steep hills on which houses seem to perch precariously. There are a quite a few tourists about, but it still has the air of a traditional seaside village, unlike the brash commercialism of Newquay.

Turning back to the house, I feel my nerves rising, but I quickly push them down and march over to the navy front door, and without giving myself time to think I ring the doorbell, and then for good measure I bang on the door. A few minutes pass with no answer, so stepping sideways I lean over the colourful window box and peer in through the bay window.

I can't see much beyond a large leather sectional sofa with bold coloured cushions and white walls covered in what look like large, bright paintings. I think of his reaction to that painting in Vence and a smile plays around my lips, which dies when I realise that the place has the still look of an empty house. Now what?

"He's not there, mate."

The Cornish drawl comes from behind me and I jerk in surprise, turning to see a tall, handsome man wearing a wetsuit and with his dark hair drawn up in a messy bun. He has a set of keys in his hand and is hovering near the house next door, so I presume that he's Matt's neighbour.

"Sorry?"

He smiles merrily, the lines around his eyes crinkling. "I presume that you're looking for Matt."

"I am," I say a little stiffly. "Do you know where he is?" I'm expecting him to be wary of giving out information to strangers, but obviously that doesn't apply to this laid-back-looking man because he smiles.

"He's down on the beach." He points back to the beach below us, in case I missed the wide stretch of sand. My lips twitch and he carries on talking. "Surf's bloody good today. He's been out there all afternoon."

"Thank you."

I move away from the house and he turns, pointing to a set of steps farther down the lane. "That's the quickest way to get down to the beach. Matt's pile of stuff is the one with the bright blue towel. Go past the house on the edge of the rocks on the left-hand side of the beach and there's a small inlet. His stuff's there. You can't miss it, as a lot of people are coming in now."

"Thanks again. Sorry, I didn't get your name. I'm John."

"Nice to meet you. I'm Jago, Matt's neighbour." He waves a casual hand and I immediately make my way down the roughly hewn, steep steps to the beach until finally I'm standing on the sand. I quickly kick off my trainers, and carrying them I set off down the beach, looking out at the sea where big waves are crashing in and the figures of the surfers are just dots in the distance as they dip and weave in the water. I realise now why Jago told me where to find Matt's stuff because it would be impossible on a beach this wide to find him, and the surfers all look the same at a distance.

Keeping my eye out for the house on the rocks I find it quickly and look for the inlet that Jago mentioned. I relax when I see it because Matt's bright blue towel is there like he said. It's easily recognisable as his because with it is the battered Quiksilver rucksack that he carries everywhere, and the blue and maroon striped VBN hoody that's his favourite item of clothing.

I sink down on the towel, looking out to sea and watching the graceful moves of the surfers who look like water birds skimming the waves, but gradually the stress of the last few days, the long hours of travelling followed by the five and a half hour drive and the sea air, combine to make me sleepy. After jerking myself awake a couple of times, I eventually give in and lie back on the towel and close my eyes. *I won't miss Matt because he's got to come back for his stuff,* I think sleepily.

I come awake with a jerk as a shadow crosses the light behind my eyes and I hear a disbelieving, "Johnny?"

I sit up quickly, hastily wiping the drool away, to find him there finally in front of me. He's wearing a black and red wetsuit that clings lovingly to his lean muscled body and he's stripped it off to the waist. In the pure pale light of a Cornish beach his skin glows with the tan that he developed in France, and his hair is a shaggy, windswept mess.

For a second his brown eyes seem to eat me up, but then he shivers and grabs the spare towel from next to me and rubs it briskly over himself. He seems to hide behind it as he wipes his face, and when he emerges he's composed and his face is set and cold. "What are you doing here?" he asks coolly as he snags his hoody and pulls it on.

Feeling at a disadvantage, I scramble to my feet, feeling the coldness of the sand and the sting of rain on the wind that has picked up since I fell asleep. "Well?" he asks, standing very still.

"I had to see you," I finally say, the words leaving my mouth and falling into the seeming abyss between us. "I had to tell you something."

He flinches and then seems to shut it down, forcing a cool smile onto his normally wide, mobile lips. "Oh, have you come for congratulations?"

"*Congratulations?*" I echo uncomprehending, and for a second his eyes flash.

"Yes, congratulations on your getting married again. Italy, wasn't it?"

"No!" I burst out, and it comes out louder than I intended. I lower my voice as he jerks. "No, I'm not getting married."

He stills. "No? Well, it's probably best to take it easy for a bit."

"I'm not taking it easy, either. I'm not with her." He looks up sharply. "We broke up, or at least I'm not sure what you'd call it when you split up from your ex-wife who you're not with anyway."

He steps towards me, and it's now that the real Matt shines through because he takes my arm gently. "I'm sorry, Johnny," he says softly. "I know that you wanted her back."

I'm suddenly overcome with emotion. "But I don't. I don't *ever* want her back. I don't know why I even wanted her in the first place."

"But you did," he says in confusion, and I gesticulate gracelessly.

"I know that I did, but my eyes are open now, and I've realised that I don't want that." I swallow hard. "I want you."

His eyes flare but then inexplicably he looks sad and angry. "You don't want me, John. You're just in the first flush of finding out that you're probably bisexual. You don't want to confuse friendship and gratitude for something more long-lasting." He looks almost pained. "You'll want to experiment and be with other people."

I steel myself. It's time. "I want to be with *you*. I don't want anyone else but you, Matt, always just you."

His face twists in agony. "You don't want me, I don't believe you. You're just confused. I won't be your experiment and I don't want to be second-best again, Johnny. I was second-best to religion with my father and to drugs with Ben. I can't do that anymore, let someone in and be cast aside, and you don't know me, anyway. Don't pin your future to someone that you don't know."

"I'm not confused, and I *do* know you."

He ignores me and goes to walk past me and I catch his shoulders to stop him, suddenly terrified that he's made his mind up and won't give me a chance. I hate the feeling that he thinks he's second-best to anything. "Look," I blurt out. "Ask me what Bella's favourite colour is."

He shrugs angrily and tries to go past me again and then huffs when I won't let him. "I don't know, John, what is Bella's favourite colour?" he intones in a fuck-off voice that makes me smile a bit.

"Fuck knows, probably yellow since she wears so much of it."

"Wow, John, that's really interesting, now let me by."

"No. Now ask me yours." Before he can speak I start babbling. "Yours is green, but the soft clear green, not emerald because that's too harsh. Your birthday is December 10th which makes you a Sagittarius, which apparently means that you're energetic, optimistic, and active. I say apparently because I don't fucking believe in any of it, apart from the bit that says that my being an Aries makes me your perfect match."

He laughs involuntarily but I carry on spewing out facts, looking nothing like a person whose job depends on him using words to make clients see things his way. I gesture at his hoody. "Your favourite item of clothing is your striped VBN hoody which you take everywhere and always put on after surfing because it's worn soft from age. Your favourite film is the 'Lord of the Rings' trilogy but the extended versions, and it *is* one film because it's the same bloody story. However, if out on a date you might say a

Quentin Tarantino film just to make yourself look clever. Your favourite food is crunchy nut cornflakes which you eat at the oddest times of the day and night. You and Bram can quote more of the 'Little Britain' scripts than David Walliams or Matt Lucas ever could. Your favourite song is 'Protection' by Massive Attack, but if Bram asks it's 'Final Warning' by Beggar's Choice. You start off sleeping curled up in a nest of covers but always by morning you are starfished across the bed with no covers at all, while I'm relegated to a tiny corner and if I'm lucky an inch of the duvet from the floor, and I *still* think that I'm lucky because I'm sharing a bed with you."

His face contorts like a small boy trying not to cry.

I pause for breath, looking at his face which shows that warm, clear expression that I love. "The point is," I say quietly, "I know everything about you, because you fascinate me, because—" I pause and swallow hard. "Because I love you, and you're so fucking *special* to me." His head shoots up, shock written on his face and then a blinding joy that relaxes and energises me at the same time. "I've never been bothered enough to know these things about any previous lovers. I really couldn't fucking care less before you, and if that makes me a bastard, then so be it, because I'm *your* bastard."

I come to a stop to find him looking at me with awe, and I puff up a bit in the face of what I'm sure will be praise, as surely I *can't* have been as bad as I thought I was.

"My God, sweetheart, do you actually argue for a living?" I sag and glare at the piss-taking fool's face. His voice is full of suppressed laughter. "No, seriously, babe, we should find you a different career where speech isn't necessary. What jobs take a vow of silence?"

I shrug helplessly, trying not to laugh, but suddenly his face transforms in front of my eyes into this soft, private, intense look, and he steps forward and cups the back of my skull until I'm so close that I can see the gold flecks in his warm brown eyes. I close my eyes helplessly for a second at the relief that runs through me at feeling his touch again, but they shoot open with his next words.

"I love you too, Johnny, so, *so* much. More than I've ever loved anyone in my life. You're my home, my best friend, my safe place."

I lean forward and rest my head against his neck, inhaling his scent and feeling an intense wave of relief and joy flood through my veins, but one little doubt niggles. "What about the best fuck that you've ever had?" I ask in a small voice. He's been with men who've got this gay thing down pat. How can I compete with that?

He chuckles, the sound reaching the base of my stomach so that I can feel it in my balls. "It's not fucking with you, John, it's making love, and everything with you is just so much better. It feels unbelievable because it just feels like *more* with you." He shrugs. "I've not fucked you yet so I can't judge that, but when you're ready it will be the best, I just know it *here*." He places my hand over his heart and I turn his hand in my grasp until I'm holding it firmly.

"I want you to," I say in a low voice. "I want you to have everything of me, Matty. I want to be totally yours."

"You already are, sweetheart. Everything that you are is *mine*. Your arrogance, your vulnerability, your ability to make me laugh harder than anyone does, your kindness and your loyalty. They're all mine and I will protect everything that you give me fiercely because *you're* mine."

"God, all yours," I whisper. "I love you so fucking much. Please don't ever leave me."

"Never," he says solidly, and his kiss on that rainy beach as we sway in the wind clutching each other tightly is both a welcome home and a vow to the future, and for the first time in my life I totally let go with someone, secure in their love.

Ten minutes later we crash through the front door of his cottage and Matt kicks it shut with a vicious swing of his leg before pinning me up against the whitewashed wall. "Oh my God, I missed you so much, sweetheart, so fucking much."

"I missed you, too," I gasp between frantic kisses which seem like he's trying to devour me. He presses his full weight against me and I moan at the feel of his hard cock pushing against my own.

I pull back, gasping, and grab his beloved face in my hands, seeing his warm brown eyes glowing with love and affection. Suddenly everything calms inside me and all the previous nerves fall away. "I want you to make love to me," I say in a low voice, watching his pupils grow large with shock and arousal, but typically for Matt he won't do anything that he thinks I don't want.

"Are you sure?" he murmurs, running his hands gently through my hair so that I tilt my head like a cat, almost purring.

"I'm sure," I say clearly. "I need it, Matt. I need to feel you inside me. It's what I want."

He closes his eyes, looking pained, but when he opens them his manner has subtly changed, his body leaning harder against me and his hands firmer as they grab my shoulders and twist me to face a set of stairs. "Get upstairs, then," he says, his voice hoarse and commanding. "I want the person I love most in the world naked in my bed in the place that I love best of all."

I shiver slightly, my cock hardening even more at the tone of command in his voice and the roughness of his hands. Who knew that I'd like to be bossed about? Not me, possibly the bossiest person on the planet.

He pushes me up the stairs, walking close behind me, pressing kisses to the back of my neck. Near the bedroom he scoops off Bram's jacket, throwing it cavalierly on the floor, and then pauses. "That's Bram's jacket, isn't it?"

"I went to see him because I didn't know where to find you," I say throatily as his busy hands reach around and pull my t-shirt off, caressing the skin of my chest and pinching my nipples as he does.

His hands pause for a microsecond. "No. Not interested at the moment," he says in a lordly fashion, and I choke out a laugh which sinks to a groan as he reaches down and slowly and teasingly lowers my zipper.

He pushes me through an open doorway into a large, light-filled room. I just have time to register a huge bed made up with white linens and a colourful throw and white walls, before he issues his next command. "Kick your shoes off," he says in a demanding voice and I comply immediately, stilling as he presses up against me from behind.

He slides his hands into my waistband and pushes the shorts off. They fall at my feet and then I arch back into his chest, giving a sharp cry as his busy hands find the outline of my achingly stiff cock under my boxer briefs and slide up and down firmly.

At the sound of my cry he spins me round and kisses me again, clutching the cheeks of my arse to pull me into him. "Not just me," I choke out. "You too." He smiles, taking my mouth in a loving kiss before stepping back.

He pulls off his hoody and then turns obediently so that I can access the long zip and get the wetsuit off his narrow hips. I kiss the tanned golden skin of his back. "This wetsuit is so fucking sexy," I murmur between kisses, and he laughs.

"You won't be thinking that in a second."

"Why?" Five seconds later I find out. "Jesus Christ," I groan, tugging on the legs of the suit. "This is like stripping a fucking sausage." He lies back against the bed laughing helplessly, his face open and loving and his tanned limbs splayed wide. Finally the wetsuit legs come loose. "Okay," I huff. "That's slightly sexier in that you're commando."

"I do my best to please," he says lazily, drawing his hand down his cock which is hard and glistening.

"Fuck, you're so good-looking," I whisper.

He raises up on the bed onto his knees and crawls across to me, grabbing my hips and sliding my boxer briefs off me. "I'm not the sexy one. It's you." He traces a firm hand across my body, his words following his hands and busy fingers. "Look at this broad chest, this muscled torso. You're wider than me and so strong. And all of that tanned, tight skin leading down to this hair." He ruffles his hands through my happy trail, one teasing finger bypassing my cock and trailing along the 'v' of my pelvic muscles. Then, just as quickly, his hand shifts and he cups my balls and I groan in pleasurable agony as he rolls them, pressing down on my taint behind them and making fireworks pulse behind my eyes.

"Get on the bed," he says in a firm voice. "Lie on your front and let me see that arse."

For a second I hesitate and he smiles gently, kissing me softly. "Nothing will happen that you don't want to, but I swear to you that you're going to like this."

"You promise?" I say in a small voice and then want to kick myself in the throat, but his expression melts and he kisses me.

"I do."

"Okay, then." I shrug and settle down and then jerk as he straddles my thighs and I feel his balls brush against my legs. Then I groan as his firm hands start a massage of my shoulders. He works his way down my back, pressing firmly and bypassing my arse to massage the tops of my thighs.

After a few moments I relax and the strokes continue, but now they occasionally tease me as with every pass he'll massage into my arse cheeks, pushing my groin into the bed and rubbing my cock against the sheets.

Soon I'm moaning and arching into his touch, pleading for more, and I can hear his soft pants and then he cups my arse. "So beautiful, Johnny, and all mine. I'm going to be the first and the last in here."

"Yes," I groan, and then pause. "I thought that you wanted me to try other men?"

His hand jerks and then grips me spasmodically. "Fucking never," he says in a fierce voice. "*Never,* Johnny. I said that because I thought that it was the right thing to do, but I don't want you to ever have another man."

I twist my head to look at him. He's crouched over me looking like a Greek god, all golden skin and a lean beauty. "And it's the same for you, then," I say in a hard voice, and he nods his head, frantic in his desire for me to know our truth.

"I don't want anyone else, ever. This is it for me, Johnny."

We exchange glances loaded with heavy feelings that shouldn't make me feel so light and safe but they do, so I nod and something seems to snap in him as he closes his eyes for a second. When he opens them, his voice is hoarse. "Spread your legs, John."

Immediately I do as he asks, spreading my legs until he'll be able to see everything. For a second I feel vulnerable because this isn't a view that I ever thought anyone would see, but then I feel his breath blow over my hole making it clench, and I feel the moist warmth of his tongue there. Surely he's not going to –

"Oh my fucking God," I shout out at the top of my voice as pleasure floods through me in a warm wave. His tongue flicks around my hole, teasing and making me wild. I never knew that this area could be so sensitive, but it's like there are twenty thousand more nerve endings here than anywhere else on my body.

"Oh, Johnny," he groans. "You're so sensitive here, love. You're going to love this."

I open my mouth to say something but my thoughts scatter as he licks over my hole and then slides his tongue inside me, his tongue wriggling and licking, and I can't speak anymore. All I can do is grunt out incomprehensible things, arching my body and forcing my ass back so that he's fucking me with his tongue.

The pleasure rides that edge between being too much and not enough to come, like all my nerve endings are on fire, and the eroticism is heightened by the sheer dirtiness and forbidden quality of the noises that he's making, the stifled groans and slurping as he almost French kisses my arsehole.

These noises are joined by my own grunts as I feel him suckle on his finger before sliding a long finger into me. For a second I tense with images of how much this is supposed to hurt, but then I relax and remember that this is Matt, and when I did it to him he went mad. Then the nerves quickly vanish because he's bringing a quickening, hot pleasure that's making me feel wild.

"You're doing so well," he praises. "Can you take another, sweetheart?"

I nod. "Do it."

He removes his finger and I feel him reach for something and then there's the sound of a cap opening. When he comes back to me his fingers are wet and he pushes two fingers in slowly, scissoring them and opening me. I'm not sure how I feel about it at first. It feels weird and alien and it burns. For a second I wonder whether this is actually for me after all, until he makes a sudden, reaching movement inside me and pleasure explodes in my arse, spreading to my cock and balls, and I yell out.

"Oh my God, what are you doing?"

"That's the prostate, sweetheart. Do you like it?"

"Ungh!" I moan. "Do it again," and he laughs, stroking again lightly.

"I like to see an intelligent man struck dumb."

I arch back, losing track of time as his busy fingers stretch me open, and when he comes back with three fingers inside me I almost welcome the burn, coming as it does with his hand stroking my cock so that everything becomes this immense ball of intense feeling and want and so much pleasure.

"Matt, please, I need it," I groan, my hair sticking to my face with sweat and my eyes blind.

He moans deep in his throat, giving my cock one last stroke, and I arch into his hand, almost humping it. "You're ready. Here, sit up," he says.

He pulls me up onto my knees, grabbing the pillows and putting them into a pile and then leaning me over them so that I arch over them.

"This is one of the best positions for a first-timer," he says in a hoarse voice, kissing the back of my neck. "You can control how much you take at a time. Are you sure?"

"I'm sure," I growl, and then grab his hand as he goes for a condom. "You said it was just us?"

He stills and then nods. "I meant it, too, John. No one else. I've never gone without condoms since Ben, and I've been tested."

I nod. "I'm clear, too." I pause and look at him. "While we're talking like this, I want you to know that I never slept with Bella."

A wave of relief flows over his face, and for a second he rests his head against my shoulder. "Thank you," he says softly. Then his head comes up, awe on his face. "So we're doing this?"

I nod, watching him avidly as he reaches for the tube of lube and squirts some over his fingers, fisting his cock and stroking it until it's coated, before reaching over and pouring some more onto my hole and pushing it in smoothly.

I swallow hard, feeling suddenly nervous. "Will it hurt?"

"No, baby," he says gently. "You're nice and open. It will feel a bit strange and it might burn a bit, but we'll just stop until you get used to it."

"I trust you," I say solemnly and his face twists, and he comes over me, kissing me wetly.

"I love you so much," he says forcefully. "I want you so fucking much."

"Then do it," I groan, and bend over my nest of pillows feeling him come close and then the wiriness of his pubic hair brushing my arse as I spread my legs. I feel him take his cock and position it at my entrance, pushing against the wet hole, making teasing little forays until it enters me slightly. He grabs my shoulders.

"You can feel it," he urges. "Now take it. Push back, sweetheart, and take my cock."

Taking a deep breath I close my eyes and push back, feeling the burn and stretch of his cock. For a second it's almost too much as the burn spreads and I feel a panic come over me, a feeling of helplessness and being held down by someone heavy.

Sensing it, he soothes me, kissing my shoulders and heaping praise onto me and telling me to push down. I gather my courage and do it, and with an almost audible pop I feel the large muscle slacken and the head of his cock slide inside me. We rest there for a second, me panting and him visibly trembling behind me.

"Are you okay?" he asks hoarsely, and I nod frantically.

"Are you?"

"God, yes," he moans. "You just feel fucking incredible, so hot around my cock and so fucking tight. I can't believe that I'm going to come in you, fill you up with my spunk until it's dripping out of you."

With these words I feel my cock which had gone soft with nerves harden so quickly that it makes me dizzy. I make a thrusting gesture with my hips and he slides all the way in until I feel the slap of his balls against my arse. For a second he rests against me and then I move, rutting against the pillows and feeling them rub against the stiffness of my cock. The feel of his prick sliding in me makes pleasure shoot through me.

"Oh, fuck," I groan. "Fuck me, do it, Matt."

"Johnny," he grunts, and then he starts to move. At first I can't get the hang of it, as I'm so used to being the one in charge and leading it. However, he grips my hips, moving me the way that he wants, and something about the way that he moves my body and takes control of the sex for our pleasure turns me on more than anything that I've ever experienced.

Then he pulls almost out and slides in at an angle and hits my prostate and an explosion of colour hits behind my eyes and I force myself back on him, grunting.

"God, baby." His voice is broken and harsh. "My John, so fucking good."

"I need to see you," I say suddenly. "Matt, I need to see your face."

He instantly pulls out and I wince and groan, feeling empty as he throws the pillows across the room violently in his need to get back in me. He pushes me until I'm flat on my back and then he kneels up, grabbing my arse and lifting me until I'm arched up, my arse resting in his lap. I wrap my legs around him as he grabs his cock and lines it up, and I arch my head back, groaning as he slides all the way in.

I run my eyes avidly over him, the visual ten times hotter than anything as I watch his intent face, the colour on his cheeks and the redness of his lips as he bites them. The muscles in his torso and pelvis twist sinuously, visible under the tight skin as he shifts his hips, slowing everything down as he moves languorously.

He's hitting my prostate almost continuously in this position and I can hear a keening in the room that mingles with his groans, and I'm amazed to find that it's me making that noise, lost in a pleasure that is unlike anything that I've ever known.

"Matty. God, move quicker," I plead and he smiles mockingly, throwing his head back and groaning as he makes another languid swipe with his hips until I lose it and push myself up more into his lap, working my anus harder against the root of his cock.

We both cry out and I groan as he reaches down, grabbing my cock which is sloppy with pre-come and milking it hard, and suddenly I'm close. "Matty," I groan. "I'm so close. I need to feel you."

He understands me instantly and backs slightly so that I'm lying flat on the sheets again, and then he folds himself over me, lying full-length on me as I twine my arms and legs around him.

"God, yes, yes," he grunts, our mouths sharing panting breaths. "I'm so close."

I grab his hair, pulling him down, and we kiss wildly, our teeth clacking together until we can do nothing except pant, and the movements are so hard and almost violent, so male and unrestrained. The stroking sensation of his cock inside me, the rubbing of his torso against my cock and the knowledge that he is fucking into me, taking me on my back with my legs spread open for him, is almost too much.

Then electricity shoots down the base of my spine and into my balls and I feel the pressure in my cock race down it, and I arch my back, rubbing my cock furiously against his wet skin as I spurt and spurt between us.

The scent of come fills the air between us, heavy and acrid, and he grunts, all the muscles tightening in his body before he arches back and gives two or three battering thrusts against me. Then I feel heat and warmth flood my body and he collapses against me and we lie, insensate but together.

After a minute I feel him soften inside me and he moans, leaning up to take my mouth in a lush kiss, sucking gently on my tongue and brushing my hair back gently. "Get ready," he murmurs. "Because this bit can be a bit uncomfortable. Take a breath."

I do as he says and then groan as he pulls out. The uncomfortable feeling passes after a few seconds and then I chuckle as I feel the liquid slide out. "Well, that's novel," I say dryly, and Matt laughs, but his face is dreamy as he runs his finger through it.

"Fuck, that's actually really sexy coming out of you."

I laugh. "You're joking."

"No, it appeals to my inner animal." He pauses and then says in a low voice, "I want to come all over you and rub it in. Mark you as mine."

To my utter astonishment I feel my cock stir, and he gives me a knowing look and a quick kiss before jumping out of bed and going into the bathroom. I hear water run and then he comes back with a wet towel and proceeds to clean me up, dropping kisses on whichever part of my body is near and uttering wordless sounds of praise. I lie back feeling utterly sated and warm and taken care of, and my eyes fill up slightly.

Finally finished, he jumps back into bed and opens his arms, and I immediately cuddle close, feeling them wrap around me and draw me to him so that we lie in a tangle of hairy, languid limbs. He presses his lips into my hair, inhaling as if he loves the smell of me. "So what did you think?" he finally murmurs.

I look up at him. "It was incredible," I say softly, and he relaxes instantly. I can't believe that he was worried. "I've never felt so connected or felt so much pleasure and the safety to be who I am. Is it always like that?"

He strokes his finger down my cheek. "It's never been like that for me before," he says solemnly.

"*Really?*"

"Yes, really. I've never felt that connection, either. Before, it's just been a way to get off and obviously I wanted my partner to get off, too, but with you I just wanted you to feel so much pleasure. Giving it to you and seeing your reactions made mine a thousand times more intense."

I reach up and kiss him. "That's okay, then, as long as I'm the best that you've ever had."

He laughs and I feel it running through his body. It's an intimate, trusting thing to feel your lover laugh while you lie against him. "Johnny, you're so competitive."

After a few minutes of lying quietly and drifting, he nudges me. "So how do you feel in yourself now that you've discovered that you're gay?"

I look up at him contemplatively. "I don't know whether I've just discovered that I'm gay so much or just that I've discovered you." I hesitate, wanting to get this right and quell any doubts that he has about influencing me. My Matty is always so concerned about never pushing me and letting me have my own mind. Finally I find the words. "You're my person and I think that I was just waiting for you. Man or woman, it doesn't matter to me. The only thing that matters is that you are mine and I am yours."

His eyes fill with tears and he hugs me hard to him for a second. "But John, it can be such a difficult thing. You will be defined now by your sexuality, not your brain or your intellect, and I know how important that is to you."

He's so serious about this, but I'm not. In this I am careless, because I know now what I want and I truly don't care about anything or anyone else.

I sit up slightly, putting my hand on his chest. "Do I care what people think? No, I don't, because I didn't have a life before and now I do. Now, I have a chance at a life that I never dreamt of and I can spend it with you." I shrug. "Am I going to let a few mindless idiots spoil it? Am I, fuck? They can go fuck themselves."

Matt laughs suddenly and pats me affectionately. "Oh, Johnny, I can see at least one area in our lives that is going to be improved by your vast reservoir of arrogance."

I come back down to him, bending to drop a kiss on his wide, warm chest. "*Our* lives," I whisper. "I like the sound of that. I never thought that my life could be like this. So safe and warm. All my life I've been looking for that feeling. I bought house after house but I never found it."

He lifts his hand, tangling his long fingers in my hair, his expression so tender and open and warm. "Sweetheart, that's love that you're describing, not a property portfolio."

I smile and touch his face. "Then I got it wrong all this time, because my home is you. I should have just looked for you."

"Well, you've found me, so what are you going to do with me?"

I stare at his scruffy face and his warm eyes that are bracketed by laugh lines that will get deeper as the years go by, and I have never felt such a strong certainty of my way forward. "I'm going to keep you," I whisper.

EPILOGUE

Two Years Later

Matt

I ENTER the lift in John's office building and fall back against the side of it, loosening my tie with a weary sigh. I've been away with Bram and the boys in New York for the last two weeks, and the minute that I got back today I'd been plunged into a day of meetings and a catch-up with my partner Lana.

I'd taken her on when I realised that the thing with John and I was serious, and he'd pointed out that if I was encouraging him not to live to work then I had to do the same. He was right, as usual, and she took to being a partner like a duck to water, and now when I leave work for a few days or longer I do so in the knowledge that the business is running smoothly, and I do the same for her. The result has been that business is booming.

I check my reflection quickly in the mirrored wall. I'm wearing a steel blue-coloured suit with a blue and white spotted tie and my hair is pulled back in a stubby ponytail, but what stands out is the look of happiness and excitement on my face. It wears it all the time now, and it's because of John. For the first time I'm in a relationship where we come first with each other, and I feel free and tied at the same time. I imagine that it's the same feeling that a helium balloon would have, full of fizz and energy.

Don't get me wrong; we argue, of course we do. We're two strong men with our own opinions, and one of us is entirely convinced that he's always right. But we've learnt to argue without dealing emotional blows. We've learnt that no matter what's said we will still end up wrapped in each other in our sheets at night, because one of the first rules that we laid down was that we always slept in the same bed. No matter how bad the argument is, we always lie down together, and the make-up sex is explosive. Our whole sex life is fantastic. We're as hot for each other as we were at the beginning, and I can't help that kernel of satisfaction in me that I will always be his first and only.

I'd moved in with him after only a couple of months of dating and it was as if we'd always been together, the adjustment being seamless. We'd quickly realised that we wanted a home that we could make our own, so we'd put our flats up for sale and bought a flat in an old grain storage building in Shad Thames, overlooking Tower Bridge. It had needed some work done to it, so once again I'd found myself project managing a renovation, only this time for the most important project in my life. I certainly never saw that coming two years ago.

Now the flat is amazing with polished oak flooring, exposed brick walls, and huge windows looking down on the River Thames. Pride of place has, of course, been given to the abstract painting that he'd bought that day in Vence when we'd slept together for the first time. The sentimental memories make my opinion of it a little less harsh, but only just.

The lift bell dings and the doors open, pulling me from my

thoughts, and I start the walk to John's office, exchanging greetings with his colleagues. They all know who I am because John has never hidden my presence in his life, and while we don't rub our relationship in people's faces, he has never been shy of touching me or being close.

I come to Carol's desk, smiling at the heaps of paperwork all over it. John may have eased up on the work hours but he's never eased up on the workload. "Matty," she exclaims, and I step forward to give her a hug. I love Carol because she's so motherly and warm and guards John like he's her son.

"Brought you something back," I say, placing some Chanel perfume and a box of Richart gourmet chocolates on the desk.

"Matty, you shouldn't have, love, but I'm not going to say no. I love these."

"I know, Johnny said so."

She smiles and grabs my hand, squeezing. "He'll be *so* glad that you're back. He's been like a bear with a sore paw the last few days, with a mood to match."

I pull a face, sitting comfortably on the corner of her desk and swinging my legs, to the obvious horror of one of John's students who run in fear of him. "Oh, dear, that sounds painful."

She chuckles, grabbing me a bottle of water from the fridge near her desk. "He told Anthony Stanton from the university that he had the legal expertise of Winnie the Pooh, and a client that if the client thought that he knew better than John, then he should hire himself and be happy taking legal advice from an idiot."

I burst out laughing, and the door to John's office pulls open sharply. We both turn our waiting faces as he ushers out some men in suits. He's wearing a pale grey three-piece suit with a claret-coloured tie, and he looks stern and distant. However, his face for a second when he first sees me makes the trip away almost worth it, being comprised of utter joy and relief.

He quickly schools his expression as the men turn to him with a question, but as they move past me he runs his hand up my shoulder, sneakily tugging on the ends of my hair. "Get in my office," he murmurs, and then sweeps past me to the elevators.

"Well, hello to you, too," I grin as Carol giggles, and giving her a kiss I wander into the office, shutting the door behind me. I smile at the sight of the desk which still faces away from the view. I'd put my foot down about the view business when I moved in with him, and insisted that the desks in his study at home and in France face the window. He'd given in on that, but insisted solemnly that he should be framed by the city when he meets clients. Apparently first impressions count when you're paying a fuck-ton of money per hour.

I notice a photo frame on his desk and pull it towards me and then smile as I see a picture of the two of us. It's a black and white taken by Sid in Ibiza. It's captured us close up, heads together. I'm laughing at something, but it's his face that catches my attention because he's looking at me and smiling, and those lines at the side of his eyes are elongated from frequent smiling, which I'd longed to see when I first got to know him.

I look around curiously, always keen to see what he's added to his office. When I first came in here when we got back from France it was a rich-looking room with expensive furnishings, but totally sterile. Nobody looking around would have had a clue about the life that he led.

Now the clues are dotted all over the floor-to-ceiling shelves against the back wall. There's a pot with bright gilded stripes from a weekend in Positano, a backstage pass for Elbow which is draped over a photo of us at Coachella, and a handful of brightly coloured poker chips from a week in Vegas. I smile at the thought of that week. We'd done a bit of gambling, but a large portion of the time had been spent rolling around in the massive bed in our suite. As John had put it, strip poker is still gambling. There are also photos of the two of us and our friends dotted everywhere, telling a story about a man who now leads a rich, fulfilled life full of friends and laughter and love.

The sound of the door clicking open makes my heart speed up, and I look up in time to see John lock the door. "My goodness,

Johnny, this is a place of work," I taunt, throwing his comment back that he'd given me when I first set foot in here.

He smiles in recognition. "Didn't stop me fucking you on that desk," he says fondly, and then in two strides he's on me, wrapping his arms around me and breathing in deeply. He kisses me deeply, thrusting his tongue into my mouth and groaning, before pushing his head into my neck and inhaling. "God, I fucking missed you so much," he groans. "Two weeks is too long, sweetheart. Let's not do that again. I'll come out to you to break it up next time."

"You'd do that?" I ask wonderingly, running my hands through his hair which is curling slightly at the ends.

"Of course I would," he says stoutly. "I can't be without you like that again. Everything was so quiet and tidy and still."

"That makes me sound like a tornado of mess and noise."

He shrugs. "Take it as it's said." Then he curls away laughing as I punch him lightly.

I catch my breath at the sight of those bright blue eyes and his wide mouth laughing, and pull him to me. "God, I missed you, too," I say quietly. "Let's definitely do that. I didn't sleep properly because the bed was so big and cold, and I turned round a thousand times a day to tell you something funny. It's not quite as funny without you."

"I love you," he whispers, and then he's kissing me and we stand burrowing into each other, our hands moving and grabbing. I feel his weight and warmth against me and I moan, sending my hands burrowing under his shirt to find the sleek skin stretched taut over his muscles. We stay that way for a while, taking comfort in the other, until he moves away slightly.

"Phone sex was fucking good, though," he says cheekily, and I laugh.

"Not as good as what you'll get tonight."

"Promises, promises."

"Yes, a promise and a certainty. Are you packed for the week-end?" I ask, looking around the room, and he nods.

"Bag's in the car, sweetheart. I packed you one, too." He checks his watch and I smile, because along with the titanium Breitling watch which is such a symbol of his position, he's wearing the leather bracelet that I bought for him in Cornwall that he never takes off. It has discreet silver beads threaded along it which are engraved with our names and the date that we came together in France, as well as a tiny hammer, a boat, and even a first aid icon, all symbols of the start of our relationship.

He looks up at me. "Are you ready to go?"

"My God, it's only two in the afternoon. No last-minute deeds to peruse? No students to frighten?" I ask mockingly and he laughs.

"No, I crossed those things off my checklist at eleven this morning. We're good to go."

I let him grab my hand and pull me to the door. "Someone's in a hurry. What's the rush?"

Something passes too quickly over his face for me to work out, and then he smiles almost nervously. "I just want to get there, Matty. You know that I love it."

I stare at him hard because he's hiding something, but then I give up because he does love the Cornish house. We go there every weekend, and although he's never got on with surfing he has developed a fondness for photography, and he and Sid always have their heads together looking at the latest cameras.

When we're in Cornwall and I'm surfing, he's either photographing something or has his head stuck in a book, which now tends to be non-work related. But wherever I am so is he, and the closeness suits us. We're our own team, backing each other up and drawing strength from the other's presence.

"Okay then, speedy, let's go."

"I'll give you speedy tonight," he growls into my neck as I pass, and I shiver.

"Not something that you should be bragging about."

He laughs. "Don't worry, I'll take my time with you. It's been a long couple of weeks. I have a lot of pent-up sexual tension to take out on someone."

"I'm volunteering," I moan as his hands come up clutching my hips and shoving his hard cock against my back.

"Not volunteering. You're conscripted." He pushes me out of the office, waving goodbye to Carol and anyone around, but with his warm hand at my back keeping constant contact with me the way that he always does when I've been away, as if reassuring himself that I'm back again.

John

He falls asleep somewhere outside Exeter and doesn't wake up until I pull the car up in the small parking area outside the house where we have a designated space. He sits up, stretching, and then reaches over to give me a deep kiss and an absentminded grope.

"We're here already. Why didn't you wake me, babe? We could have shared the driving."

I shake my head. "You were knackered, love, and I don't mind the driving. It lets me decompress a bit, and get my relaxed head on and put work away." He likes that because he smiles. He'd insisted when we got together that work was work, but life is life and it takes precedence. He doesn't mind the hours that I work as long as I park my arse on a chair next to him to eat dinner, and that when I'm with him, I'm *with* him. I'd used this journey, however, to try to calm my nerves about the talk that I want to have.

He distracts me from that thought when he rotates his neck and yawns. "Fuck, I'm hungry."

I smile. "Great minds think alike," I say as I motion to the back seat. He cranes over and cheers.

"Fucking hell, fish and chips. Best idea yet."

"I have far too many for you to choose from," I remind him modestly, and he laughs.

"Where shall we eat them?"

I nod down at the beach where the sun has gone down, leaving a wild twilight sky of lemon and lilac. "Where else?"

"Perfect," he smiles. "Are the towels in the back?"

I nod and he gets out to get them while I gather the bags of salty-smelling food, and then we traipse down the hill to the beach with his arm slung companionably round my shoulders, a familiar and beloved weight that always makes me happy.

Pausing only to take our shoes and socks off, we wander over to what we now call our spot where we always gravitate to on the week-ends. The beach is mainly deserted now, apart from some dog walkers moving away in the distance. He laughs, looking at our expensive suits. "We look like a right couple of townies."

"Shut up and eat." I smile, chucking him his bag, and we fall on our food eating hungrily while we catch up with each other's news and he tells me funny stories from the promotion tour. When he's finished eating he grabs the wrappers, putting them into a carrier bag, and then lies down with a deep, happy sigh, putting his head into my lap. For a while we both stare out to sea at the now melon and indigo sky, feeling the salty breeze in our faces and listening to the cries of the hungry gulls as they ride on the wind.

Previously I let life pass by, seizing and celebrating only the victories, but now, with him, every day contains another memory that I want to hoard. I love him utterly and deeply beyond anything that I've ever felt for a living person, and he makes me happy beyond anything that I believed I was capable of feeling.

He sighs contentedly. "I can't believe that two years ago we were on this beach and I was listening to your insane babblings."

I snort out a laugh. "I think that you meant to say my carefully considered and beautifully worded argument."

He pshaws. "Whatever you say, babe." He pauses and then says softly, "I'm glad that I did listen, though. I've never been happier with anyone than I am with you. Every single day just waking up next to you makes me content."

"Content," I murmur. "Such a small word for such an encom-passing feeling."

He nods and settles farther into me with a happy sigh, and I release his hair from its short ponytail and run my fingers through it, feeling the soft silky strands catch and wrap around my fingers. He'd had it cut a bit shorter a few weeks ago, but it's still long enough for me to run my hands through it. I love doing that because it calms me. I let out a deep sigh and suddenly the nerves vanish and I know exactly what to say and feel a deep certainty over the answer.

"Matty, will you marry me?"

For a second I think that he hasn't heard me, but then he twists and rises up to a half-crouch. *"What?"*

"Will you marry me?" I say it more quickly now with a bit of uncertainty creeping in, and then I'm off babbling again and it's two years ago all over again. "I mean, I wanted to ask you in a really romantic place, but where's more romantic than here on our beach where we got together, where we're always just Matt and John and happy together?"

He stares at me, his mouth open slightly, I hope in amazement and not in dismay, but I plough on regardless. "I love you so much, Matt. You're everything to me. You've given me a home for the first time in my life and it isn't where we stay, it's you. You've given me a family of friends, and every day you make me laugh and make me think. You challenge me, but best of all you give me peace and joy and the freedom to be me, because you love me in all my guises. You're my best friend and my lover and my sounding board all rolled into one."

I reach into my pocket and pull out a small box. "I had these made because I wanted something totally different for you, because you're utterly unique and irreplaceable to me."

I extract the rings which are beautiful wide hammered bands, copper on the outside with smooth silver inside. "Look, I had yours engraved, sweetheart." I point to the words *'Grow old along with me. The best is yet to be.'* "It's Robert Browning. I read it and thought of you." His face twists as if under some strong emotion, but I can't read him at this moment so I babble on. "But if you don't like them or don't want to do it ... Oh God, I hope that you do want to do this, because otherwise I'm going to feel like a gigantic twat."

I falter to a stop when his eyes fill. "Well, Jesus, I didn't mean to make you cry," I groan. "This fucking beach, I swear that it's cursed my vocabulary. Only here does this happen."

I stop because suddenly he's on me, sliding his arms around me and wrapping me in the tightest hug. His lips find mine and he kisses me deeply and wetly until I'm lying on the towel under him, my thoughts blown away like sand in the wind. He pulls back suddenly and I groan, going after his lips, but he grabs my face.

"Yes!"

"Yes?" I query, raising up and chasing his lips, wanting them on me now.

He laughs. "Yes, I'll marry you, Johnny. I'd like nothing better than to be yours."

I smile, tears in my eyes now. "You'll always be mine, love. This is just the icing on the cake."

"I like the icing, particularly if you're naked and wearing it." I laugh until he seizes my lips again with a throaty groan, and it fills me inside instead like a bottle of champagne shaken up. We kiss with open mouths, our tongues tangling and hands beginning a groping that is a bit too obscene even for a deserted beach. I pull back when his hand goes down the back of my underwear, and suddenly he pauses. "Did you get a ring made for you as well?" I nod and he smiles. "I know what I'm having engraved on yours."

I smile up at him. "What?"

"'*I carry your heart. I carry it in my heart.*' It's E.E Cummings."

I smile, emotion a lump in my throat. "You do carry it. I love you."

We kiss for ages and then I pull back. "You do know what this means, don't you?"

His pupils are blown and he watches my lips as I talk. "What?"

I laugh triumphantly. "I've still got it. This beach is not cursed. We are free to have life-changing conversations out here whenever we want without the fear that I'll turn witless. Life is good. I am once again the Lord of Words."

He smiles pityingly at me. "Walk, don't run, babe. You did use the words gigantic twat in your wedding proposal."

"Well, shit!"

THANK YOU

Thank you to my wonderful, funny husband. Thank you for providing the answers to very personal questions about your penis! I know now that the Bread and Cakes aisle in Sainsburys on a Saturday afternoon is not the best place for asking these questions. Thank you for answering and then shrugging and saying, "You've asked me weirder questions!"

Thank you to Natasha Snow for such a beautiful cover. You took all the information that I gave you and created something that was better than anything I could have imagined. Plus, you did it with a great deal of patience with the seemingly endless search for the perfect cover model and my eternal muttering of, "He just doesn't look like the man in my head." I'm sure that you often needed a strong drink after one of my emails but I never knew it!

Lastly, thanks to you, the readers. Thank you for taking a chance on this book. I hope that you enjoyed reading it as much as I enjoyed writing it. The story would never have happened if it wasn't for all those readers who wrote to me asking for more Matt. Matt was never intended to be more than a one-line character when I started writing 'Keep Me,' but somehow he kept working his way into scenes and ended up being one of my favourite characters, so I loved giving him his happily ever after! As a thank you I've written a short story about Matt and John's wedding and it can be found on my website in the Extras section.

I never knew until I wrote my first book how important reviews are. So, if you have time please consider leaving a review on Amazon or Goodreads or any other review sites. I can promise you that I read every one, good or bad, and value all of them. When I've been struggling with the writing, sometimes going back and reading the reviews makes it better.

CONTACT ME

Website: www.lilymortonauthor.com
This has lots of information and some fun features on here, including some extra short stories. I've written a short story about Matt and John's wedding and you'll find that here.

If you'd like to be the first to know about my book releases and have access to extra content, you can sign up for my newsletter here

If you fancy hearing the latest news and interacting with other readers do head over and join my Facebook group. It's a fun group and I share all the latest news about my books there as well as some exclusive short stories.

www.facebook.com/groups/SnarkSquad/

ALSO BY LILY MORTON

Mixed Messages Series

Rule Breaker

Deal Maker

Risk Taker

Finding Home Series

Oz

Milo

Other Novels

The Summer of Us

Short Stories

Best Love

3 Dates

Made in the USA
Middletown, DE
26 November 2020

25315339R00132